THE THEORY OF EVERYTHING

PHILOMEL BOOKS
A division of Penguin Young Readers Group.
Published by The Penguin Group.
Penguin Group (USA) Inc., 375 Hudson Street, New York, NY 10014, U.S.A.
Penguin Group (Canada), 90 Eglinton Avenue East, Suite 700, Toronto,
Ontario M4P 2Y3, Canada (a division of Pearson Penguin Canada Inc.).
Penguin Books Ltd, 80 Strand, London WC2R 0RL, England.
Penguin Ireland, 25 St. Stephen's Green, Dublin 2, Ireland (a division of Penguin Books Ltd).
Penguin Group (Australia), 250 Camberwell Road, Camberwell,
Victoria 3124, Australia (a division of Pearson Australia Group Pty Ltd).
Penguin Books India Pvt Ltd, 11 Community Centre, Panchsheel Park, New Delhi—110 017, India.
Penguin Group (NZ), 67 Apollo Drive, Rosedale, Auckland 0632, New Zealand
(a division of Pearson New Zealand Ltd).
Penguin Books (South Africa) (Pty) Ltd, 24 Sturdee Avenue,
Rosebank, Johannesburg 2196, South Africa.
Penguin Books Ltd, Registered Offices: 80 Strand, London WC2R 0RL, England.

Edited by Jill Santopolo. Design by Amy Wu.
Text set in 11.75-point Kennerley.

LIBRARY OF CONGRESS CATALOGING-IN-PUBLICATION DATA
Luna, Kari.
The theory of everything / Kari Luna.
p. cm.
Summary: When fourteen-year-old Sophie Sophia journeys to New York
with a scientific boy genius and a giant shaman panda guide, she discovers more about
her visions, string theory, and a father who could be the key to an extraordinary life.
[1. Fathers and daughters—Fiction. 2. Visions—Fiction. 3. Supernatural—Fiction.
4. Friendship—Fiction. 5. Physics—Fiction. 6. Science fiction.] I. Title.
PZ7.L9787157The 2013 [Fic]—dc23 2012018791

ISBN 978-0-399-25626-4
1 3 5 7 9 10 8 6 4 2

THE THEORY OF EVERYTHING

KARI LUNA

PHILOMEL BOOKS | An Imprint of Penguin Group (USA) Inc.

To Kai and Noah,
who have always believed in everything.

The most beautiful and most profound emotion we can experience is the sensation of the mystical. It is the sower of all true science. He to whom this emotion is a stranger, who can no longer wonder and stand rapt in awe, is as good as dead.

—Einstein

PROLOGUE

Once I saw a guy's heart roll right off his sleeve. Mom and I were sitting in a booth at Sal's sharing a sausage calzone when I saw it—a big red heart sitting on the outside of his arm instead of the middle of his chest where it belonged. When Mom left for the bathroom, I saw it move, slowly down his biceps until it got to the elbow, rolled off and landed on the floor with a thud. Right next to his bright green sneaker.

The heart stood still. The guy twirled spaghetti on a fork with one hand and gestured excitedly to his date with the other. And she just sat there, sipping soda through a straw and looking totally uninterested in whatever he was saying, which was too bad. Considering the heart and all, it was probably important.

"Cut it out," Mom said, sliding back into the booth. She had a smear of red-orange lipstick on her teeth. "How would you like to be on a date and have some kid look you over?"

"I'm too young to date," I said, staring at the floor where the heart had been. "And you might want to blot."

Normally I would have been mortified by her lack of grooming skills, but I had bigger things to worry about. Things like seeing something that wasn't there. Just like Dad.

"I know you miss New York," Mom said, leaving her lip print on a white paper napkin. "But San Francisco is the New York of the West, remember?"

It wasn't the New York of the West because people walked too slowly, ate burritos the size of their faces and rode trollies, but whatever. I was less interested in our most recent move and more into the fact that I was maybe, possibly turning into my father.

"How old was Dad when he saw something?" I asked, smearing sauce around the plate with my fork. Wondering if he was twelve like I was.

"You know we don't talk about your father," she said, tapping her nails against the laminate. Her hands hadn't stopped moving since Dad left. "Let's get out of here."

She grabbed her coat, slid out of the booth and forged ahead, heels clacking. I lagged behind her until I got to the heart guy's table, where I froze, staring at the heart, which was now back where it belonged: next to the I and above the NY on his white tourist T-shirt.

"You'll have to excuse my daughter," Mom said, pulling me away with one hand and pointing at their cheesecake with the other. "She's just mad we didn't order dessert."

I was mad I saw something no one else did. But more than that, I was mad Dad wasn't there to explain it to me.

The front door chimed as she held it open.

"Come on," Mom said. "I'd like to get home before Christmas."

And I'd like to go back to New York, back to when Dad was around, but I doubted either of those things was going to happen.

"Sophie Sophia!" she said, waving me toward the door. Her breath froze in little clouds before her.

"Coming," I said, tightening my black-and-white-striped scarf around me. I knew I'd never tell her what happened. But I wished—desperately and secretly—that it would happen again.

ONE

My head is full of magic, baby, and I can't share this with you.
—Love and Rockets, "So Alive"

Most people don't mourn their dads through a mixtape.

Boyfriends, maybe, but then it's usually a playlist. In my world, though, grief was best served analog. Especially when the dad in question bailed when I was ten, leaving only a handful of mixtapes behind. I was a fan of the music, but not him. Four years of returned letters and a total lack of phone calls can do that to a person. It can also make you smarter and emotionally inept at the same time. I could hold my own in a conversation about Depeche Mode but was a total mess when it came to anything else.

"Excited?" Mom said, backing our '87 maroon Volvo station wagon out of the driveway. "You're a sophomore now."

"Yes, in another new school. In another new town! You're too good to me," I said.

"Enough with the sarcasm, Soph," she said, flipping her chocolate hair off her shoulders. She'd been growing it out since we left New York, while I chose to chop mine off, leaving me with a short-bob-with-bangs kind of thing. "It's not like Chicago's devoid of civilization."

"True, but we're fifty miles north of there," I said.

"I know," Mom said, grinning as we passed the WELCOME TO HAVENCREST sign. "Isn't it great?"

The streets were so wide you could fit an entire New York neighborhood in them, and massive trees hung down like parasols between row after row of Victorian houses.

"This place is one gigantic doily," I said. "I should have worn white gloves."

"It might have improved your outfit," she said, giving me the once-over as we pulled up to a stoplight. "What *are* you wearing, anyway?"

"I'm going for nautical," I said, twisting the long strand of fake pearls around my neck. "It's in. And these represent the treasure you find while out at sea."

I was a fan of theme dressing, and today's theme was oceanic: floor-length navy skirt with a large whale pocket on the front, blue-and-white-striped boatneck T-shirt, striped kneesocks and black twelve-eye Doc Martens. It was part sailor, part adventurer, all survivor.

"You look unique," Mom said, flashing a half smile. "Like your very own person."

"I actually *like* the way I look," I said, regretting the snark as soon as it came out. She meant it as a compliment, not the insults I knew were coming the minute I was inside the school.

"Of course you do," she said, shifting in her seat. "What's not to love? Besides, when have you ever taken fashion advice from me?"

"Touché," I said, poking her shoulder. "Do I detect a shoulder pad?"

"You do *not*," she said, smiling. Mom could be superannoying like most moms, but at least she was smart, like whip-smart. I guess you had to be if you were married to a physicist.

"This is just a regular work suit, not a power suit from the eighties."

"Aaaah, the eighties," I said, caressing the Walkman sitting in my lap. I turned on the radio, but some alterna-teen crap blared out of it, so I changed the station. "I don't know why new bands even bother. Why anyone thinks they can do better than The Smiths or The Cure is beyond me."

"Some would call it progress," Mom said. "Like those digital music player thingies?" She glanced at my Walkman like it was offensive.

"They're called iPods," I said. "Besides, digital is totally overrated. It's not like you can find amazing MP3s at Goodwill."

"Okay, but what about CDs?" she said.

"Still digital," I said. "Analog is cool. It has history, like a pair of cuff links or a love letter. Besides, it's your fault. You and Dad got me started."

"Your father got us both started," Mom said, waving her

arm out the window. The fresh air felt good, like maybe things would be okay. Like maybe moving to a suburb would keep me from seeing things that weren't there. Mom called them "episodes," just like she did with Dad. And even though the word *hallucination* never crossed her lips, I'm sure it crossed her mind. I know it did mine.

"Angelino made the best mixtapes of anyone I know," she said. "And now they don't even *make* tapes."

Neither does Dad, I thought, which meant they were all I had of him. He and Mom fell in love over Echo and the Bunnymen and Joy Division and passed their passion for eighties music on to me. That's why the Walkman was my weapon of choice. You could learn a lot about a person from a ninety-minute Maxell tape.

The car slowed and stopped in front of a sign that read HAVENCREST HIGH SCHOOL. Kids hung out on the steps in pairs or in groups. Singles were nowhere to be seen, because that's what you did when you were alone. Out of sight, out of target practice.

"You ready?" Mom said.

I wasn't ready when Dad left us in New York four years ago. I wasn't ready when I started a new school in San Francisco two years later. I wasn't ready when I saw the heart roll off of the sleeve, records flying around at Record Mania, or Sting serenading me in the soda aisle. I wasn't ready for a mind I couldn't control, a reality that didn't seem real and friends I couldn't keep. No one wanted to bond with the strange girl, including my last school. A suspension was followed by an expulsion and our station wagon, loaded with boxes, picking me up in the middle of the day. I wasn't ready when we headed toward Illinois with Balzac, my Siamese, in my lap, but I made it. So maybe the secret to survival was *not* being ready.

"You know I adore a challenge," I said, shoving my Walkman and tapes deeper into my bag.

"Then leave the Walkman here," Mom said. "At least while you're at school."

"I hate to break it to you, but cassettes aren't what make me weird," I said. If only it were that easy.

Mom took off her tortoiseshell sunglasses. Her eyes were red and watery, like she was about to lose it. But since she was starting a new job and I had a new school to conquer, we didn't have time for a Hallmark moment.

"Mom," I said, "everything's going to be okay."

I walked up the stairs and when I looked back, she waved, tentatively, like even her hand wasn't sure about me going in there.

"Good luck!" she said, even though we both knew it would take a lot more than luck for my episodes to wait until after school.

I took a breath, opened the door and stepped into my new life. Outside, the Volvo sped off—Mom fleeing what she couldn't control, me knowing it might follow us wherever we went.

TWO

"You're late," the physics teacher said as I walked into class. He looked more like a French teacher, with his navy blazer, purple bow tie and curly hair that almost touched his shoulders.

"Sorry," I said, looking around the class for a seat. "I got lost."

In my dreams I was on time and people clamored to sit next to me, asking me about my unique outfit and what music I was into. "What was R.E.M.'s early work like?" they would ask. "What's so special about The Smiths?" I'd invite them to eat lunch with me, and we'd discuss Voltaire or Salinger over chutney or mochi. Before I knew it, I'd have a whole fan club dedicated entirely to me.

"You must be Sophie Sophia," he said, looking at his list. "I'm Mr. Maxim. Take a seat."

I sat in the front row—the only one open—and turned around to check out of the rest of the class: a sea of fluffy-haired girls mixed with normals mixed with the occasional guy in a sports jersey. And a few punk kids. I tried to make eye contact with the punks, but their heads were down. A few of the blondes snickered, but all in all, none of them looked like future members of my fan club.

"So that just about covers the syllabus," Mr. Maxim said. He was sitting on the front of his desk, which meant he was either *actually* cool or just thought he was. "Does anyone have any questions?"

"Are we going to discuss M-theory?" a kid in the back row asked.

Mr. Maxim hopped up from the desk so fast one of his feet landed in the trash can.

"We have a physics enthusiast in our midst!" he said, trying to shake the trash can off his foot. "Is anyone else familiar with M-theory? String theory?"

I had to sit on my hands so I wouldn't raise them or hug Mr. Maxim, who'd suddenly turned physics class into an afternoon with my dad.

"I thought we were studying gravity," said one of the blond girls. Judging by the amount of hair spray she'd used, I was pretty sure she was familiar with the concept.

"We are. We're not getting to theoretical physics until the end of the semester, but most of physics *is* theory," Mr. Maxim said, freeing the trash can from his foot but leaving a red lolli-pop stuck to the side of his loafer. "Think about the possibility of extra dimensions. Think about black holes and time travel. Think about the millions of things we don't understand. Physics could hold the answers."

Answers were why I was there, but all the other kid's heads were down, earbuds in ears. Mr. Maxim slammed a book on the desk, and people popped up.

"I get it," he said. "Not everyone is into science. But phys-ics is more than measuring things. It teaches you to look at the world in a new way. And whether you're hanging at the pool or pondering mortality, physics will make you ask questions. And believe that anything is possible. If you learn nothing else from high school, that will be enough."

"So I can skip the rest of my classes?" asked one of the ear-bud guys.

"That's up to you," Mr. Maxim said. "But as Newton said, actions have reactions."

"Like detention?"

"Like every action has an equal and opposite reaction," I blurted out. Some people grew up with the Lord's Prayer, but I'd been hearing Newton's Third Law of Motion since birth.

"Bravo," I heard from the back of the class, followed by clapping.

And there he was—the first person I'd seen who didn't look like everyone else. His blond hair flopped in front like Morrissey's from The Smiths, and he was wearing one of those little-old-man shirts from the fifties, the kind that buttoned up the front. The kind that made me feel like I was back in New York, just like his wing tips and black Buddy Holly glasses. I christened him Fab Physics Guy.

"Well, well," Mr. Maxim said, smiling. "I think we've found your lab partner, Ms. Sophia."

The bell rang and people ran from the room, but I took my time, reveling in the fact that I hadn't freaked out. It was just one class, but it was a start. I felt victory down to my bones. And then I felt the eyes of a certain Fab Physics Guy burning a hole between my shoulders. In the tradition of searching for answers, I had to ask: did anyone know the scientific equation for awesome?

I was supposed to take chemistry. That was where they put sophomores, especially ones with science grades as nonstellar as mine, but I talked my way into physics. I used the Dad Bomb, something I usually left alone, but since Angelino Sophia was a theoretical physics professor at NYU, it held some weight. Weight that the guidance counselor promised not to share with my future science teacher. I got in on her recommendation, and I was going to absorb as much as possible. There was no way I was going to pass up a chance to find out what was so enticing about the whole physics thing. Why Dad spent more time in the lab than he did with us. And why, in the end, his job won and we lost. Mom always said he left us because of work, but I wasn't sure. Even my friends with Wall Street dads saw them every once in a while or got a text. But I received nothing, which made me develop a little theory of my own, a theory unfounded in facts but based solely on feelings. Dad didn't leave because of work. He left because of me.

The rest of the day was uneventful, which is exactly what I wanted out of the first day of school. Mom was right—Havencrest was less stimulating than other places, even San Francisco. There, indie kids were everywhere wearing shirts they'd screen-printed that morning or tweeting about the next biggest band. They were nice, but exclusive. Brooklyn was more inclusive, either because I grew up there or because we wore uniforms. It evened things out a bit, or at least made them more obvious. If someone didn't like you, you knew it. In San Francisco, girls would be nice to your face and giggle as you walked away, especially if you were the weird girl. Like me.

So far, the most ironic thing I'd seen in Havencrest was a football player wearing a Sunkist T-shirt, probably from Urban Outfitters. And a few drill teamers wearing Converse with their uniforms, like they were rebelling against Keds. No one had been mean, but no one had been that nice, either. The day was strictly monotone—nothing too high, nothing too low. I couldn't think of anything less stimulating than that. But I had my rules, just in case.

How to Survive a New School
by Sophie Sophia

---

1. Don't see things that don't exist. At least not until after three P.M.

2. If you *do* see things that don't exist, deny it.
3. If that doesn't work, act like you don't
   speak English.
4. Or that you were doing a performance art piece.
5. And if all else fails, throw candy and run. Enough
   chocolate and most people will forget anything.

The last bell rang and kids swarmed the halls, rushing for the red doors like it was the apocalypse. I followed them and stepped out into the back parking lot, enjoying the sunshine for the first time since that morning. I was walking along the fence that bordered the football field when I heard my name.

"Excuse me, Sophie?"

There, in all his vintage glory, was Fab Physics Boy. Saying my name. A small part of me wanted to stay and talk to him forever, but the larger part knew I had to leave. I was a ticking time bomb of potential freak-show-ness, and the only way to avoid it was to go. But I couldn't move. My Doc Martens melted into the concrete like they knew something I didn't. Like maybe this year was going to be different.

I looked at him, sun bouncing off his glasses, and smiled. Started to answer. So it's no surprise I heard drums in the distance. And as I looked out onto the football field, I saw a band of giant pandas, marching and drumming with massive lollipops, keeping the beat.

THREE

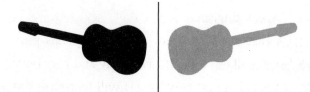

The field looked the same, except instead of being covered with kids, it was filled with a dozen pandas moving like pros, marching right, left and all over the field, forming everything from circles to the letter W. Or maybe it was an M—it was hard to tell. But they looked amazing, like a White Stripes video. There were a dozen of them decked out in tall red hats with white plumes and red-and-white-striped drum straps that draped across their chests like peppermints. They even carried red and white swirly lollipops instead of mallets—pandas and pops on parade. Too bad the greatness of their outfits didn't match their musical ability. And too bad Fab Physics Boy wasn't there to see it.

"No, no, no," the lead panda said, stopping and adjusting his black Ray-Ban sunglasses. His hat was the opposite—white with red plumes—and he carried a baton.

"Would it kill you to stay in tune? This is New Order, not rocket science."

Except it *was* rocket science, at least that's what Dad said. He compared New Order's music to some of the greatest equations ever written, which is why "True Faith" drifted up from the basement, filling the house with the sounds of science.

"Let's try this again," the panda said, putting a whistle in his mouth. "Tweet-tweet-tweet-tweet!"

At his command, a dozen pandas filed behind him and started playing, badly, as they headed straight toward me. I was half nervous and half curious. I mean, the closest I'd ever been to a panda was at the Bronx Zoo. When I leaned toward it, the guide had told me to be careful, that even though he looked like he wanted a hug, he might deliver a strong left hook instead. That's how powerful they were.

"Tweet!" the lead panda blasted, and then stopped quickly, ten feet in front of me, sending a pile of pandas and the sound of cymbals crashing behind him.

"Hello," he said, removing his sunglasses and extending a giant paw. "I'm Walt."

It's not like I hadn't seen anything weird before. I'd been surprised by talking birds and chairs that flew. Rock stars who sang in elevators and gargoyles who came to life, giggling. My episodes were more *Fantasia* than anything else, but still. Things could change. Things always changed.

"I'm Sophie. Sophie Sophia."

I offered my hand and watched it disappear inside a mound of fur.

"Nice name," he said. "Did you enjoy our little performance?"

Since he was a million feet tall and I liked to find the positive in things, I focused on that.

"You guys can *march*," I said. "Seriously."

"I knew it," Walt said, rocking back and forth on his heels. "We stink. Merv over there has two left paws."

The panda picking up the xylophone shrugged.

"Sorry, boss," he said. "I told ya, music ain't my thing."

I liked how relaxed he was, how relaxed all of them were, which made me think they were more on the hugging side and less on the punching side. Besides, when had I ever gotten hurt inside of a hallucination?

"No matter," Walt said. "We'll get it, eventually. But according to my internal clock, it's poker time. Care to join?"

"I've never played," I said, following them back onto the football field, feet sinking into fake grass. Mind blown.

"I'll teach you," Walt said. "I'll teach you a lot of things."

The pandas made a circle around the fifty-yard line and plopped down simultaneously, making the entire field shake. I went down with them, landing in between Walt and the panda with the trumpet.

"Larry," he said, extending his paw.

"Sophie," I said, shaking it. "Thanks for having me."

Walt shuffled and dealt, and Larry mixed drinks, pouring from one flask then another, adding a bamboo stirrer at the end. He handed one to me, which I handed to Walt.

"I'm a Manhattan man, myself, but Merv likes mint juleps," Walt said. "They're a bit of a girly drink, but he's an old friend, so we make an exception."

"They're all soda with a stick of sugarcane," Larry whispered, handing me a cup. "Don't tell Walt."

I sipped and smiled. It tasted like the time I ate several sugar packets at a diner, only better. Walt pushed a pile of jelly beans over to me, the apparent poker chip of choice, and the game began. I folded almost immediately, every time, but I didn't care. According to Walt, the best way to learn was to lose and then start again. Kind of like surrender.

"Why am I here?" I said.

"Humans are funny," Walt said. "Never content to just enjoy this Manhattan, this poker game, this pack of pandas."

He held up his cards. "Can anyone beat a full house?"

The rest of the pandas groaned and shook their heads.

"That's what I thought," he said. "It's the Walt show, baby!"

We surrendered our jelly beans on the bass drum in front of Walt, and he scooped them up. But instead of keeping them, he poured them into my whale pocket, red, green and yellow cascading into its gray body.

"He looks like he gained five pounds," I said.

"But at least you have snacks," Walt said.

"How do you know I like snacks?"

"You're fourteen," he said. "Besides, sometimes you just know things."

Like how I knew my dad wasn't like other dads. He lived somewhere other fathers didn't, a place filled with lions and lollipops, Bernoulli and bowling balls. He was either in his basement inventing something or off on an adventure trying to prove theories that existed only in his head. I was too young to understand physics, but Dad had taught me the value of believing in things you couldn't see. Just because I didn't see the same things Dad saw didn't mean they didn't exist.

Walt stood up and tapped the sugarcane stirrer on the outside of his cup.

"Everyone? Can I have your attention? I'd like to make a toast to our newest friend here."

The pandas stopped talking and turned to face me.

"Sophie, you showed up today whether you wanted to or not. And you did it with curiosity, a big heart and a willingness to learn. From all of us to you, welcome to our tribe, of which you'll always be a member."

He raised his cup. "To Sophie."

A chorus of white and black paws went up in the air, red cups waving.

"To Sophie!" they yelled, voices echoing across the field.

To me, I thought, feeling like I belonged for the first time in forever. Even if it was only for a few minutes. Even if no one could see them. Even though they were pandas, they were my friends—reminding me that I still had the ability to make them.

Wind hit me in the face, and the concrete curb was cold against my skin. Colder than the fake grass I'd been on, colder than being surrounded by pandas. I wasn't sure how long I'd been gone—sometimes it was minutes, other times hours—but the parking lot was empty except for a few kids hanging out in the doorway and football players filing out on the field. The same field where I drank soda with sugarcane and played poker. The same field where I'd found my tribe, only to have them disappear. Typical.

I heard a whistle, but it was just the coach, gathering the guys for practice. I stood up and my pearls swung forward, hitting another necklace. A whistle on a chain, like the coach wore. Like Walt wore. I put it up to my lips and blew it once, twice, three times.

"Walt? Larry? Merv? Anyone?"

I don't know why I thought the pandas would come back, since it had never happened before. My episodes were always different, which is what made them so unnerving. Maybe if they'd contained a cast of recurring characters like any sitcom, I'd have been more amused than unsettled. I took off the whistle and turned it over and over in my hand as if it contained a clue. And then I spotted Fab Physics Guy leaning up against the fence. Since I wasn't sure how long I'd been gone, I had no idea how long he'd been there or what he'd seen.

"Hey, there," he said, walking toward me. "Are you okay?"

I had been until he showed up. So I took a deep breath. Remembered my list. And since it was too late for steps two, three and four, I picked up my bag and resorted to step five—tossing jelly beans and running like a New York Marathoner until I reached my house.

FOUR

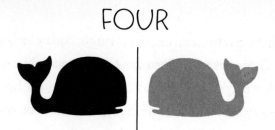

I was craving some serious headphones-wearing, Bauhaus-listening time, but Mom attacked me as soon as I walked through the door.

"You're home!" she said, shoving a Chinese takeout menu in my face. "Ready to celebrate your first day with a little General Tso's chicken?"

When I started kindergarten, Dad decided that we should celebrate the first day of school like a rite of passage with Chinese food and old movies. The idea was that whether the day was good or bad, at least you'd have egg drop soup and Audrey Hepburn to look forward to.

"Pass your plate," Dad said on the eve of my first day of second grade. He poured sauce over my moo shu and root beer into a plastic goblet and placed egg rolls on our plates.

"One, two, three!" he said, and we bit into our egg rolls simultaneously. It was part of the ritual, like a prayer that contained cabbage. So was the speech that followed.

"I'd like to make a toast," Dad said as we raised our goblets. "To second grade. Be nice to Sophie. She sees the world differently, and that's a good thing."

He winked at me and then he stared like he was sizing me up, seeing how different I was from the year before.

"And to Sophie, I say, be free," he said. "Be curious but thoughtful, adventurous but kind, led by your imagination but guided by your heart."

"Hear, hear!" Mom said, bringing her glass to meet ours in the middle, plastic thudding, affirming the idea that we were in it together. Mom hopped up and threw her arms around us, squeezing, her tears dropping onto the egg rolls.

"Mom!" I said, moving the plate away.

"Sorry, sorry," she said, wiping her eyes and smiling. "You know how I get with your father's speeches."

Dad grabbed her and kissed her cheek. Those were the days before the fights. Before Dad disappeared all the time. Before craziness came in and didn't leave until he did. After that, Mom kept up the first day ritual, anyway. At first I complained, but after a while, I got it. Just as Dad predicted, it was nice to know that whatever evils the first day of school contained, at least I knew I'd get plum sauce and movie stars out of it.

"Longest. Day. In. Existence," I said, tossing my backpack on the floor. I would have thrown it somewhere else, like a chair, but we didn't have one. Mom called it the minimal look, but I called it "Sir Moves-A-Lot," named after the famous '90s rapper. It was also because we only owned the essentials—rust-colored sectional couch, long teak coffee table, kitchen table, dressers and beds. Oh, and Dad's red beanbag chair, which I had in my room. Dad used to sit in it and verbally plot how he was going to unleash his greatness into the world.

"First days are always long," Mom said. "My day was long, too. Do you want to talk about it?"

"That's pretty much the last thing I want to do," I said. "Would you care if I took a quick nap?"

"Not at all," she said, sneaking in a hug. I was too tired to resist. "I'll wake you when the food's here."

Balzac and I went up to my room, and he joined me in a group flop on the bed. Emotional roller coaster of a day? Meet my dear friend: the nap.

One hour and three magical words later, I was awake.

"Egg roll time!" Mom's voice floated up the stairs.

My eyes flew open and I rolled over on Balzac, who screeched and jumped off the bed.

"Sorry, buddy," I said, swinging my legs around. A red jelly bean fell out of my pocket and landed on the blanket. It was a souvenir.

Souvenirs were physical objects that I brought back from my episodes. I didn't steal them, they just appeared when an episode was over, like a whistle around my neck, which wasn't there anymore. Or jelly beans in my pocket. I called them souvenirs because they reminded me of where I'd been. That's what souvenirs were for, but in my case, the places I visited didn't exist for other people. It's not like I went to the Grand Canyon and brought back a magnet or something. I played poker with pandas on a football field. I brought back jelly beans and a whistle.

Most of the time, souvenirs were small, like a pocket watch or a feather, but sometimes they were bigger. That was why I started sewing extra-large pockets on my clothes, to give the souvenirs a place to go. And since I loved fashion—and squares were boring—I ventured out a bit. I sewed cloud-shaped pockets and tree-shaped ones. Squirrel pockets and guitar pockets and, one time, part of the Pacific Ocean. Pretty soon every pair of pants, every skirt was well equipped with a hiding place—and a story.

"Sophie Sophia!" Mom called. "These egg rolls aren't going to eat themselves."

I went downstairs and saw our own moveable feast.

"There's moo shu pork, General Tso's chicken, veggie lo mein and two orders of veggie egg rolls. With extra plum sauce," Mom said.

Her chopsticks were already sticking out of the moo shu, and she held a pancake in one hand.

"I even convinced them to bring us jasmine tea."

She pointed to a paper cup sitting in the middle of takeout boxes and sauce packets, curls of steam rising like a salute.

I'd survived my first day of school. Now I just had to survive this town.

How to Survive a New Town
by Sophie Sophia

1. If you move to a big city, throw this list away. You won't need it.
2. Order Chinese food, specifically moo shu pork. Evaluate.
3. Find a diner that serves coffee. Chains are a last resort.
4. Locate and frequent the following: bookstore, music store, thrift shop, cheap movie theater, Goodwill or Salvation Army.
5. If the above don't exist, rely on the library.
6. If a library doesn't exist, move to another town with haste and without apology.

Mom sat on the couch, but I sat on the floor, Indian style, so I could be eye level with the food. I opened the veggie lo mein and dug in. It was salty and sweet, on the edge of perfection. For a few minutes, hunger won out over conversation.

"Don't put those there," Mom said, breaking the silence. She nodded at the small pile of celery I'd started on the table next to me. "It's disgusting. Just push them to the side of your dish."

"No way," I said. "If I ate one, the strings would stick in my throat and I'd choke and die."

"You're so dramatic," she said, smiling. "Maybe we should watch *Whatever Happened to Baby Jane?*"

"I'm in more of a Tim Burton mood," I said.

"Of course you are."

Mom picked up an egg roll with her chopsticks, dipped it in sauce and brought it to her lips. She used to be a dancer, which explained the graceful thing, but it was annoying. If I'd tried that, the egg roll would have dropped on the floor halfway to my mouth.

"How about an Asian film?" she said.

"Too predictable." I nodded at the cartons littering the table.

"Then you pick," she said. "I don't care what we watch, I'm just glad you survived your first day. Sure you don't want to tell me about it?"

"Amazingly sure," I said, erasing the day by shoveling noodles into my mouth. "How about *Roman Holiday?*"

"Perfect!" Mom said. "Audrey goes with everything. Could you pass the pork?"

I woke up with my cheek stuck to my arm, courtesy of the lo mein sauce. At some point, I'd eaten so much I laid my head on my arms, which were on the coffee table, and fell asleep. I grabbed a napkin, cleaned myself up and rubbed my eyes. The movie was still playing, but it was near the end, the press conference scene where Audrey goes back to being a princess and Gregory Peck asks questions like nothing happened. I was thinking about how hot he was for an old guy when Walt plopped down on the floor beside me.

"Isn't this a great movie?" he said. "You can't get better than Hepburn. I could look at her face all day."

"Could you keep it down?" I pointed to Mom, sleeping with a carton of moo shu in her lap.

Walt pretended to zip his lip with a big black and white paw.

"What are you doing here?" I asked.

"You missed me," he said. "Besides, wherever egg rolls appear, so do I."

Walt grabbed the last one, dunked it in the remains of the plum sauce and tossed it into his mouth.

"I haven't had time to miss you," I said.

"Okay, then I missed *you*," he said. "Where's the love?"

"More like where are your friends?"

"So many questions," he said.

"And so few pandas," I said. "Why is it just you? And why did you come to me, instead of the other way around?"

I usually popped into episodes already in progress, like when you hate the movie you paid for and sneak into another one. It was already playing, only now it was playing with you in the back row, confused about the plot but happy about the popcorn. The movie didn't come to me; I went to it. But now a panda from the football field was in my house, eating all the egg rolls. Nothing about that could be a good sign.

"Allow me to formally introduce myself," he said, twirling both chopsticks in one hand. "I'm Walt, your shaman panda."

I didn't know everything, but I learned about shamans in seventh-grade history. Shamans were messengers between the visible and invisible spirit worlds. They also had the ability to heal, which, judging from Walt's chopstick drumming on the coffee table, wasn't his forte.

"If you're some kind of shaman, prove it," I said. "Heal me."

"You want to be more specific?"

"Make my episodes go away," I said. "You're charming and all, but I'd like to quit seeing things now."

Walt stopped drumming, and Mom started snoring, softly, like someone running her hands up and down a set of mini blinds.

"That's not how it works," Walt said, speaking quietly.

"So enlighten me, enlightened one," I said. "Are you a healer or what?"

"I am, but sometimes the healing is internal. I'm here to guide you, not make things happen or prevent things from happening," he said. "I'm more like a guardian angel without wings. Unless they're chicken wings, of course."

He picked up a carton of fried rice and emptied it into his mouth.

"I didn't ask for a guardian panda or shaman or whatever you are," I said, standing up and pacing back and forth in front of the television. "I didn't ask to see things or to move away from New York, but those things happened anyway. So here's some guidance for you. Leave. I don't want you here."

But as soon as I said it, I knew it wasn't true. Maybe having a giant, invisible shaman panda as my first friend here wasn't the best choice, but maybe it was. Walt was in on the joke. I'd never have to lie to him, to tell him I had a headache when really I was just reeling from returning from an episode. I didn't have to explain how scary it was to try to live on shifting ground, never knowing if I was safe in my own head, much less a math class. And if he wanted to guide me, as he said, or watch over me like some black and white furry angel, I was in no position to pass *that* up.

"I'm a jerk," I said. "Also known as a brat, prima donna or pariah. I'm sorry. Peace offering?"

I handed Walt the small white bag from the middle of the table. It was the same bag that came with Chinese takeout in every city and contained the usual suspects: soy sauce, duck sauce that no one ever ate and two fortune cookies. Maybe that's why Dad made Chinese food a part of our ritual. If you wanted to commemorate something, you couldn't do much better than food that came with fate at the end.

Walt shook a fortune cookie into his paw and presented it to me.

"I know you didn't ask for me," he said. "But look at it this way: there is nothing you can tell me that will freak me out. No one else can see me. And the best part? You never have to come to me. I'll come to you."

"Plus, you have a killer smile and impeccable wit," I said, giggling and taking the cookie out of his hand. I broke it in two and stuck a piece in my mouth. Stale mixed with vanilla.

"Depart not from the path that fate has assigned," I read from the slip of paper. "You have *got* to be kidding."

"What? I didn't write it," Walt said. "And I never used the word *path*, thank you very much."

"But you're going to," I said. "If I let you be my shaman

panda, Zen words are going to start popping out of your mouth like a slot machine."

"Zen is in!" Walt said. He smashed his cookie on the table, sending pieces—and Balzac—flying around the room. I grabbed his fortune off the table and there, in tiny black letters, was his destiny. Even though it sounded a lot more like mine.

"A friend is a gift you give yourself," I said. "That's corny."

"But true," he said, sticking his paw in the plum sauce and then in his mouth. "Admit it. You know you like talking to me."

I didn't hate it. And even though he ate all the takeout, showed up without warning and was a panda, he didn't stare or ask questions; he just accepted. Like I used to do with Dad.

"I'll do a trial basis," I said.

"Yes!" Walt said, throwing his arms in the air and shaking his butt around.

"But no more of that," I said. "We only go-go dance around here. And no more sneaking up on me. I hate that."

"Got it," Walt said. "Mod dancing and a megaphone. Anything else?"

I thought about hugging him, partially to make sure he was real, partially to get lost in that black and white fur, but I wanted to be cooler than that. So I raised my knuckles and made a fist.

"Sophie Sophia, keeping it real," he said, bumping his paw against my fist like an agreement. "I like it."

I pulled my hand back, and Walt was gone. The only evidence that he'd ever been there was a panda butt imprint in the carpet and a chewed stick of bamboo next to it.

Mom sat up, rubbing her eyes.

"Did I hear you talking to someone?"

"Nope," I said. "Must have been the movie. Or Balzac."

I stacked cartons, attempting to clear the table and distract her with my impeccable manners.

"Sophie, are you seeing things again?" She yawned. "You can tell me. There's nothing we can't work out."

And by "work out," she meant move where no one knew us. Where no one cared.

"I was talking to Infinity," I said, instead. "It was fascinating, as usual. Now I'm going upstairs to talk to Dreamland. I'll tell you all about it in the morning."

I tossed a handful of cartons in the trash and held my breath as I walked upstairs, hoping she wouldn't figure things out. Praying, even though I never prayed, that she hadn't heard me with Walt.

FIVE

Today was Thursday, the day that deserves to be kicked out of the calendar, completely. Most people loved Thursday because it was almost Friday, which was practically the weekend. But for me, Thursday was a reminder of something else: that day when the fun and games forgot the fun; when someone I loved terrified me; and when I ended up in one cop car, waving, while my dad rode away in another one.

"It's TYRANNICAL THURSDAY!" Dad said one Thursday, emerging from the basement in red long underwear. "And as the tyrant, I have decided that today we will go to the zoo in our pajamas."

I laughed so hard chocolate milk sprayed out of my nose.

"It's too cold for pajamas, Daddy," I said, wiping my face on my sleeve. I was five, and the only thing I wanted more than going to the zoo was staying warm. I hated the cold. It was a phase I was going through.

"So we'll warm ourselves with our minds!" he said, running circles around the table. "We're the smartest people I know. If anyone can create heat with thoughts, it's us!"

"Angelino, put some clothes on," Mom said when she walked in.

"I would if I could," he said. "It's Tyrannical Thursday, and Sophie and I are going to the zoo in our pajamas."

Mom poured coffee into her blue mug, the one with the chip on the side.

"Sophie has school," she said. "You know that."

"What can she possibly learn in a classroom that I can't teach her? Am I right?"

He looked at me, and I nodded yes as he piled a waffle on my plate and poured a syrup smile on top of it.

"Of course she's going to agree with you," Mom said, ruffling my hair. "Sophie is nothing if not a fan of monkeys."

"Which is why I'm taking her to the zoo," he said.

Mom took a waffle off the plate and ate it plain.

"Fine," she said. "But no pajamas. And wait until after school."

"Deal!" Dad said, winking at me. "I don't know why you worry so much."

At the time, Mom knew something I didn't: Dad was sick. Which meant he wasn't the best person to take care of me. But that didn't keep him from showing up at school at noon with a doctor's note in one hand and a pair of pajamas in the other.

As we walked around the zoo, he told me his theories on why parrots mimic, why polar bears like ice and what makes elephants majestic. I was shivering but acted like I was fine until he stuck his arms through the bars, trying to catch a capuchin monkey. He wanted to take him home because, evolutionarily, the monkey was my brother, but the guards didn't like that answer. They also didn't like it when they asked him to "come with them" and instead of going, he pulled a stainless-steel eggbeater out of his jacket pocket and charged at them. Assault by scramble.

Before I knew it, he was sitting in the back of one of the police cars and I was sitting in the back of another, wrapped in a blanket. Scared. Sirens blared as they drove away, Dad waving frantically, me wondering if I'd ever see him again.

I knew Mom was mad because she kept yelling—at the police station, in the car and in the living room. I wanted to yell back and ask her why every time Dad and I were together, she had to ruin it. Now I understood it wasn't the pajamas or the zoo that made her angry, it was all of it. Including a lot of things I never saw. But at the time, I thought if she stopped happiness every time it appeared, it would think it wasn't welcome. And in my five-year-old mind, that meant it wouldn't show up anymore.

"Showing up is ninety percent of your grade," Mr. Maxim said as I slipped into class. I was late because Mom had done the whole ambush-by-orange-juice thing. I hated it when she interrogated me over breakfast.

"Preferably showing up on time," he said, looking at me while I checked out his red gingham bow tie. "Labs start next week, so until then, ponder what we covered today. Velocity, which is a vector measurement of the rate and direction of motion, has exciting possibilities."

Mr. Maxim handed me the list of lab partners. I found my name and ran my finger directly across from it to find my probably better half: Finny Jackson. I had no idea who he was—who anyone was, really—but I hoped he was more into physics than the Urban Outfitters catalog, unlike my lab partner in San Francisco.

"There's nothing more rewarding than asking a complicated question and coming up with an elegant solution," Mr. Maxim said, tripping over a book and flying forward. As he caught himself on the file cabinet, I couldn't help but wonder: was there an elegant solution for him?

"See you tomorrow," he said as the bell rang. I grabbed my books and dashed out before Fab Physics Guy saw me. I spent the rest of the day dashing, hiding, ducking and avoiding. I knew I'd have to see him eventually, but it didn't have to be today. Which is why I kept my head down and combined walking with ducking. Dwalking.

"Hi."

I looked up and practically knocked Fab Physics Guys' Buddy Holly glasses off his face.

"It's Sophie, right? Sophie Sophia?"

I stepped back as people filed around us, heading for the real world.

"I have to go," I said. "I'm going to be late for class."

"The last bell just rang," he said, grinning. "School's out. But I don't want to keep you. I just wanted to say hi, since we're going to be lab partners. I'm Finny Jackson."

Look up the origin of anyone's name and you'll find something familiar. Whether they're born with it or grow into it, names oddly fit the people carrying them. Finny was probably short for Phineas, which means "oracle." Hopefully the oracle of physics. And my name is two versions of the same name stuck together, both of which mean "wisdom." Why I couldn't just skip high school and go straight to college was beyond me.

"Pleasure to meet you," I said, and then I curtsied. I had no idea why I did that.

"And you," he said, bowing. "Are you secretly British?"

"The most British thing about me is my love of Monty Python and The Smiths," I said.

"Me too," he said, pointing to his T-shirt. It was vintage, from *The Queen Is Dead* album. I had seen one like it in a store in San Francisco and wanted to buy it and sew a pocket over the word *queen*.

"Nice shirt," I said. And then, out of nowhere, I felt my friend-making mechanism kick in. "Are there any good parks around here? I'm dying for some scenery without lockers."

"I know just the place," he said. "And I wanted to give you this."

He reached in his jacket pocket and pulled out a whistle on a chain. Walt's whistle.

"Where did you find that?" I said, snatching it out of his hand.

"Near the football field where you dropped it," he said. "You know, the same place where you saw me, ran away, came back and ran away again? All in the span of, like, fifteen minutes?"

"I was probably just lost," I said, smiling, thrilled he hadn't seen anything more than some wacky girl behavior. "So how about that park?"

We walked forever until the houses gave way to thick, glorious trees, a little lake and a path that wound in between it.

"It's no Central Park, but it's pretty cool," Finny said. We'd been walking and talking long enough for me to know he had a love affair with New York. Just like I did.

"How can you like a place so much when you've never even been there?"

"It's the mystique of it," Finny said. "Broadway? Radio City Music Hall? Running into Ethan Hawke at a Starbucks? Truman Capote?"

"Capote was born in Louisiana," I said.

"Whatever. He hung out in Greenwich Village, and he was fabulous."

"He was," I said. "So was Andy Warhol."

"Oh, wow, did you know him?"

Two kids flew by on skateboards, followed by two jogging women with strollers.

"Um, hi," I said. "We're the same age."

"Did your parents know him? Maybe he ate at your kitchen table, and you don't even know it."

"Doubtful," I said. "My parents ran in different circles."

"Which circles were those?"

I remembered hanging out in Dad's office at NYU. Meeting Mom after work at Katz's Deli. Seeing a matinee of *The Lion King* on Broadway with Mom, and The Donnas at a small club in Brooklyn with Dad. Sitting on our stoop, looking at the stars. Listening to Mom and Dad fight through the window.

"They ran in the smarty-pants academic circles" I said. "Dad was a theoretical physics professor at NYU."

"Oh my God, oh my God, oh my God," Finny said, hyperventilating.

"Breathe," I said, patting him on the back. "Sit on the curb or something."

"Quantum," he said, panting. "String theory. It's my life."

"I know," I said, looking down at his white Converse, which were covered in equations written in Sharpie.

"Why didn't you tell me? Is your dad into M-theory? If your dad is involved in cutting-edge research—"

"He's not," I said, interrupting him. "He's not on the cutting edge of anything."

"Right," Finny said. "Top secret and all of that, I get it. You can't tell me. But if he's a big-time physics guy at NYU, why did he move to Havencrest?"

I felt my mouth get smaller and my heart along with it.

"He didn't," I said, hugging my knees to my chest.

I didn't remember the night Dad left four years ago, but I remembered when I realized he wasn't coming back. My upstairs neighbor gave me one of her Catholic charms—Our Lady of Sorrow—and I pressed that thing in my palm so hard it left a mark. I wasn't sure why the lady was sorry, but I knew why I was—my best friend was gone. I wrote Dad letters and even though I never heard from him, I still missed him. He used to make flowers out of paper and waltz around in wacky hats while sharing his newest theory about cupcakes and quantum. "Angelino, stop it," Mom would say. "You're scaring her." But I saw the ends of her mouth curl up when she said it, like she was trying not to laugh. Mom wanted me to stay grounded. But how could I when Dad was always lifting me up?

"Wow," Finny said. "That's rough." His glasses slid down his nose and he pushed them back up.

"It's not like he's dead or anything," I said, although I wasn't sure about that.

Finny opened his backpack and pulled out a pack of black licorice, my second-favorite candy next to chocolate. "Would this help?"

I nodded, grabbed it and shoved a piece in my mouth.

"I'm sorry about your dad," he said.

"And I'm sorry the world's not made of this stuff."

I grabbed another piece. As long as I was eating, I didn't have to explain.

"It doesn't compare, but my family's pretty weird, too," Finny said. "My mom is obsessed with pink carnations. They've pretty much invaded our house—the couch, rugs, plates, towels, everything. She even put carnation stickers in my shoes."

He took off a Converse and there, at the bottom, was a bright pink flower.

"No way," I said, laughing.

"Yeah, and she cooks the same things, over and over, until you want to die," he said. "Fish sticks on Monday, chicken enchiladas on Tuesday, meat loaf on Wednesday, tuna salad on Thursday, and Friday night is Taco Night."

I was laughing so hard I had to stop eating licorice. "What about the weekend?"

"Saturday is pizza or takeout, and Sunday is Leftover Night, where you make a sandwich out of whatever is left. Even if it's enchiladas," Finny said. "It's gross."

Not only did it sound disgusting, it sounded completely foreign to me. We never had a routine when I was growing up because Dad said predictability was the death of life. And whether we believed it or not, Mom and I kind of ran with that theory.

"I have to get home," I said, looking up. The sun was setting, leaving streaks of cotton candy against a darkening sky. "My mom's a worrier."

"So call her," he said. "That's what cell phones are for."

"Which would be awesome if I had one."

Finny tilted his head.

"Mom wants to give me one—it's not that," I said. "It's more of a Walden Pond thing. I don't want to be reachable twenty-four seven, you know? Sometimes it's nice to be alone."

What I didn't say was that while everyone else was obsessed with the communication of the future, I was still thinking about the past. Dad and I had had walkie-talkies, and we got along just fine.

"We'll work on that," Finny said. "Because texting is awesome. In the meantime, want to use mine?"

I took his phone but then realized I didn't even know my new phone number.

"Let's just get out of here," I said. "I have no idea where I am. Wanna walk me?"

Finny popped up and grabbed his bag. "Human map, at your service."

We reached my house about twenty minutes later and Finny stood on the porch, like he was waiting for something to happen. Was there a new friendship code that had developed in the two years since I'd had a friend? Was there supposed to be a wave? A high five? A handshake?

"Okay, bye," Finny said, leaning in and kissing me on one cheek and then, before I could object, the other. I just stood there, staring at him.

"That's how the Europeans do it," he said without an ounce of embarrassment. "Friends kiss hello, good-bye and all of the times in between. It's a lip-obsessed culture. Isn't that weird?"

"It would be weird if it happened again," I said, smiling.

"I know, right? But it was worth a shot," he said. "Don't worry, we'll find our ultimate greeting."

Sometimes, without warning, you find a member of your tribe. Someone who speaks your language instantly. Understands the way you see the world. And knows that high school can be a mean place, especially when you travel there alone. You have this instant connection like you've known them for a million years, even if it's only been a day.

"We're going to make great lab partners," Finny said. "And partners in crime. Do you like coffee?"

"Coffee and I have a long, sordid relationship," I said. "Know where I can get a decent cup?"

"Café Haven," Finny said. "We should go sometime."

"Yeah," I said. "We should."

He started to say something else, but I turned around, quickly, and gave a little wave. Not because I wanted to, but because I had to. The tears were coming too hard, too fast for me to cover them up. In spite of it all, in spite of everything, I might have made a friend.

SIX

Rock, rock, rock, rock, rock 'n' roll high school.
—The Ramones, "Rock 'n' Roll High School"

A week later I stood in front of my closet, yawning. Mom started calling it the Great Volcano because it was packed so tightly it was about to blow, but I thought it was perfect. What was life without a few thousand costume changes?

"It's stress," I said, leaning down and rubbing Balzac's ears. "That has to be what's making me see things."

He was my number-one confidante, pre-Walt. He was also the silent type, which meant I got to ask the questions *and* answer them.

"Do you think a spa weekend would solve anything?" I said, not really knowing what that meant but hoping it included seaweed wraps, green juice and a distinct lack of episodes. Balzac purred and wrapped his body around my left calf like the stress whisperer.

"Sophie! You need to leave in ten!"

Mom was *definitely* not helping my stress level, but maybe the perfect outfit would.

"Nature's calming, right?" I said, taking my tree skirt off the rack. Balzac batted it with his paw, a sign of feline approval.

The skirt was my favorite—gray wool, A-line style with a green tree pocket on the front and a brown trunk whose roots wrapped around the edges like trim. I threw on a black turtleneck, added a Clash *Combat Rock* T-shirt over it and ran a comb through my bangs, straight as Cleopatra's. Green-and-brown-striped kneesocks, my Army Navy jacket, a green knit beret, and I was ready—just in time to save Finny from the Nosiest Mom on the Planet.

"Sophie has a curfew, especially on school nights," I heard Mom say as I walked down the stairs. "Do *you* have a curfew?"

"Of course," Finny said. "There's nothing to do here at night anyway."

Except listen to music and watch movies, which was what we'd been doing the past week. As it turned out, school wasn't so bad when it came with Finny afternoons and evenings. Mom was so shocked that I had a new friend she hadn't even insisted that she meet him, mostly because she hadn't been around.

"And we're off!" I said, rushing in and grabbing Finny's arm.

"Not without breakfast you're not," she said, producing two Pop-Tarts on paper towels from behind her back.

"Moooom," I said. I wanted to crawl under the coffee table and die.

"What?" she said, flipping her hair, trying to charm my new friend. "Growing minds need nutrition."

"Fine," I said, grabbing the paper towels. "But we have to go."

"You know you two can hang out here anytime," she said. "I can't cook, but I make a mean frozen pizza."

"Basil," I said, dragging Finny away from the door. "She adds fresh basil. Bye, Mom!"

"Au revoir," she yelled, waving. "Come back soon!"

"Your mom is cool," Finny said.

"That's because she's not *your* mom," I said, kicking leaves as I walked, leaving a trail of red and gold in my wake.

We munched on Pop-Tarts (brown sugar: me, strawberry with sprinkles: him) and talked about the White Stripes' best album (*Elephant*: me, *Icky Thump*: him). When I mentioned Balzac, my talking cat, Finny choked, spraying sprinkles everywhere.

"It's not like he speaks English," I said. "He just meows on cue."

"Adorable," Finny said, wiping his mouth. "Kind of like your skirt."

"I sewed the pocket on myself," I said, twirling.

"No way," he said. "Who taught you to do that?"

Kim Gordon from Sonic Youth helped me sew a button once, but it wasn't like I could tell him that.

"My upstairs neighbor in New York," I said, which was partially true. Martha gave me sewing lessons, occupying the endless, lonely hours after school or when my parents fought. But within a few months, I found a ten-dollar Singer at the flea market and began modifying my clothes myself, headphones on. I started with extra fabric and buttons and eventually moved on to pockets.

"That's cool," he said. "But I think this might be even cooler."

Finny opened the door and ushered me into Café Haven like we were attending a ball. He wanted to go last week, but it had been closed for renovations, which were totally worth it. A bright red counter stretched across the front, barstools gleaming underneath; ceilings reached for the sky, spotted with twinkling lights and chandeliers; blue vinyl booths lined the middle, filled with people; and there, in the back, was a sitting room, elegant Victorian stuffed couches and curvy-legged coffee tables between them. I wasn't sure which part was considered the haven—or if one room was a haven from the other—but I loved how it went from diner to coffee shop and back again.

"It's amazing," I said, looking up at the lights. And then, as I brought my eyes down, they got stuck on a cute guy in a sparkly blue booth. He held a mug of coffee in one hand, *On the Road* by Jack Kerouac in the other and was dressed like he'd just stepped out of the book: white T-shirt, skinny leg jeans and ankle boots.

Finny nudged my arm.

"Looks like coffee isn't all you want this morning."

"Very funny," I said, grabbing my vanilla latte off the bar. "I was just checking the place out."

"The place or the patron?" Finny might be a scientist-in-training, but he was also romantic—just not toward me or anyone else of my gender, I suspected. And I was more than fine with that.

"I'll be outside," I said, "warming up with Love and Rockets."

I put my earbuds in and stood by the door, bopping my head to "All in My Mind" while I waited. I looked inside, hoping to see Finny, but I saw Literary Loner instead. And before I had a chance to look away, he saw me. And smiled.

"Ooooh!" Finny joined me on the sidewalk. "He loves you."

"More like he busted me," I said, but I smiled back.

And then I hurried off, Finny in tow, racing away from one embarrassing situation and—if my history was any indication—probably into another one.

Since I'd met Finny, I'd discovered having a best friend was like having a boyfriend without all the drama. It was great until I realized it wasn't entirely true. Finny had plenty of drama, it just wasn't about people. It was about physics.

"Isn't it amazing that my view of time and space could be different than someone else's view of time and space?" Finny asked, his voice bubbling like carbonation.

We'd just come from a class lecture on special relativity and Finny was freaking out about it.

"What Mr. Maxim was saying was that space and time are relative to velocity. Which means you can't say that time is something different than space."

"Your point would be?" I said, trading my physics textbook for global studies, which was just as heavy.

"Relativity is applicable to real life," he said, almost squealing.

"At this moment, someone is especially relative to you. And he's right over there."

He pointed, I turned, and there was Literary Loner, sans the coffee, standing ten lockers away. Smiling at me.

"Omigod, that makes three," Finny said. He was more clued in to my budding social life than I was. "Three smiles, Sophie. That means he's going to ask you out."

"Crap!" I said, turning around as quickly as I could. "What do I do now?"

"I'd run like crazy, but I'd like to think you're more skilled at this," Finny said.

"Well, I'm not. My class is that way," I said, pointing in Loner's direction. "But I'm going this way."

I turned and walked away from him, not sure how I was going to get to history, but at least I'd avoided Confrontation with a Crush.

"Come on, Sophie," Finny called after me. "You're a city girl! Be brave enough for the both of us!"

Thanks to a recent recurring panda, I wasn't strong enough to carry anyone but myself.

"I'll see you in the cafeteria," I said, dreading it. "That's bravery for you."

As a rule, I avoided the cafeteria. Most new kids did. But since Finny was the first real friend I'd made since New York, and since he'd told me he loved Pizza Fridays more than anything, I was going to make a concession. That's what you did for members of your tribe. Even if it was only a tribe of three. And even if one of those three was technically a cat.

"Cheese or pepperoni?"

A cafeteria lady with a crooked hairnet waved a spatula at me. I'd been waiting for Finny for ten minutes but finally got in line. And now, instead of arguing about realities, I was being accosted by a common kitchen utensil.

"Pick one or move on," the cafeteria lady said, tapping her spatula on the metal pizza tray.

"Cheese," I said. I could have gotten one for Finny, but he wasn't there. And people who ditched didn't get rewarded.

"You're lucky—that's the last one," she said, handing me cardboard covered in tomato sauce.

"Oh, man," said the guy behind me. "They're out of cheese!"

He said it like his life was ruined, even though he was on the football team and had tables of people waiting to sit with him. Without Finny, I had no one, only the emptiness that came with leaving the line and having nowhere to go. The best I could hope for was that the floor would open up and swallow me whole.

"Walk much?" Heather, the head cheerleader, said as I bumped into her, spilling soda all over my tray.

"More like get dressed much," Stacey said, pointing at my tree skirt.

Stacey was second in command. She was also only half as funny, which was probably part of Heather's plan. She knew what all evil leaders knew: the best way to stay on top was to surround yourself with those closer to the bottom.

"It's pathetic," Heather said, laughing, brunette ponytail bobbing as they both walked away.

"Environmental is in," I wanted to say, but I just stood there, arms trembling, mouth closed. Saving all my witty comebacks for later when they wouldn't help me at all. And since Finny wasn't coming, there was no reason for me to stay. I headed for the door, which is when I heard it.

Clang.

Metal on metal.

The pizza lady banged her spatula on the metal tray not once, but twice. Three times. Ten times—in a rhythm I knew all too well. Soon all the lunch ladies joined in with spoons and spatulas, beating on cookie sheets and countertops. When a woman popped out of the trash can strumming a saucepan as a guitar, I knew I was in trouble.

"*Well, I don't like pepperoni—cheese, cheese, we're out of cheese pizza,*" she sang. "'*Cause that's not what I want to eat—cheese, cheese, we're out of cheese pizza,*" she continued as the hairnet band kept the beat.

"*I just wanna have my pick, eat some lunch, just a little bit, cheese, cheese, cheese, cheese, we're outta cheese pizza . . .*"

I tried to control myself, but it was hard to stand still while the lunch ladies covered "Rock 'n' Roll High School" by the Ramones. So I didn't. None of us did.

Math nerds hopped on tables and played air guitar, sending their iPhones flying; cheerleaders swung their collective ponytails in circles, littering the linoleum with scrunchies; drama kids mimed the lyrics, showing shock and awe with the "out of cheese pizza" line. When the football players formed a circle and ran around slamming into each other like punks, I danced just outside of them. It felt good to be a part of something, even if it was only a mosh pit.

"*Bum, bummer, outta cheese pizza.*"

"*Too bad, we're not gonna eat ya.*"

"*Guess I gotta have a burri-taa . . .*"

The guitar wailed. The drums pounded. And as the chorus built, I knew I had nothing to lose.

"*Cheese, cheese, cheese, cheese, we're outta cheese pizza,*" the woman sang as I ran up onstage in front of my fellow moshers, gave the rock-and-roll symbol and dove, headfirst, into the welcoming arms of my new friends.

Time slowed, skipped and jumped as my body flew through space, arms outstretched like a superhero. The sound of the Ramones faded, and the deafening clatter of the cafeteria appeared instead—dishes clanging, girls squealing and one voice, in particular. It belonged to Heather.

"Holy crap, you broke my arm!" I heard her say as I slid down the brown laminate table until I was stopped by a bowl of cottage cheese and peaches. *Her* cottage cheese and peaches.

"Get off of her!" Stacey said, rushing in and pushing me to the side. "Heather, are you okay?"

She was, but I wasn't. Somehow, I'd managed to land directly in the middle of the table, ruining my skirt (dipped in French dressing), my shirt (flung in tomato sauce) and, of course, my face (covered in cottage cheese). Luckily, no cheerleaders were harmed in the making of this episode.

"Maybe it's just sprained," Heather said, cradling her arm.

"Nobody worry about me, I'm fine," I said, hopping off the

table. I had a massive stomachache and my skirt was turned around backward, so on top of everything else, I had a tree on my butt.

"Were you trying to commit suicide?" Stacey looked at me, big eyes blinking.

"Social suicide, maybe," Heather said.

At least her mind was intact.

I smoothed down my hair, which felt like it had gone through a wind tunnel, wiped my face with a napkin and looked around the cafeteria. It was obvious I was the only one who had witnessed my stage dive. The rest of them only saw the new girl, crazy as they came, doing a belly flop into the cheerleaders' table.

"Ms. Sophia? Would you come with me?"

Ms. Shipley, the school nurse, extended her hand. I didn't take it, but I followed her out of there, away from the scene of another episode and, after a quick checkup, on to the scene of another one: the principal's office. It was like San Francisco all over again. I didn't have much on my side, but I did have a little something I'd created last time I went to a principal's office: my list.

SEVEN

How to Survive a Visit to the Principal's Office
by Sophie Sophia

---

1. Compliment her on her hair.
2. Use innocence to your advantage and act like you've never been in trouble before.
3. Leave the snarkiness at home. (Or at least in your locker.)
4. Nod a lot and respond emotionally. Adults love to feel like they're "reaching" us.
5. If you have to, lie for the greater good and let karma sort it out.

"May I help you?"

I plopped down in a drab olive-green chair outside the principal's office. It was the international color of high school, which seemed weird. Weren't most of us depressed enough already?

"I'm Sophie Sophia, here to see Principal Pattison."

"You're her!" the secretary said, scooting her chair back. She was wearing enough colors for both of us, with her rainbow earrings and scarf. It was tie-dyed like the bag on the floor next to her. "Do you need some water or something?"

"I'm good," I said, feeling the small spatula in my pocket. I wondered if I had time to hide my souvenir before anyone saw it and accused me of stealing, too.

She leaned toward the phone and pressed a button. "Principal Pattison, I have Sophie Sophia for you."

"Who?" a loud voice blasted through the intercom.

She looked at me, leaned in and whispered like she was talking about a terminal illness.

"It's that girl," she said, "from the cafeteria."

"Then speak up!" the voice boomed. "And send her in."

The door opened and Literary Loner stepped out of the office as I walked toward it. We were so close I could smell his hair as he passed. It smelled like oranges.

"Hi," I managed to croak.

"Hi," he said, giving me the same smile as before. This now qualified as the best day ever, even if I got suspended.

The secretary pushed him toward the exit. "That's enough

out of you, Romeo," she said as she pushed me toward the door. "Go on in, Juliet."

"Well, if it isn't our very own Greg Louganis," Principal Pattison said, peering at me from behind a massive walnut desk. I sat down across from her and in front of a small brass monkey who was perched on the corner, laughing.

"Who's Greg Louganis?" I said.

"A famous diver," she said, opening my file. "Just like you are, I hear."

"That was an accident," I said.

"Let's start from the beginning." She cleared her throat and sat up taller, even though she was probably a foot taller than me already. "Your scholastic history is impressive, but your behavioral record leaves much to be desired."

She had no idea.

"For now, let's leave the past in the past and focus on the present. The why behind the what."

"The what?" I said.

"We know the what," she said. "I'm interested in the why."

And I wished I knew what the heck she was talking about.

"Sophie, why did you dive into a table?"

When she said it like that, it *did* sound like I had a death wish.

"It wasn't premeditated, if that's what you're thinking," I said. "I didn't know what I was doing."

"Really," she said, smiling. Her mouth kept moving, but I was distracted by the painting hanging behind her. It was a portrait of a horse with huge teeth, kind of like hers. I couldn't stop staring. I knew people's art said a lot about them, but I had no idea what this said about Principal Pattison.

"Sophie?" She snapped her fingers. "Are you with me?"

"I like your hair," I blurted.

"Thank you," she said, fluffing her short puffy bob. "I was trying something new."

She cleared her throat.

"Back to you, though. Are you really going to plead insanity here?"

I'd been trying not to plead insanity to myself for years, but it was always out there, lurking. Like if I saw too many things or messed up too many times, it would claim me, the way cancer claimed other people. Dad might have been a combination of genius and insanity—the jury was still out—but I wasn't him. And I was trying, desperately, to keep it that way.

"Not at all," I said. I leaned forward, put my arms on the desk and practically whispered. "Can I tell you a secret?"

"Of course," she said, leaning forward. "This room is nothing if not confidential."

I paused. I had no idea what I was going to say, so I looked to the carpet for inspiration, but it was just brown with blue flecks. Boring. And then I had it.

"I sleepwalk," I whispered.

Principal Pattison sighed, came from behind her desk and sat in the chair next to me. I thought she was going to take my hands in hers, but luckily it didn't go that far.

"Sophie, are you bored?"

I was in high school. Of course I was bored.

"I see this all the time with smart kids. You're not challenged enough, so you act out in odd ways," she said. "Maybe if you took a few more Advanced Placement classes. Or maybe you could play in the band! I hear the oboe is challenging."

My hourly existence was a challenge.

"I'm not lying," I said. And then, because I stayed up one night researching sleep disorders when I couldn't sleep, I laid it on her. Authority armed with Wikipedia.

"I'm a sleepwalker. Most people think it only happens at night, but it happens during the day, too. That's the kind I have. So I didn't intend to stage dive into someone's table. And I didn't even know I'd done it until I landed, which, of course, woke me up."

She leaned back in her chair. "Why isn't this in your file?"

I knew I had moments to convince her or risk expulsion.

"Have you ever been the new kid at school?"

"Many times," she said. "My father was in the navy."

"Then you know how hard it is to make friends," I said. "There is no way I would dive into the most popular girls' table on purpose. Not only is it weird, it would also ruin any chance I'd have of making friends."

"It's true," she said. "New kids are *desperate* to fit in."

"So when I told you I was sleepwalking, I meant it."

She wrung her hands like they had the answer, as if squeezing them would make it pop out.

"I'll have to confirm it with your doctor," she said.

"Of course," I said.

She got up and walked back behind her desk, sitting down.

"And your mother."

"To be expected," I said. That was why I'd given them a fake cell phone number when I enrolled. And then she leaned forward like she was going to tell me a secret, too. Like a slumber party in the middle of the day.

"Does this happen a lot? This sleepwalking thing?" she said.

"Not anymore," I said, making a note to thank my brain later. "I have medicine for it, I just forgot to take it this morning."

"Oh!" she said, her voice brightening. "Okay, then. That's an easy fix. You know how I remember to take my pills?"

This was going to be good.

"How?"

"I make my secretary remind me," she said, laughing, and then she pressed the intercom button and yelled, "Millie! Water!"

Seconds later, the door opened. Millie rushed in while I walked out.

"Sophie, wait," she said, taking a few pills from an orange bottle and popping them into her mouth. "I can't have you walking around unmedicated. Go home. You can bring the necessary paperwork when you return on Monday."

"Thanks," I said. "I'm sorry for any problems I might have caused."

"You smart kids are a hoot!" she said. "So polite, even when you're in trouble. Now, go home and read *War and Peace* or something."

I loved how Tolstoy was the go-to reference for nerd. But I hated that I couldn't get that painting out of my mind, which meant there was a reason for it. Maybe Principal Pattison had a portrait of a horse on her wall for the same reason I wore the tree skirt. It was calming because plants and animals were just that—not human. And even though we could be pretty great, it was nice to take a break from people, once in a while.

"Sophie, wait up!"

Finny ran toward me, his black courier bag lagging behind, hitting him in the butt.

"I'm late," I said, opening my locker and filling my backpack with books.

"I wanted to apologize," he said, panting. His face was red as the pepperoni he'd missed at lunch. "I never meant to stand you up."

"It was fine," I said. "No big deal."

"That's not what I heard," he said. "Are you okay?"

I wanted to tell him. In reality, he'd probably think it was cool and want to study me, like an experiment. But I couldn't risk losing him. Not yet.

"Never been better," I said. "Knowing Heather, the story that's going around is way worse than what actually happened."

"So what *did* happen?"

I couldn't lie. Not one more time, and not to Finny. So I did the next best thing.

"We'll talk later," I said, slamming my locker. "I have to go."

"Then I'll go with you," he said, walking beside me. "Look, I got caught up in this chemistry experiment and totally lost track of time."

"Can we just forget about it?"

"Nope," he said. "But maybe this will make up for my extreme ineptitude. Close your eyes and open your hand."

I felt something small and circular pressing into my palm. I opened my eyes and saw The Smiths *Meat Is Murder* button.

"Finny!" I said. "This one's your favorite."

"You're my favorite," he said. "There's more. Look under it."

Underneath the button was a piece of paper the size of a fortune. It had numbers written on it. Lucky numbers separated by dashes.

"I gave Kerouac your phone number, too. His name is Drew. Whoever calls who is up to you guys," Finny said, grinning.

"I should be so mad at you right now," I said. My shoulders relaxed. Heart lifted.

"Yes, but isn't it more fun to be excited?"

I don't know how he knew, but he did. Nothing cures the aftermath of an episode like a crush.

I slammed the front door, and Balzac came running.

"Sophie? Is that you?"

Mom was home. Early. And since it wasn't a holiday and she couldn't have gotten fired yet, that meant one thing. The school realized the cell number was a fake, did a little digging and called her at work.

"Hey," I said, walking into the kitchen like nothing was wrong.

She was standing over the stove stirring the contents of a pot with a wooden spoon. It smelled like onions.

"Surprise!" she said. "I took the afternoon off. I thought it was time we had a home-cooked meal like the rest of Middle America."

"Strange, but acceptable," I said, relieved. "Is that spaghetti?"

"Sauce for the meat loaf," Mom said.

"Better meat loaf than pot roast," I said.

Mom turned her back to me and hummed. Pot roast was a reminder of one of the bad nights, one of the nights Dad went crazy, and we didn't talk about those. That night, Mom had just made my favorite meal—pot roast with baby carrots and potatoes—when Dad showed up, threw it all on the floor and announced that we were going out for Indian food instead.

"Grab your coats!" he said while I stood next to Mom, tears in my eyes, wishing I could trade a thousand nights of naan for just one of those potatoes. Dad opened the door and put on a top hat.

"Let's go, ladies! Adventure in the city awaits!" he said.

I held Mom's hand tighter, a silent plea to let me stay. She stood firm.

"Thanks but no thanks, Angel," she said. "Sophie and I feel like staying in."

Dad looked confused, but then dashed out like a superhero, oblivious to the pool of tears and perfectly good pot roast he'd left behind.

"Nothing a little extra spice can't fix," Mom said, and picked up our dinner off the floor. She rinsed what she could, added things from glass shakers and threw it back in the oven.

"This is not how you'll cook when you're older," she said, "but I'll be damned if I'm going to waste a good dinner. I spent three hours in here."

She rarely cooked, and I knew it, so I didn't mind if the stuff she said was pepper was actually dirt. It tasted good, even without Dad. Even though that was the first night of many where there were two at the table instead of three.

"Can you set the table?" Mom said.

"Sure." I grabbed the napkins and headed for the coffee table.

"How was school?" she called from the kitchen.

"Educational," I said. I folded the napkins in little paper squares like at a restaurant.

"That's not what your principal said."

And there it was. She *never* took an afternoon off. Especially not to cook.

"What did she say?" I asked. "Did she mention that I'm a scintillating conversationalist?"

"Not exactly." Mom walked into the living room and wiped her hands on her apron, staining her front with red sauce. "The other night, you told me you weren't seeing things."

"I'm not," I said. "Just sometimes."

"Okay," she said. "We'll deal with that later. Just tell me what happened today."

"The cafeteria ladies covered a Ramones song."

"And?" She tapped her bare foot on the carpet.

"Everyone danced like a music video, and I got excited and dove into a table and some girl's cottage cheese," I said. "It was no big deal."

"You almost got suspended," she said. "It was a very big deal."

I didn't know I'd almost been suspended. I didn't know what the night would hold, much less next week, because I didn't trust myself. Or Mom. I'd seen it before. She was the spa weekend, the tree skirt, the calm. Which was always followed by the storm.

"Meat loaf!" Mom said as the timer dinged.

Meat loaf, I thought, wishing that normal food could help me live a normal life.

I cleared the plates, and Mom said something she'd never said before.

"I think you're grounded."

I grinned. Discipline wasn't her forte. She was better than Dad, but after he left, she wasn't mean to me because she thought I'd met the meanness quotient for a lifetime.

"You *think* I'm grounded, or I'm actually grounded?" I said.

"Very funny," she said as I took our dishes to the kitchen. The cell phone she'd given me the week earlier buzzed in my pocket.

"Sophie? We're not finished here," Mom said, her voice booming from the other room.

"Just a sec," I said, looking at the screen. I'd never been happier to have a phone—or a text—in my life.

DREW: Café Haven? Monday?

Wow. Not even a hello? Just straight to asking me out? Maybe he wasn't into texting, which was fine. I wasn't either. So we'd keep it short and sweet. That was probably a good thing, considering I was an inadequate texter.

"Sophie?" Mom called again.

"Almost finished," I said, turning on the faucet. I let the water run while I composed my masterpiece.

SOPHIE: Sure. After school?

DREW: Unless you're feeling delinquent.

Oh, I'd feel whatever he wanted me to feel.

SOPHIE: Always. But I'll be good.

DREW: Okay, see you then.

SOPHIE: See you then!

I regretted the exclamation point as soon as I typed it, but it was true. A thousand exclamation points couldn't even begin to express how excited I was.

"Nice job on the dishes," Mom said, appearing in the doorway.

I turned off the faucet.

"You are definitely grounded," she said. "Phone, please."

"Mom! You just gave it to me. Plus it's the weekend. I have plans."

"Not anymore," she said. "I need to keep tabs on you until we figure this thing out."

As if "this thing" was something to be figured out, especially by someone who thought the only problem I had was an overactive imagination. At least, that's what Mom told herself and, by association, me.

"But this is my first offense," I said, handing her the phone. "Don't I at least get a warning?"

"What about me?" Mom said. "Where's my warning? I never know what's going on with you, and you won't tell me, so I have to hear it from your principal. From now on, I want the truth. And I want to hear it from you."

Mom thought she wanted the truth, but she didn't. No one did, because once it was out there, you couldn't take it back. I wanted nothing more than to tell her that, without warning, I played poker with a panda marching band. I saw the lunch ladies cover the Ramones. And I had a shaman panda who thought that all of this meant something, that I was on a path. I wanted to tell her how hard it was to have a reality you couldn't count on, especially in another new town. But more than that, I wanted to make her promise not to leave like Dad did. I wanted her to tell me I'd never be alone.

"That thing in the cafeteria wasn't my fault," I said.

"Oh, no?" she said, shaking her head. "That's what your father used to say. You can do better than that."

Balzac meowed and hopped in my lap.

"What if I don't want to?" I said, stroking his fur.

"Then you'll sit in your room and think about it until you do," she said.

"Fine," I said, hopping up, sending Balzac flying.

"No going out, no phone, no Internet until I say so."

"How am I supposed to do my homework?" I said, already missing the chats I was planning with Finny in my mind. I couldn't wait to tell him about Drew.

"Use that old typewriter you love so much."

"This is so unfair," I said. Especially now that I had a boy who liked me, a potential date and gossip to convey. This was the first time in my life I'd actually needed technology, which meant her penalty was even more punishing than she realized. I was hoping she'd cave in, but instead she used the same line as every other parent in America.

"Life is unfair," she said. "Go to your room."

I marched upstairs, slammed my door and played Bauhaus at full volume. In seconds, my room filled with the droning sound of bass, Peter Murphy and the energy of my own anger. So instead of fighting it, I gave in to it, taking off my shoes, flopping on my bed and bemoaning my fate. Just like a normal teenager.

EIGHT

"Can I come in?"

Mom knocked on my door and then opened it.

"You're already in," I said, yawning. At some point, I had fallen asleep, record sleeves and books all around me.

"In bed already?"

"Incarceration is exhausting," I said, popping my arms out of the covers. "What did you bring me?"

"Chocolate chocolate chip or toffee swirl?" she said, taking ice cream out of a bag. Anytime she punished me, which wasn't often, she always showed up a few hours later with ice cream. Two pints, one conscience, cleared.

"Chocolate," I said. "I think I'm supposed to be giving you the silent treatment, though."

"And you will," she said, handing me a pint. "It's hard to talk with ice cream in your mouth. Scoot over."

Mom climbed into bed with me like she had for the first few weeks after Dad left. I'm sure it was supposed to be the other way around—me coming to her—but she always beat me to it, curling up behind me. Jeans brushing pajama legs. Her sobs never as soft as she thought they were.

"You told the principal you were a sleepwalker?"

We sat side by side, legs out, backs propped on pillows.

"It seemed brilliant at the time," I said. "I didn't think about having to get a doctor's note. Or the fact they would eventually figure out your work number."

Mom scooted closer so that her leg touched mine.

"Quite the elaborate plan," she said. "You must really like it here."

"I do," I said. And then I looked at her, really looked at her, for the first time all night. "Don't you?"

She licked ice cream off her spoon. "I like that you have a friend."

"So we'll figure it out?"

"For now," she said, her words like storm clouds, gathering. "There's one condition, though," she said. "Lie for your safety, if you have to, but don't lie to me."

She had no idea those were one and the same. One mention of my shaman panda and the car would have been packed by morning, the three of us hundreds of miles away by noon.

"Okay," I said. "But I have a condition, too. I need you to tell me what was wrong with Dad."

"Nothing was wrong," she said. "He had an overactive imagination, just like you do. The facts haven't changed."

"But I've changed," I said. "I'm older. Maybe I'll hear things differently."

"Not tonight," Mom said. "I can't take any more pain right now."

Neither could I, I thought. Pain was having a crush that would never happen. Pain was being broken and not knowing how to fix it.

"So tell me something else," I said. And even though I knew the story, I asked for it, anyway. "Tell me how you and Dad met."

Mom put the lid on her ice cream and set it, along with the spoon, on my nightstand. I was eating mine slowly, letting the chocolate chips melt on my tongue before spooning more in.

"We met at NYU," Mom said. She was using her dreamy voice. "Your dad was studying physics, I was studying modern dance, and he showed up at my class every day for a month, trying to join the troupe. Just to be close to me."

"But he didn't dance," I said, which I knew. He had like a hundred left feet.

"But he kept showing up," Mom said. "After a while, the teacher was so enamored with him, she made him an understudy. He never performed, not once, but he didn't care."

"Because you were there," I said, thinking about Drew. Wondering if he'd text before Monday, even if I couldn't read it.

"Yes, but I ignored him," Mom said. "The difference was,

your father never gave up. And after a few months of strawberry-ginseng-banana smoothies, I fell in love."

"That smoothie sounds like the *opposite* of love to me."

"It was the eighties," Mom said, laughing. "We all drank that stuff. Besides, things like that don't matter when you're in love. You'll see."

I wondered if I was going to be seeing anytime soon. I handed her my ice cream and sank deeper into the bed, pulling the covers up to my chin.

"Most of the time I hate him," I said, thinking about Dad. But I couldn't help thinking about other things, like Sunday mornings and the crossword puzzle, the way I hung on to their banter like air, words flying back and forth, kisses in between. I ate cereal until I popped, just so I could stay in the room with them.

"But sometimes you miss him." Mom smoothed the hair off my face. "That's okay," she said, voice shaking. "Sometimes I miss him, too."

She leaned in, kissed my forehead, and a tear dropped onto my face. I told myself it wasn't my fault she was sad, that she got there on her own, but I knew it wasn't true. Dad put both of us there, whether he meant to or not.

NINE

My family never did the church thing, but Dad said saints were an exception. He had this massive book about them, and I devoured it, repeating names over and over like the lyrics to a good song while sitting in his green leather chair, feet dangling. Saint Francis of Assisi, bird preacher. Saint Lydwina, protector of ice skaters. And my favorite, Saint Christina the Astonishing, patron saint of mental illness. She proved you could be flashy and holy at the same time. She also hated being around people because she could smell sin on them. So instead of wearing perfume, she climbed buildings and trees. Hid in cabinets and cupboards. And when there was nowhere else to go, she levitated.

I used to want a saint who would bring me an endless supply of striped socks, but lately I'd been thinking about Christina. I found her card stuck in one of my books this morning and put it in my pocket. Christina probably couldn't stop my episodes completely, but maybe she could at least teach me how to levitate out of them. It was number one on my list.

How to Survive Going Back to School
After an Episode by Sophie Sophia

---

1. Levitate out of any uncomfortable situation.
2. Since you can't actually levitate, ignore people.
3. Tell them you weren't sent home early,
      you went to Paris.
4. Why Paris? Why *not* Paris?
5. Redirect attention to your outfit. Wasn't it
      inventive?
6. Repeat the following: I am more than my episodes.
      (It's true.)

Mom barged into the bathroom as I was getting ready. Normally I would have demanded my private time, but after a weekend spent in communication lockdown, I was happy to see her.

"Pardon *moi*, I'm working on my visage," I said in my best French accent, a mix of Peter Sellers and Pepé Le Pew.

"That's right, you have French this morning," Mom said.

I wasn't even taking French, but my face was covered in an oatmeal-citrus mask, so I couldn't exactly correct her.

"Did you know that your great-grandfather was from Lyon? You practically have French in your blood."

I laughed and cracked my mask. "That's gross," I said. "It's like ooh! Get them out! The French are in my blood, invading me with their poodles and café au laits!"

Mom sighed and grabbed my brush off the counter. She moved behind me and ran it through my hair. It was one of the few rituals we still kept, so I let her do it.

"You must be a hit at school," she said.

"Not yet," I said. "I try to lay low the first semester. And then—when they least expect it—my wit and I attack."

I saw one of her eyebrows raise in the mirror.

"That's no way to make friends, Soph," she said. "And you might want more than one."

I scowled and my mask crumbled and fell into the sink.

"For your information, I have two friends," I said.

"Really?" Mom took the brush away from my hair and then looked at me like she'd just discovered a new species.

"Aha," she said. "What's his name?"

"How do you know it's not a girl?"

"Please," she said, brushing her own hair. "Look at what you're wearing."

The theme was wisdom, and I had on my red, orange and blue owl pocket skirt, a pair of plaid tights and little owl earrings. Adorable? Check. All I had to do now was talk about love and Mom would let me go anywhere.

"His name is Drew," I said. "And I know I'm grounded, but he asked me to study with him after school." I wanted to be prepared with an irresistible outfit and freedom. "Can we make an exception?"

She sighed and looked at me in the mirror.

"Mom, please?" I said. "He wears vintage clothes like I do, his hair smells like oranges, and he's practically a Kerouac scholar . . . plus he's perfect and cute and seems to genuinely like me."

I took a breath in, puffed up my cheeks and held it until she answered. It was one of my favorite tactics. Sometimes I turned bluish and had to let the air out before she responded, but most of the time it worked. Like curing hiccups, only I was trying to cure my social life.

"Okay," Mom said. "But just for an hour."

I let my breath out and then inhaled deeply, the oxygen of victory.

"If something happens, you call me," she said, handing me back my phone. "Promise?"

"I promise," I said, but I wouldn't need to call. I had a good feeling about it, like that part in the movies when the heroine is dressed up and looks amazing and her date is on time. There are no awkward silences or, in my case, hallucinations, and everyone lives happily ever after. For a moment, I actually believed I could be that girl.

I made it through a weekend of grounding, which meant no Finny, which also meant he accosted me as soon as I sat down next to him in physics.

"Did he call? Did he call?"

"He texted," I said. "Friday night."

"Eeeeh!!!!" Finny said. "Did he ask you out?"

"Of course," I said. "We're meeting this afternoon."

"So you're not grounded anymore?"

"Oh, I am," I said. "But Mom gave me an hour pass. I think she's sick of seeing me."

"This is so exciting," he said, waving his hand in front of his face like he was fanning himself. "You know this makes me Cupid, right?"

"Calm down, Cupid," I said. "He might not even like me once he gets to know me."

"Oh, he'll like you. But whichever way it goes, you have to call me when you get home. I want to hear *everything*!" Finny said, forgetting to use his inside voice.

"I want to hear everything, too," Mr. Maxim said. "Everything sounds right up my alley. Would you care to elaborate?"

Red crept up Finny's neck, threatening to take over his face.

"We were talking about parallel universes," I said. It was the first thing that came to mind, since it was actually *on* my mind.

"In relation to string theory, of course," Finny said, glancing at me.

"Someone read ahead," Mr. Maxim said, straightening his tie. He'd gone from bow ties to polka-dotted real ties, which I didn't think was an improvement.

"It's only a theory, of course," he said, going to the board and writing as he spoke. "But string theory posits that there are ten dimensions of space and one dimension of time, even though we can't see them all."

"That's because they're curled up inside of themselves," Finny said, practically jumping out of his chair. I loved it when he got into a physics frenzy.

"Precisely," Mr. Maxim said. "And some scientists speculate that this theory also makes the idea of parallel universes possible. There's no way to prove this yet; that's why they're theories. But Einstein was all about theories, and look how well that worked for him!"

He laughed, and Finny followed. They might as well have just had a class for themselves.

"Come on, people, how exciting is the idea of parallel universes?" Mr. Maxim said. "Like a universe that's just like here, except everything is half the size. Or monkeys walk around with jobs and houses, just like people."

"That's not exciting, that's disgusting," the hair-spray girl said. "Monkeys are gross."

"It doesn't have to be monkeys—it can be anything," Mr. Maxim said. "Caterpillars or cats. Porcupines or pandas. Like a panda-verse."

My bag fell out of my hands and crashed to the floor.

"We'll cover this later in the semester. But since we can't see the extra dimensions or prove that parallel universes exist, the floor is still wide open for discussion."

Mr. Maxim walked over and looked out the window. "Anything is possible, people. Just use your imagination."

I walked in the bathroom, and Walt was sitting on the counter, swinging his legs.

"Hello, gorgeous."

"Hi!" I said, giving him a hug. I was so excited to see him I didn't even check under the stalls like I usually did, but the room was empty anyway.

"You're an enthusiastic little elf. What gives?"

"I'm happy," I said, reapplying my lip gloss. "Plus, we were just talking about you."

"You and Finny?"

"No, Mr. Maxim in physics class."

"If I'd known I was making an appearance, I would have called my stylist," Walt said, smoothing the fur above his eyes with his paw.

"Not you, specifically," I said, smacking my lips together. "He was talking about parallel universes. Specifically, a potential panda universe. He called it a panda-verse."

"Cute," Walt said. "Did he say where it was? I'd love to visit."

"I think you're from there," I said.

Walt laughed and turned his back toward the mirrors.

"Well played," he said. "You're pretty crafty for a girl who wears lip gloss."

I poked his arm. "You're going to have to tell me about it sometime. Along with why you're here and what it has to do with me. Or maybe, since I'm so crafty, I'll just find out myself," I said.

Walt grinned. "That's kind of what the whole path thing is all about."

"Hey, if the path includes extra dimensions, parallel universes and infinite possibilities, I'm in."

"You might want to think about bringing someone with you," Walt said. "What about Finny?"

"I can't tell him yet," I said. "He likes me the way he thinks I am."

"He also likes physics," he said. "He could help you."

"Help me figure out that my episodes are more than episodes? I already knew that," I said. "Especially after you showed up."

"You know what they're not, but you don't know what they are. Don't you want to find out?"

I did. More than anything.

"Is it synchronicity that your first friend is into physics, just like your dad? Or is it something bigger?"

"I hadn't thought about it," I said.

"So think about it," Walt said. "Tell him about the Ramones. Tell him about me."

"No way," I said.

"Why not?" Walt said. "What do you have to lose?"

"My best friend, possibly."

As soon as I said it out loud, though, I changed my mind. That was what having a best friend was all about—being honest and sharing everything, even the bad things. So if we were really friends, or if I wanted us to be, there was only one thing to do.

"You're right," I said. "We're Sophie and Finny. I'll tell him."

"Bravo!" Walt said, raising his arms and cheering. "I raised you well."

As I watched him do his victory dance, I wished I could do more than tell Finny. I wished I could show him.

"First things first, though," I said, dancing with him. "I have to get through my date."

"What's to get through?" he said. "You're adorable. You have nothing to be nervous about."

"Nothing?" I said, stopping and staring at him.

"I'm not going to ruin your little rendezvous, if that's what you mean," he said, standing still. "Contrary to popular opinion, I actually want you to be happy."

"What about my episodical tendencies?"

"I can't predict or control those," he said.

"But you can give advice," I said. "And I don't mean telling me to be myself."

"Deep breaths," he said. "Try to ground yourself in the moment. But more than that? Have fun. I'll give you a head start."

Walt started at one end of the bathroom and did high kicks to the other end, making me smile. He ended with a spin and bumped into one of the hand dryers, turning it on.

"Whoa!" he said. And then he bent down, put his mouth under it and spoke.

"Whoooooaaa," he shouted, his voice vibrating off the tile. "Do you ever do this?"

"Not since I was little," I said.

"It's ridiculous!" he said, taking a breath. "You have to join me!"

It reminded me of Dad, the way he always asked me to join him. The way he believed there was so much more to our reality than what we could see. I bent down beside Walt and held his hand like a pact. And then I put my arm around his middle and leaned in as he pushed the button again.

"Whooooaaaa," I shouted, hearing my voice in a new way.

"Whooooohhh," we continued, sending the voices of panda and possibility through space.

TEN

Come back, come back, don't walk away.
Come back, come back, come back today.
— The Cure, "In Between Days"

After physics class and Walt, I was so excited that I rushed to Café Haven, forgetting that I wanted to be fashionably late.

"Hi," I said to the barista at the counter. She was wearing a black shirt, black skirt and a diner name tag that said "Callie."

"Can I get a vanilla latte for here, please?"

"Sure," she said. "And I like your tights."

She nodded at my plaid ones, which is when I noticed her black and white argyle ones.

"Thanks," I said. "I like yours, too. And your shoes."

We compared Doc Martens and laughed.

"You kids," an older waitress said, walking by and smiling. "You're so eclectic."

"That's Judy," Callie said. "She owns the place and is actually awesome. She lets me wear whatever I want, eat whatever I like and play whatever I'm feeling."

"That's cool," I said. "What kind of music do you like?"

"Everything," she said. "That's why I go from Sinatra to The Clash to Tchaikovsky, even though he's a little repetitive. I'm a fan of musical open-mindedness."

I was glad she didn't have x-ray vision, because if she had, she would have seen the stack of mixtapes in my bag and busted me for being stuck in a singular decade.

"You're a friend of Finny's, right?" she said, handing me my latte. It smelled like heaven in a cup.

"Yeah," I said, walking toward the booths. "You've heard of me?"

"Are you kidding?" she said, walking beside me. "You're the best thing that's happened to him since forever. Sophie, right?"

"Right," I said. I set down my cup and slid into the booth. "Sophie Sophia."

"Great name. Should I put in Finny's order? Double chocolate milk shake with strawberries and bananas?" Callie said. "He's pretty predictable."

"He is, but he's not coming," I said. "I'm meeting someone else."

Callie opened her mouth, so I put my earbuds in and let The Smiths serenade me with "Ask" before she could ask questions. It was part of Dad's *Questions and Quantum* mixtape, which also included "Destination Unknown" by Missing Persons and "Just Like Honey" by The Jesus and Mary Chain.

"I like your skirt," Callie said, pointing to my owl pocket.

"Thanks," I said, yelling through my headphones. I'd picked it out that morning because it made me feel smarter. I turned my music down.

"You know Finny and I are just friends, right?" I said. "We're not dating."

"Of course," Callie said. "I know how much he likes you, but it's good to have more than one friend."

"Especially since Finny's so busy with science."

"Havencrest's little Einstein," she said, grinning. "He's going to surprise all of us one day."

Truth was, Finny was already pretty amazing. He was president of the Young Einsteins Club, had a head start on his science fair project and was constantly scribbling some new theory down in his notebook. While I was busy being in survival mode, he was busy changing things, setting the stage for the next big discovery. I couldn't wait to have the brain space to think about something other than how to get through the day.

I had just turned my music back up when I felt a tap on my shoulder.

"Hi," Drew said.

"Hi!" I shouted. He held his ears and sat down across from me.

"Oh!" I said, taking my earbuds out. "Sorry."

"My fault. I think someone once said never interrupt a girl and her music. Is that a Walkman?"

"Yeah," I said. "I'm a fan of the mixtape generation."

"That's cool," he said. "I like analog."

"Me too!" My insides melted. I wanted to immediately ask him what else he loved besides Kerouac and vintage clothes, but I controlled myself.

"What's on the tape?" he asked.

"Mostly eighties music," I said. "I was listening to The Smiths."

"The Smiths are epic," he said.

"I know, right?" I sat up taller in my seat. "There are all of these bands who can't write their own music, so they just steal riffs from Johnny Marr. It's embarrassing."

For the next half hour, we bonded over Bauhaus and Beat Happening, The Psychedelic Furs and The Pixies. Drew and I clearly loved the same music. As it turned out, we liked a lot of the same books, too, like Salinger and Beat literature and the one he was named after: Nancy Drew. His mom was a librarian, which meant he was living with books while I was living with crazy. There was finally a pause in the conversation, and he asked the question I'd been dying to ask.

"Are you hungry?"

"Fiercely," I said, leaning back and putting my arms up on the booth. "I'm a grilled-cheese-with-tomato kind of girl. You?"

"Grilled-cheese-without-the-tomato guy," he said, flipping his hair out of the way. He had dark wavy bangs that hung down over one eye. "Want more coffee?"

"Yeah, but I better switch to decaf."

I handed him my mug and he sauntered to the counter. It wasn't like he was arrogant or anything. I think he was just so relaxed he had no choice but to move that way. I couldn't imagine ever feeling that calm—not with shaman pandas lurking around every corner. He practically floated back to our table like a god, coffee in hand.

"You like Sonic Youth, too?" he said, setting down my mug and pointing to the speaker above us.

"Show me a girl who doesn't like Kim Gordon, and I'll show you a girl who doesn't know her," I said.

"It's pretty obvious we have the same taste," he said. "Stage-diving music, right?" He grinned in a way that gave it all away.

"You heard about that?" I leaned my head back against the seat.

"I saw you in the office," he said.

"Oh, yeah," I said, trying to be nonchalant. "Why were you there?"

"I was trying to start a literature club," he said. "But mostly I heard about you from other people. I don't do gossip, but the whole school was talking about it."

"Right," I said. "And what did they say, exactly?"

"That you stage dove into the cheerleaders' table trying to kill some girl named Heather."

I laughed. It sounded ridiculous when you said it out loud.

"And you believed them?" I asked.

"You don't seem like a killer," he said. "Besides, I like a girl who shakes things up."

Goose bumps covered my arms. The same thing happened when we were texting.

"I get that from my mom," I said. It used to be the other way around—Mom holding things down while Dad shook things up—but after he left, they switched roles. He was consistent—gone—and Mom did everything she could not to stay in one place.

"So what do you get from your dad?" he asked.

"You don't want to know." My throat tightened.

"What, an awesome pancake recipe? The ability to change a tire in a single bound?"

"Good tries," I said.

But you really should stop guessing now, I thought. Because you don't know a darn thing about it.

"Whatever it is, he did a good job," Drew said, grinning.

I was so panicked I missed my mouth, sending coffee flowing down the front of my shirt.

"I inherited his clumsiness," I said, leaving coffee-soaked napkins on the table. "I'll be right back."

I closed the door to the bathroom, put my hands on the sink and breathed. The Cure's "A Night Like This" blared from the speakers while I counted backwards from ten. Anything to stop my hands from shaking. Robert Smith sang about love and loss, about wanting things to be the same, like they were before. Like before Dad left. Drew was a good guy—even better than I'd imagined—so I knew I had to pull it together. I blotted my shirt with paper towels. I had a cardigan I could wear to hide the stain. I also had free will. I could choose to think about Dad, freak out and ruin my maybe-date or I could focus on other things. Like the cute boy waiting with a grilled cheese sandwich.

"You can do this," I said to myself in the mirror. I smoothed my bangs, took another deep breath and opened the door. I heard people cheering, smelled sweat and cigarettes and saw that the room was dark, like a club. And then someone handed me a guitar.

"Okay, Sophie," said a guy wearing all black and sporting an English accent. "This is your moment. Are you ready?"

I didn't know why I was supposed to be ready, but I knew I wasn't on a date with Drew anymore. The steps in front of me led to a stage packed with guitar stands and amps, drums and a keyboard. Excited girls lined the front, girls who looked like me but with more eyeliner. And guys like Finny, only with bigger hair. Some of them even wore lipstick.

"I think there's been a mistake," I said, holding the neck of the guitar. "I don't even play this."

"Nerves." The guy chuckled. Even his laugh had an accent. "You'll be fine. Follow me."

The lights went off, and I followed him onto the stage with the others by flashlight. I threw the guitar strap over my shoulder while he plugged me in, handed me a guitar pick and nodded to the row of pedals in front of me.

"Watch your vibrato," he said. "And if you're unsure, look to Robert for cues."

"Robert?"

As soon as I said it, the lights went up, the crowd screamed, and a figure rushed by me, a silhouette I'd know anywhere. I'd spent hours with his trademark teased hair and baggy clothes, swooning over the way he had with sadness. Wishing I could reach through my Walkman and shake the hand of the guy who knew my life better than I did—and had the guts to sing about it.

Blue lights went up, the crowd completely freaked and Robert Smith turned around and smiled—smudged red lipstick and all. I was onstage with The Cure.

The drums started and my hands were on the guitar, playing the first line of a song I knew all too well, a song that had gotten me out of bed some mornings when I wanted to stay in. I switched to chords, strumming while the keyboard came in and then, like in a dream, Robert started singing "In Between Days."

I played wildly, dancing around like I saw them do on YouTube. In their music videos, The Cure seemed sullen but excited at the same time, as if hitting particular notes caused actual pain. He sang about love and loss, about wanting someone to disappear and then, as soon as he said it, wanting them back again. I could totally relate.

As soon as that song ended, another one started, the bass and piano taking over as they kicked into "The Lovecats." I wondered if anyone had gotten lost inside an episode yet, because if not, I would volunteer to be the first. I bounced up and down like Dad and I did when the song came on the radio, only this time I was in it. Totally in sync with the audience for three minutes and forty seconds in a way that doesn't happen with anything else. My hands kept playing, and I felt connected, like I wasn't then—nor would ever be—alone.

I didn't recognize the next song on the set list, not that it mattered. My hands did things without my brain even knowing about them, fingers on the frets like I'd been playing my entire life. Instinct had gotten me this far, and since I wasn't sure how long I'd be there, I wanted to do something that mattered. Something to help Robert Smith remember the small dark-haired girl who'd shared his stage *and* his vision of the world.

He looked back and nodded, the handoff signal for a solo. Forget my mom's approval, I had the go-ahead from the lead singer of The Cure. So I stood wide, lifted my arm high and circled it around, doing a windmill. The keyboardist made a face, either because I was missing my notes or because I looked weird, but I kept circling anyway. The crowd cheered, the bass held down the song, and I swirled around once more, with great force, hand heading toward the strings.

But instead of the deafening, beautiful trio of notes, I heard the din of the diner. People chattering, not cheering. And the sound of bone making contact with concrete.

Concrete making contact with bone.

Crack. Snap. Scraping the bathroom wall.

Bodies shouldn't be allowed to make sounds like that.

At least, that's what Dad said.

I held my knuckles, scraped and bloody.

In the mirror I saw his knuckles, scraped and bloody.

And then I moaned and crumpled, my body thudding, my heart breaking as it fell to the floor.

"Daddy?"

A nurse held me back. "Honey, you can't go in there."

"DADDY!" I screamed, hoping my voice would penetrate the space between us as they dragged him down the hall.

"They're helping him," she said, holding on to me.

I knew what helping looked like, and it didn't look like that.

"It was an accident," he said, flailing his arms. "Let me go!"

Daddy had left me on the corner of 125th Street. I knew he didn't mean to leave me there, that he'd be right back. Only it took a while, longer than it usually did. Enough time for someone to see me. I should have stood farther back, but it was dark and I was scared. So I camped out under the streetlight with my backpack, watching cabbies and people walk by. Ignoring the policeman when he approached me. What are you doing out here so late? Why are you alone? he wanted to know as Daddy showed up out of nowhere and grabbed me. I was his, after all. He could do that. Except he couldn't. That's what the policeman said as he put both of us in the back of the police car. He also threw around words like *abandonment* and *public nuisance.* Daddy was talking a lot about other worlds that were like ours, but different. Chattering about things that didn't make sense. Are you drunk? the officer asked. High? I said no, he doesn't do that stuff, and I was old enough to know what that stuff was. I thought he was taking us home, but we ended up in the emergency room instead.

"Why don't we sit over here until your mom comes?" the nurse said, pointing to the waiting room.

Her hands were cold. I wanted her to let go of my arm, wanted the nurses to let go of his arms. But when they did, Dad flung himself around, wildly, hitting the wall hard with his hand. Time slowed as I stood there and watched him look at his hand, knuckles scraped and bloody. Then he turned and looked at me, eyes wild. Like it wasn't even him anymore.

"NOOOO!" he screamed as they slammed him down onto a gurney and tied his wrists and ankles, restraining him so he couldn't move. Someone put a needle in his arm and he went limp.

"Daddy," I sobbed, my body crumpling. The nurse held me.

"He'll be okay now," she said, pouring me into a blue cloth chair. "Your daddy's going to be just fine."

Fine meant a seventy-two-hour hold. *Fine* meant Mom cradling me in her arms, apologizing for working late. Sleeping beside me in my bed the rest of the night. I used to think *fine* was the same thing as *good*, but now I knew better. Daddy came home a few days later, and while he didn't seem great, I never saw anything like that again. At least, not until I saw it in myself.

ELEVEN

And she gave away the secrets of her past
and said I've lost control again.
—Joy Division, "She's Lost Control"

"Sophie?"

The door swung open and Finny stood there, not Drew. People had been banging for a while, trying to get in. Callie knocking, talking about a master key. I knew I was supposed to get up. I knew I should answer the door and walk out, and everything would be okay, except I couldn't. Walking into the world made it real, and I'd have to admit, whether I wanted to or not, that I was turning into my dad.

Finny bent down beside me. I was curled up in the corner, by the sink. Back to the wall, head bowed, arms hugging my knees.

"Are you okay?"

In my head I said yes, but it never left my mouth. Only grunts and moans, the sounds of a wounded animal.

"Let's get out of here," he said.

Finny's hand hovered above my back like he wanted to touch me, but he wasn't sure it would be okay. But it was—and it was the only way I was getting off the floor. I grabbed his hand and started to pull myself up, pretty much forcing him to support me under my arms. I leaned on him as we left the bathroom, winding down the hall and out the back door. He propped me up against the back wall of the café.

"If you want to make it to your house, we'll need chocolate," I said.

"Back in a sec," he said.

I looked at my hand and wiggled my fingers. They looked bad but didn't seem to be broken. Not like my insides.

Finny returned with a brown paper bag full of Café Haven's infamous (according to him) brownies. He broke one in half, put half in my mouth and the other half in his. We leaned against the wall, chewing. We ate another one the same way. And then another, passing a bottle of water back and forth, swigs in between bites. By the third half brownie, I felt my strength return. And not just in my body but in my mind, too.

Sometimes you faced the truth because it was time, because you waited or did the work or whatever it took to get there. But other times you were forced into it. Something happened, and you couldn't stand in the dark anymore, not knowing what you knew. All the saint cards and shaman pandas in the world couldn't help me if I wasn't willing to help myself.

||||||||||

Finny and I squeezed through a chain-link fence three doors down from his yard and trekked through the grass to the little house I'd only heard about, nestled up high inside of a tree. It used to belong to the Peterson kids, but when they went away to college, they gave it to Finny.

"Watch your step," he said, climbing up the small ladder to the top of the tree. I followed him.

"Welcome to The Lab," he said, waving his arm around. "Like it?"

It was unbelievable. Most tree houses are just slabs of wood, but this was like an actual house—smooth, stained wood walls with real windows. There was even a fake fireplace with a white fake fur rug in front of it, plus fluffy orange floor pillows, empty soda cans and an old wooden desk. And a red and orange cartoon owl hung over the fake mantel with a word bubble that said "Whooo's there?" It was cozy and cabiny and as far away from science as you could get.

"Why do you call it The Lab?" I said. "It looks more ski lodge to me."

"Because it's where I do my most important work," Finny said. "Over there."

He pointed to the desk covered with test tubes and measuring cups, note cards and Hershey bar wrappers. Clutter, just like in my head.

"Excuse the mess," he said, opening a drawer and shoving wrappers into it. "If I'd known you were coming, I would have cleaned."

I grabbed a big orange pillow and leaned against the fire-place, hands behind my head. If I turned just right, I could see the bluest parts of the sky.

"I need your help," I said, looking at the clouds for courage. "This is going to sound weird, but I see things."

"Me too," Finny said, leaning back in his chair and looking around. "I love it when the leaves turn. Even the sky is a differ-ent color right now."

This was going to be harder than I thought.

"No, I mean I see things other people don't see."

"I *know*," Finny said. "You have a different point of view. That's what makes you so awesome."

I sat up and put the pillow in my lap, hugging it.

"Let's try this again," I said, frustration winning out over fear. "I see things other people don't see. I call them episodes, but those in the medical profession prefer the term *hallucination*."

"Wait," Finny said, looking away from the sky and directly at me. "What?"

"I hallucinate," I said.

"Are you schizophrenic?"

"No," I said. It was the first place people always went.

"Okay, then you have bipolar disease," he said.

"Wrong again," I said. "It might help if you had more information—"

"Do you have a personality disorder?" Finny asked. When he was nervous, he went into Super-Solve-It mode, even though he didn't really understand the problem. "Is it epilepsy? Do you have seizures?"

"No," I said. "And I'm not mentally ill. At least I don't think I am. Could you stop for a second?"

Finny walked circles around the tree house. You could almost see his scientific wheels turning, his head filled with interlocking gears.

"You have hallucinations that aren't hallucinations," he said. "Could you be a monk and not know it? When monks become highly evolved, they can travel through consciousness."

"I can barely meditate for a second," I said, closing my eyes, which popped right back open. "I doubt I'm enlightened."

"Maybe you're psychic. Or maybe they're auras. Do you have migraines?"

"No," I said. "But keep asking me these questions, and I'll get one."

"I'm a scientist," Finny said. "Questions are my go-to, like an automatic setting."

He was wearing a vintage Boy Scout shirt with band buttons on it instead of badges. In all of his walking around, the New Order button had fallen to the floor. He finally stopped pacing, and I picked it up.

"Hold out your hand and close your eyes," I said.

He sighed as I pressed the button into his palm and then closed his fingers around it.

"I don't need you to worry," I said. "I don't need you to look like I did in that bathroom. I don't need you to put a label on something that hasn't had a label since it started, two years ago, either. I just need you to be who you've been the past few weeks. My friend."

I knew he'd still want to solve me, which was one of the reasons I'd told him in the first place. I wanted to be solved. I just didn't want him to have a nervous breakdown doing it.

Finny opened his eyes, looked down at the button and smiled.

"You said you needed my help," he said. "How may I be of service, Ms. Sophia?"

Over the next half hour, I told Finny the specifics of what I saw and when, where it started and how often it happened. I started with the first thing I'd ever witnessed: the heart rolling off that guy's sleeve. Then I skipped ahead, telling him about seeing stockers perform Duran Duran's "Hungry Like the Wolf" in a grocery store and witnessing my wallpaper come to life, giant sunflowers peeling off, waving their arms at me. I told him about the lunch ladies covering the Ramones, and by the time I got to the marching band pandas, I thought his eyes were going to pop out of his head. I decided to save The Cure, Walt and Turning into My Father for another afternoon.

"Why now?" he said. "Why didn't you tell me before?"

"Maybe for the same reason you haven't told me something," I said. "I had to wait until I was ready."

Finny stood up and looked out one of the windows. A red leaf blew in and landed on his shoulder. Maple.

"I'm gay," he said.

"Awesome!" I said. I almost clapped, but that felt inappropriate. "Really."

"Wait, you knew?"

"I guessed," I said. "You gave me, like, a thousand clues."

Finny wore wing tips, never talked about girls and used more hair product than I did.

"Do you think anyone else knows?"

"Doubtful," I said immediately. "I picked up on it because I'm from New York. Our gaydar is much more advanced."

He giggled, and I joined in. We laughed until we fell on the floor, rolling around the tree house. Leaves blew in, so we threw them at each other, red, yellow, gold. Maybe it was the chocolate that made us giddy or maybe it was the truth, sneaking out of the shadows and into the light. Ready to play.

"Episodes, you're going down!" I said as Finny scribbled on the butcher paper hanging by the fake fireplace.

I was less concerned with why they happened and more concerned with stopping them, but Finny said the two were connected. He also said if I wanted his help, I had to listen to him. And stop using catchphrases.

"Not even Sanity or Bust?"

Finny shook his head.

"I'm just excited," I said. "Instead of wishing my episodes would go away, I'm actually doing something about it."

"*We're* doing something about it," he said, smiling. "Besides, I needed a final science project, anyway, so this works out great. And don't worry—the subjects are always anonymous."

I wasn't thrilled about being the topic of an experiment, but I also knew Finny couldn't leave a puzzle alone. So if helping his science project meant helping me, I was in.

"Let's do it," I said. "What's first?"

"Establish a constant," he said.

"I don't have one," I said. "My life is totally random."

"You are, but your episodes are not," he said. "They're consistent. They're the constant."

"Okay," I said, even though hearing it out loud made me cringe. "What's next?"

"We gather data, recognize patterns and develop a theory."

I remembered Dad doing the same thing, working on problems he never seemed to solve. Developing theories that never went anywhere. Maybe I would be the exception.

"So here's the deal," Finny said. "You live your life the way you always would, listening to music, hanging out with me, making cool clothes, having episodes, normal stuff. I just need you to do one thing."

"You just called my episodes normal," I said. "I'll give you my KLM Airlines bag if you want it."

"I love that bag, but no," he said. "Just buy a journal and document everything: what you ate for breakfast, how you're feeling, what you see, that kind of thing. Then I'll analyze it and hopefully identify a pattern."

"And if we identify a pattern, we can prevent it, right?"

"In theory," he said. "That's why they call it an experiment."

"Experiment Sophie?"

"More like the Normalcy Project," he said, smiling. "Based on the idea that everyone is abnormal until proven normal."

"I love it," I said, feeling like I could breathe again. "I could totally see that on a T-shirt."

I could also see myself without episodes one day, with Finny to thank for it. He was a genius at science. But as he paced around the tree house, stopping to scribble on the butcher paper, I noticed something else. Finny was also a genius at being my friend.

"It's getting cold up here," I said. "Want to take the big experiment to my house?"

"The Normalcy Project," he said, drawing his hand across his shirt like it was printed there. "Also known as your life. And yes, let's get out of here."

Finny threw a few things in his bag, I grabbed mine, and we climbed down the stairs, one rung at a time. One step closer toward normalcy. When we got to the bottom, we linked arms and headed down the street, dusk at our backs.

TWELVE

I unlocked the door of my house, ready to endure whatever Mom was going to dish out. Since I was, like, three hours late and hadn't bothered to call, it was going to be major. Good thing I had Finny as a buffer.

"Mom?" I said, looking around. "Hello?"

"Is she here?" Finny said.

"Nope," I said, pulling him into the kitchen. "Let's take advantage of it." I grabbed a bag of carrots and cans of ginger ale out of the fridge and headed upstairs, Finny and Balzac following. I flopped on the bed, and Finny stood in front of the collection of black and white postcards, staring.

"Warhol and Nico," he said, touching one of them. "That's new. How is it I could notice that but totally miss that you hallucinate?"

"Have episodes," I said.

"That's not a scientific term," Finny said. "Can we say hallucination, just for the sake of the experiment?"

I traced the circles on my bedspread with my finger. "As along as you understand that's not what they are," I said.

"You're going to have to help me with that," Finny said. "But first: when are we going to redo *my* room?"

I called my bedroom New York Meets Everywhere Else because it was full of found things like a sad-eyed dog painting, a floppy red felt hat and a collection of vintage sunglasses hanging on a ribbon on the wall. Anything that inspired me, basically. My favorite was a sculpture Dad made out of tin cans, bicycle gears and broken bits of an old Supremes 45 record. It sat next to his beanbag, which was now occupied by Finny, who flipped through a stack of cassettes on the floor.

"Want to listen to *Black Holes vs. Sunday Afternoons?*"

"Sure," I said as he put it in my boom box. If we were going to discuss my mental state, we might as well have music to go along with it.

"So what are hallucinations like?" Finny asked, pressing Play and then sinking into the beanbag chair. "Do you see a bright light? Step through an opening?"

"It's not Narnia," I said, throwing a pillow at him.

"I don't know," he said, ducking. "That's why I asked."

I lay on my back and hung my head off the side of the bed, letting all the blood rush to it. Making my face turn red.

"Sometimes I get a headache," I said. "Or hear things. My body reacts more post-hallucination than pre-hallucination."

"So there are no warning signs," he said.

"Nope," I said. "Welcome to Randomland."

"Does stress make them worse? Can you leave whenever you want? Can you control them at all?" Finny asked.

I remembered the time Dad tied cans of chili to his ankles with rope. When I asked him what he was doing, he said he was trying to weigh himself down so he could stay with me. At the time, I didn't understand—I just knew that no matter what he did, he'd disappear anyway. I thought about that instead of the words that were coming out of my mouth.

"I can't control them, but I'm not alone," I said. "Dad couldn't control his hallucinations, either."

I was jumping on my mini trampoline when it happened.

Bounce. Bounce. Up in the air, face to the sky, then face-to-face with Daddy holding a red paper parasol, floating in the air. He popped out of nowhere, like in cartoons, and then he landed on the grass.

"Hi, sweet pea," he said. "Having fun?"

"Hi, Daddy," I said, still bouncing. "Where did you come from?"

"Somewhere too far for little girls to go," he said.

"Like Chinatown?"

"Something like that," he said, twirling his parasol. "I brought this for you."

I hopped off the trampoline and took the parasol, spinning it above my head.

"It's magical," he said. "They call it a Dream Director."

"Why?"

"Because, according to legend, it directs your dreams."

"How does it work?" I wanted to know how everything worked.

Dreams have a system, Daddy said. They started in the sky and moved toward our heads, but direction determined whether the dreams were good ones or bad ones. Good dreams were creative and happy and traveled like a triangle, sliding down the side of our heads and going into the ears. But bad dreams were angrier; they shot down out of the sky like rain and headed straight for the middle of the forehead.

My hands flew up to my own forehead. "Does it hurt?"

"Of course not, silly," he said. "You're asleep. But that's why we have the Dream Director. We'll hang it upside down over your bed so it can catch the bad dreams before they go in."

"So I'll only have good dreams?"

"I hope so," he said, ruffling the top of my head. "Just because I travel a lot doesn't mean you shouldn't have the best dreams possible."

"Why can't I go with you?" I said, tracing my finger along the edge of the parasol. It was the color of cherries.

"Who would do your job?" he said, kissing my cheek. "You have to stay home so I have someone to bring souvenirs to."

"So you can remember where you've been?"

"Yes, pumpkin pie," he said, pulling me close and almost crushing the parasol. "But also so you can remember *me*."

Finny stood and looked around my room, his eyes stopping on the parasol in the corner.

"Is that it?"

"Yes," I said. "One and the same. And no, I'm not going to hang it over my bed."

Finny touched it and withdrew his hand quickly, like it was on fire.

"You know this changes the game, right?"

"Dad hallucinating or the fact that he brought something back?"

"Both," Finny said. "But unless your hallucinations are hereditary, the souvenir thing is more important. If this were all happening in your mind, you wouldn't bring something back."

"I know," I said. "Something like this."

I took the whistle from around my neck and handed it to Finny.

"Whoa," he said, grinning. "This is from an episode? It's like holding *history*."

Most people would have flipped out on me a long time ago, but Finny just rolled with every new thing I told him, even though each piece was stranger than the last. Maybe Mr. Maxim was right. Physics blew the doors of the mind wide open, giving you plenty of room to wander.

"And every event produces a souvenir?" he asked.

"Yes," I said. "They help me know I'm back." I always checked my pockets immediately.

"You know we have to talk about your dad," he said.

I fell back on my bed. He still didn't know exactly what happened after The Cure. Or Walt. I wondered how many more pieces he could hold before he broke.

"Of course," I said, fake perking up. "Gathering data has to include everything, I get that. But don't you have enough to work with for now?"

Finny turned the whistle over and over in his hand.

"Definitely," he said, handing it back to me.

"Are you sure you're okay with this?"

Finny threw an arm around my shoulder.

"Of course," he said. "I'm a scientist. I'm a fan of the unexplained."

Which meant he was fan of me, too.

"SOPHIE SOPHIA!"

We froze as Mom's voice floated up the stairs.

THIRTEEN

Her feet sounded like packing up, like hitting the road, like panic. She wasn't coming to my room to tell me a funny story or tuck me in for the night. She was coming to take me away again.

"And there I was, calling hospitals, driving all over town, while the whole time you were in your room?"

My bedroom door flew open.

"Hi, Mrs. Sophia," Finny said, waving.

"I think you might want to leave now," she said. Her chest rose and fell quickly. "There could be consequences for the accomplice."

Finny grabbed his bag, whispered, "Good luck," and ran down the stairs.

Mom stood there silent, like a giant, until the door slammed.

"Downstairs," she said. "Now."

She stormed off and I looked around my room, taking it in just in case it was the last time.

"It's okay," I said, rubbing Balzac's ears. "Maybe she'll give me a pardon or something."

I blew my room a kiss and took each step as slowly as possible. No point in rushing to the execution. When I finally got there, Mom was sitting on the couch with a glass of red wine.

"Was your phone broken?"

"I don't know," I said. "You just gave me the thing. I don't know how to work it, so if it was off, it wasn't off on purpose. Besides, this isn't Brooklyn. You don't have to be so worried."

"You were three hours late. Besides, I'm your mother," she said, slamming her glass on the coffee table. "It's my job to worry."

"I was at Café Haven with Drew," I said. "And then I was with Finny."

"Did you forget what being grounded means?" she said. "I gave you a free pass for an hour, not for the entire afternoon."

"I know," I said. "And I'm really sorry. I lost track of time."

Mom walked over to the stereo and turned on the radio. New Age music filled the room.

"Gawd, this is awful," I said.

"I need to relax," Mom said. "I don't want to say anything I'm going to regret."

"I could say a lot of things about this music that I'd never regret," I said.

"It's calming!" Mom said in a voice that was the opposite of calm.

I tried not to smile, but I couldn't help it.

"Okay, okay," she said, smiling, too. "See? I guess it works. Music is subjective, anyway. Who are we to decide what's right and what's wrong? Maybe it just *is*."

"And this music *is* terrible," I said, getting up and changing the station.

Mom took a deep breath and patted the cushion next to her. I sat beside her, and Balzac jumped into my lap, purring.

"I've been avoiding this conversation, but I think it's time to have it," she said. "You're getting to be that age."

"What age?"

"Teenage years," she said. "When things start to show up."

Great. We were going to have the sex talk.

"Sophie, you have to be more careful than other people," Mom said. "You have this imagination that runs wild and gets you into trouble. And now, with the hormones coming in, it could be a difficult time."

"Uh-huh," I said. Was she talking about the terrible teens or something else?

"I lived through the whole episodes thing with your father," she said. "And I see you, and I don't know."

Wait a minute. "Don't know what?"

Mom sighed. "I don't know if I have the strength to live through it with you."

And there it was. I got up and went to the kitchen. I couldn't be in the same room with her, not right then.

"Come back," she said. "Let's talk about this."

I didn't want to talk, I wanted to feel safe. I wanted to feel like, no matter what, Mom would chalk it up to my imagination and act like everything was going to be okay. Like she always did. Denial had worked well for us so far. And just because I told Finny the truth didn't mean I was ready to tell anyone else. Especially not when it could leave me homeless.

"Sophie, please," Mom said. "I think you misunderstood me."

That's when I saw it, a brochure for teenage mental illness and a psychiatrist's card to go along with it. Sitting by the phone.

"I don't think I'm going to misunderstand this," I said, marching into the living room, thrusting the card in her face. "Care to explain?"

"It's exactly what it looks like," she said.

"Mom?"

"What am I supposed to do?" she said. "All the articles say that mental illness shows up in the teenage years, and you're there. And then you almost got suspended? I thought we were through with that. So if you're hallucinating—"

She'd never used that word. Not once. Not even when talking about Dad.

"I don't hallucinate," I said.

"Have episodes," Mom said. "Whatever you and your father call it. If it's happening, and you're not telling me, I can't keep you safe."

"I'm fine," I said. "I told you what I saw."

"So tell someone else," she said. "I want you to talk to this doctor."

"No way," I said. "Are you forgetting about California?"

"I'm remembering California," she said. "That's why I talked to a friend at work about you—not specifics—but she's having trouble with her daughter, and she gave me this brochure and referred me to this doctor. It helped them. Maybe it could help us. Because I don't want a repeat of San Francisco."

"And I don't want to be locked away," I said. "One appointment, and you know that's what will happen."

"We don't know that," she said. "It's just one appointment. Don't be so dramatic."

And just like that, it came tumbling out of me. All of it.

"Dramatic is seeing a marching band made up of giant pandas," I said. "Or stage diving to a Ramones cover. Or playing with The Cure in a café only to hurt my hand while doing a guitar windmill. Dramatic is *Walt*."

"Who's Walt?" Mom scooted toward the edge of the couch, tapping her nails on her knee.

"My shaman panda," I said, wishing I could control the words coming out of my mouth.

"Your shaman panda."

I could see her unraveling.

"He's more of a guide," I said. "It's his job to help me."

"Oh, really? Is he the one who helped you stage dive during lunch? "He sounds like a great influence. Maybe next time he'll help you walk on broken glass or jump off a bridge."

"It's not like that," I said. "Those things were accidents."

"Wait, I've got it!" she said, ignoring me. "Maybe your panda could help you pull off a stunt at my office and get me fired. Or at school so you'll get expelled. Yes! And then we can move again, and you can start a new school again, and we'll act like nothing happened. Except *everything* will have happened and your panda won't be there to explain it to me or clean up the mess because *I can't see him.*"

"Mom," I said. I tried to take her hand, but she pulled it away. Her face was red. "It's not like that."

"Tell that to your new doctor," she said. "Because I don't want to hear it." She ran her hands through her hair. They were shaking.

"I'm not going to that doctor," I said.

"You are," she said. "I can't control what you see. And I have no say in whether or not you take your shaman panda to school with you. But I'm your mother. I can make you get help."

"I don't need help," I said, even though I did. I just didn't need it from a psychiatrist. "This is ridiculous. I'm being persecuted because I see the world differently than everyone else."

"Not differently," Mom said, sighing. "*Insanely.* Everyone else walks through the world with their sanity intact."

I felt blood rushing up against my bones.

"Including Dad?"

"Your father had problems," she said, her voice softening. "Sophie, he was very, very far from normal. You had to have known that."

I sank to the floor like a stone thrown into the ocean.

"I didn't know that," I said, sitting cross-legged, leaning

against the couch. Tears flowed down, covering my face. "To me he was just Dad."

That was why we never talked about him, why Mom had been avoiding the subject for years. If I'd known how she felt about him—really and truly—then I would have known how she felt about me, too.

"That came out wrong," Mom said. "I didn't mean it."

But she did, and she knew it. And now I knew it, too, which meant nothing would ever be the same. I grabbed my backpack off the floor and headed toward the door.

"Put down your bag," Mom said. "It's dark out there."

"I know," I said. "But I can't be in the same space with someone who thinks I'm crazy."

I slammed the door and popped the *Delirious Dusk* mixtape into my Walkman and hit Play. Dad loved walking around New York City at night. He said there was something about the sky and the way the light hit the buildings that made the city come alive. That was why he made a soundtrack to go with it, full of brooding music that was dark, like the fading night, but inspiring—Tones on Tail, Bauhaus, Jesus and Mary Chain. It featured driving guitars to match the driving thoughts in my brain.

How to Survive Having a Mother Who Thinks You're Crazy by Sophie Sophia

---

1. Put it somewhere deep in the back of your mind and ignore it.

2. When it comes back up, and it will, cry it out.
   Sometimes that's the only thing that works.
3. Confide in your real friends, not your shaman
   panda one.
4. Remember Lewis Carroll and van Gogh.
   It wasn't sanity that made them great.
5. And, most importantly, prove her wrong.

"Ooof!"

I tripped on a horse apple on the way to Finny's house and almost fell flat on my face. Just like I'd been doing all day in one form or another. I picked it up and hurled it against the concrete wall of an office building. It left a satisfying print on the wall, so I kept throwing them.

Smash, a slider for Dad. *Crash*, an overhand for that psychiatrist. *Smack*, a fastball for hallucinations in general. I threw several more to get into the rhythm of it. Getting rid of whatever was inside of me. And then I wound up my arm, like I did with The Cure, and threw one as hard as I could. It blew apart when it hit the wall and scattered mealy bits all over the parking lot, white chunks glistening under the streetlights.

"That was for you, Mom."

I gathered more apples in a pile at my feet threw them, horse apple after horse apple, covering the ground with muck. I saw chunks of green and white everywhere. And then I saw part of a Converse, right in the thick of things.

"You look cute when you're angry," Finny said, standing beside me.

I glared at him.

"Your mom called. She thought you'd be with me, so I told her you were."

I glared again.

"Can I at least join the party?"

"No," I said. I picked up another horse apple.

"That's cool. Just pretend I'm not here," he said. "Unless, of course, you want to talk, because I'm here. You know that, right? Come hurricane or earthquake or anything?"

I nodded.

"Can I spend the night?"

"It's already approved."

I wanted to say thanks, but the words stayed stuck in my brain. Like the horse apple cradled in my hand.

"I'll leave you to it, then," he said. "Be there in fifteen and there's a chocolate soda in it for you."

He left and there was silence, like before I began. And then there was the sound of horse apples, crashing against the concrete.

FOURTEEN

I walked by my house before I went to Finny's. I didn't realize I was going that way until I was already there, standing outside the window. I saw Mom upstairs, sheer white curtains revealing a silhouette hugging her knees to her chest, rocking back and forth on the bed. I heard U2's "With or Without You" at full volume, which meant she was thinking about Dad. She had probably assumed we'd moved on—new town, new school and the appearance of actual friends. But then I almost got expelled again, reminding her that no matter how far she went, his crazy would always be with her—in the form of a living, breathing, fourteen-year-old me.

"I thought Peeping Toms were supposed to have fun," Walt said, appearing beside me.

I threw my arms around him, fingers sinking into fur.

"Hello to you, too," he said, holding me, replacing my frustration with calm. His hugs were the ultimate Zen move. "Rough night?"

"You have no idea," I said, letting go and wiping my tears on my sleeve. "Or maybe you do."

"Sorry," he said. "I had a gig in Vancouver."

He pointed to the black bandanna tied around his head. I hadn't even noticed it, or the black leather wristbands with tassels that he twirled around.

"How'd it go?" I asked.

"Two encores," he said. "Walt and the Pandas rocked it. But how was your night?"

"I told my mom about you," I said.

Walt stood back and put his paws over his chest. "I'm honored, truly."

"It was an accident," I said, bending down to smell a flower that had no smell. "She wasn't ready to hear that I was seeing things again, much less that I like to stroll the suburbs with my second-best friend who's a panda."

"Again," Walt said, bowing, "*honored.*"

"I'm glad you feel that way," I said. "Because I need a favor."

"Name it."

I stopped in front of the yard that had two angel fountains in front.

"I need you to appear to my mom," I said.

He laughed. "And I need you to play guitar in my band. It would be awesome, but it's not going to happen."

"Why not?" I asked.

"I don't have the authority to appear to anyone but you," he said. "It's against the rules of the High Panda Council."

"Wait, you have a boss? And there are *rules*?"

"First, everyone has some kind of boss," he said. "And rules are there to protect people. You're my client, not your mother, so I can only appear to you. Unlike pizza with sausage and mushrooms, I'm not meant to be shared."

"But you're evidence!" I said. "Like souvenirs. That's what convinced Finny these are more than hallucinations."

"So show your mom a souvenir," he said.

"They're too common," I said. "You see keys, whistles and guitar picks everywhere. And while I know they're from somewhere else, I can't prove it to my mom. You, on the other hand, are irrefutable."

"And scary," Walt said. "She would completely freak out."

"Yeah, but at least she'd know there was something else going on," I said. "She was married to my dad, so she's familiar with the unexplained. One whiff of that, and she'll call off the whole psychiatrist-leading-to-loony-bin thing."

"Would that I could," he said, waltzing along the sidewalk. "But I cannot."

The calmer he was, the more agitated I became. "You're supposed to be helping me," I said. "How is this helping? And don't give me some crap about how the best guidance is within myself."

"But it's true," he said. "There's always a solution. Just because I'm not it doesn't mean that a solution doesn't exist."

"I couldn't be less in the mood for your fortune cookie wisdom," I said, kicking a row of bushes.

"I know you're angry," he said. "But rules are rules."

"You never struck me as a goody two-shoes," I said, walking ahead of him.

"Only when it comes to this stuff," he said. "But I'm not going anywhere. I'm here. It's still my job to guide you."

He stood under a streetlamp, which gave him an angelic glow, although I knew better.

"Guiding me where?" I said. "I don't need to know where Finny lives, we're here. What I don't know is where to go next."

"You know how this works," Walt said, putting his hands together in front of him like a prayer. "It's up to you to pave the path. I'm just here to point out markers along the way."

He bowed and then he was gone, but there, through the window, was Finny. Waving. Standing smack-dab in the middle of my path.

"Chocolate soda?"

I walked through the back door and into the kitchen to see Finny standing by two parfait glasses half filled with chocolate syrup.

"You waited for me," I said, but I wasn't surprised. Waiting wasn't so bad when you knew the other person would show up. "Can I help?"

"Get the ice cream," Finny said, motioning to the freezer.

Mrs. Jackson's kitchen was the epitome of a happy home-maker's house—matching flowered wallpaper and curtains, mixing bowls and tea towels. It was hard to imagine living in a place where things happened like clockwork—chicken enchiladas on Tuesdays and tuna salad on Thursdays. A place where aprons were worn while baking to keep messes to a minimum. I was the girl with cake batter in her hair, egg on her shirt and her foot in her mouth. Always.

Finny poured club soda into each glass and stirred. Then he scooped two small mounds of vanilla into each, making the concoctions bubble and fizz.

"What happened with your mom?"

I shrugged as I squirted a generous helping of whipped cream in each glass.

"Really?" he said, adding straws. "That's all I get?"

I took a sip of my soda.

"She wants to send me away."

"To camp? Boarding school?"

I took the straw out of my mouth, raised my hands above my head and waved them around, making a kooky face.

"To Crazyville?"

"Almost," I said. "She wants me to see a psychiatrist."

"Oh," he said. And then it sank in. "*Oh.*"

"I'm as good as locked up," I said, slurping. "You and I both know souvenirs won't keep me out of the mental ward."

"Your mom wouldn't do that to you."

"No, but a psychiatrist would," I said. "And you didn't see Mom. It was the worst fight we've ever had."

"Whatever she said, I'm sure she didn't mean it," he said.

"She meant it," I said. *Very, very far from normal.* "She just didn't mean to say it."

I drained the rest of my soda and then, when it was empty, I spooned ice cream into my mouth like a panacea.

"What are you going to do?"

"What are *we* going to do?" I said, smiling. "I can't go home without a plan, which means we need to put the Normalcy Project into overdrive. Can you handle it?"

"Handle it? I'm already on it."

"Like a pro," I said, raising my parfait glass so we could toast, which we did. "So what's next?"

"That's easy," Finny said. "Your dad."

Thanks to The Cure, Mom and Finny, Dad was no longer on the no-talk list. He was everywhere. We put our glasses in the sink and, high on chocolate and whipped cream, moved the party to the dining room. I don't know if it was the flowers on the rugs, curtains and chairs (Finny wasn't exaggerating) or the chocolate, but I was feeling inspired. And somewhat ready to talk about Dad. Finny brought out lined paper and colored pencils for charts and legal pads and pens for taking notes.

I told him everything about my dad that he didn't already know, which didn't contain much in the science department. Most of the information about my dad happened after work or on breaks from inventing, so it was more crazy than scientific. Finny was convinced the two were related, though.

"We have to think bigger," he said. "Where Western medicine fails—"

"Physics prevails?" I said.

"Hopefully," he said. "Since your hallucinations aren't of the normal variety, I shouldn't be using basic theories to solve them."

"So what's the most controversial theory out there?" I said.

"In theoretical physics? Anything having to do with string theory," Finny said. "Did your dad ever mention it?"

Dad worked on lots of stuff like model trains made out of tin boxes, lectures about lollipops and poems about space written on scraps of paper. I was sure there was some string in there somewhere.

"Not specifically," I said. "All I know about it is what we've learned in class so far."

Finny stood up, letting his chair fall to the floor. "Follow me."

He sat on the couch, I sat beside him, and he got a ball of purple yarn out of the drawer in the coffee table.

"Are we making friendship bracelets?" I said. "I'm touched."

"No," he said. "String theory."

He cut off a piece of yarn with scissors and tied the two ends together, making a loop. He put one end of the loop around his thumbs, the other around his pinky fingers and stretched and then flexed his fingers, pulling the string taut.

"This is the universe."

"I always knew it was purple," I said.

"Now, imagine the universe is made up of small strings," he said, taking his right index finger and picking up the string that ran across the left palm and pulling it across. Then he did the same thing with the left side until the yarn crossed back and forth in the middle, making big Xs. Just like cat's cradle.

"These strings—gazillions of them—vibrate in the eleven dimensions we can't see," he said, shaking his hands like jazz hands.

"Like we talked about in class!" I said, plucking one of the strings in the middle.

"Exactly," he said. "And they're constantly splitting and reconnecting with other strings to form even more particles that make up, well, everything."

"It's cool," I said. "I'm just not sure what it has to do with me."

Finny looked so excited I almost regretted saying it.

"Physicists—like your dad, probably—believe that if we can understand the way strings move, we can understand nature itself. And if we can understand nature . . ."

His logic fell over me like rain.

"We can understand everything," I said. "Including my episodes?"

"That's the idea," he said. "At least, that's *my* idea."

"Yes!" I said. I went to hug him, but he held his hands taut, like he was afraid of destroying the universe. So I pinched the two Xs, one in each hand, and pushed them down and outside, opening up the center. I'd played this game before. Then I pointed my fingers down and scooped them through the middle while Finny let the universe slide from his hands to mine.

We played cat's cradle back and forth while Finny reminded me of things I'd heard from Dad but forgot, like how Einstein explored atoms and stars with his theory of relativity and space warps, the big bang and black holes with his theory of general relativity. He also told me how string theory was often called the ultimate theory, or the theory of everything. I loved the idea that everything, even hallucinating, could be explained by a single equation. As if all the chaos in my life could be solved with a word problem.

Dad liked crosswords because they were word problems and equations because they were numbers problems. He never heard a question he didn't try to answer or meet a puzzle he didn't attempt to solve, which was annoying and amazing. No matter what it was, though, he always used the same tool: science. Just like someone else I knew.

"It's a part of the path," I said.

Thunder boomed and then huge raindrops fell, hitting the roof like drums.

"What path?"

"Someone has a theory that my episodes are part of a bigger picture," I said. "That I'm on some path and they're actually part of it."

"Whose theory is that?" Finny said.

"I'll tell you later," I said. "What's important is that the path led me to you. And you—my little Einstein—are leading us to Dad."

I wasn't sure where Dad would lead, but at least it would be forward.

"Dad's the only other person on the planet who seems to have experienced what I'm experiencing," I said. "He may not know what it is or how to stop it, but I have to think he knows more than I do."

"And I have to think it will have something to do with string theory," Finny said. "See? Scientists can have internal guidance, too. So what's next?"

Year One I pleaded with Mom to take me to him, to give me back my dad.

Year Two I begged a little less.

Year Three we moved to San Francisco, and I entered the angry phase. If he didn't need me, I didn't need him. But then I had an episode, and I wanted him to appear, for a moment. When he didn't show up, I returned to the angry phase and never looked back.

I guess it was time for Year Four.

"We have to find my dad," I said. Which meant I needed to forgive him.

How to Forgive Your Dad So He Can Maybe Save Your Life by Sophie Sophia

---

1. Forgive him.
2. Say it out loud so you mean it.
3. It's okay if you don't feel it yet. It takes time.
4. Remember it's not for him, it's for you. Forgiveness with an agenda.
5. Since the agenda is saving your life, fake it if you have to. Maybe one day you'll actually feel it.

"It's late," Finny said, opening a pine chest and pulling a carnation-covered comforter and pillow out of it. He threw them on the couch, setting up camp, but I protested.

"I'm way too amped to sleep," I said. "Can I sleep out here and watch a movie on your laptop instead?"

"Sure," he said, handing me his backpack. "But don't stay up too late. I want to start early. I think you're on to something."

"I think I am, too," I said. I had to be. Straitjackets weren't my style. Neither was a padded room. "Good night, Finn."

"Good night," he said.

The door to his room clicked, and I leaned against the side of the couch, legs stretched out long under the comforter. It was cozy down there, surrounded by all those flowers, which was perfect. I had work to do. I opened Google and typed in two words I never thought I'd type: *Angelino Sophia*.

Dad's name, Angelino, meant "the spirit messenger God sent to men." He loved to tell people that, like it excused the crazy stuff he did. "Give me a break," he'd say. "I'm a spirit messenger." But I always wondered—what kind of message did he send by leaving us? And more than that, what kind of God sends a message to a ten-year-old girl that her father doesn't want to be with her anymore?

In addition to my father's name, I Googled *academics, physics, thesis, dimensions, hallucinations, brain studies, Einstein, string theory, psychosis, NYU professor, controversial theory. Episodes. Eccentric. Abandoner.* And *Where the heck are you?*

The Internet made it way too easy to find someone, which is why, when you couldn't find them, it was more frustrating than usual. Even if he didn't do social media or blog, Dad should have been somewhere, in a group shot on Flickr or an alumni list. But he wasn't anywhere, which made me think the same held true for the real world. Except if he'd died, at least there'd be an obituary.

I set the laptop on the coffee table and snuggled under the covers for a minute. Think, Sophie, think. If you wanted to hide, where would people go to find you? The library? The thrift shop? The museum? The record store? If I disappeared, the best way to find me would be to go to the most interesting place in the area, the spot where curiosity and inspiration collided. There were tons of sites like that on the Internet, but only one that was doing it before the web was even invented.

"Got it!" I said, opening a new window and going where I always went when I wanted to find anything: the *New York Times*. Not only did it have the best stories, it also had the best search option, one that should have made all the other search options run away in shame. I typed in Dad's name plus *theoretical physics* plus *NYU*. And then I hit the button I hoped would change everything: *All Since 1851*.

Since none of the links were an exact match, I skimmed the stories, looking for clues. And when I clicked on "Quarks and Professors, Reunited," I found one. It was a photo of a bunch of older guys standing in three rows holding a poster with a colored circle on it surrounded by lines and other colored circles. It said "The Quarks Society," and there, in the back row, was my dad.

He was smiling, the kind of smile you give when you're really happy, hanging out with friends. According to the article, this group was formed in the late eighties to focus on theoretical physics. I scanned the photo, looking for more clues, but none of the members looked familiar except for the guy standing next to my dad. The list said his name was Dr. Perratto. He had let me nap on his couch when Dad wasn't ready to leave campus yet and given me bags of chips from the vending machines. It was nice to have another place to hang when Dad was running late or forgot about me, which happened more than it should have.

According to the article, Dad was a founding member but hadn't been at the reunion. Luckily, the reunion had a website, but it was pretty basic. It didn't tell me much more than the article had, but it did have something the article didn't: a contact list. I clicked on it, scrolled down—and there it was: Dad's name and phone number, with an area code I knew well because I'd had it, too: 718.

I grabbed my phone and dialed, but luckily I hung up before anyone answered. The website was old. He probably didn't have the same number anymore. And even if he did, what was I going to say? Hi, it's your daughter. I know it's six o'clock in the morning, but would you mind if I came to New York? It was smarter to use the number to get his address and show up. Maybe he didn't live there anymore, or maybe he did, and it would be this big homecoming, complete with apologies and answers. Offers to help and solutions. Everything I'd ever wanted to know about myself and all my episodes would come out in one glorious afternoon.

I imagined Dad explaining things to me, and it was exactly what I wanted to hear. There were reasons for everything, explanations that put things into place and—most important— would keep me out of the psych ward. We'd drink pink lemonade and float away on clouds and spend the rest of the trip getting to know each other again. He wouldn't be crazy, and I wouldn't be crazy, and Mom would fall in love with him again. They'd get back together, and the last four years would seem like a blip in an otherwise extraordinary life. Crossword puzzles and cereal, zoos and pancake faces, parasols and popcorn. No more fights, no more being apart—just us, like we used to be. Before the disappearing started.

I knew reunions were very rarely like that.

But I was going to New York anyway.

FIFTEEN

The next morning I snuck into Finny's room. It was early, but I couldn't wait. I sat on his bed and leaned in.

"How would you like to thrift in Greenwich Village?" I whispered in his ear. "Eat artisanal bread in Brooklyn? Feed the ducks in Central Park?"

"Stop teasing," he said, groaning and rolling over.

"I'm serious," I said. "MoMA. Real bagels. We could even find some famous physicist's house or something."

Finny bolted up and threw off his plaid wool blanket, which matched his pajamas. He was so adorable I wanted to die. Hopefully he would want to die, too . . . of joy in a vintage shop on Bleecker.

"It's another day in Havencrest, not one of your fabulous episodes," he said. "You can't choose where they're set, right?"

"Nope," I said. "I'd actually have to be in Times Square to have an episode there. So let's do it."

"Do what?"

Finny made his bed and piled it full of pillows. He called his room Escape from Carnation Palace, but I thought it was more boarding school chic.

"Go to New York," I said.

"If we're going to New York, I better wear something good," he said, pulling a mustard cardigan out of the closet. "And by New York do you mean getting a slice after school?"

"I mean I found Dad's phone number," I said, putting his laptop on his desk. "He's not in Timbuktu or Tanzania, Finny. He's in New York."

Finny opened the laptop and there, on the screen, was what I found last night.

"Whoa," he said. "Did you call him?"

"No," I said. "I think it's better just to show up. We can do a reverse lookup to get his last known address, but I need a credit card."

Finny opened the top drawer of his dresser, and there, underneath a pile of argyle socks, was the answer to our problems, packed in a blue plastic rectangle.

"Forget Saint Christina," I said. "I'm going to have to start saying all of my prayers to Saint Visa."

"Hallelujah!" he said, typing, while I remembered the two hundred dollars Mom had stashed in her sock drawer for emergencies. Enough for a train ticket.

"And then, like magic, he appeared," Finny said, scooting back from the screen. It showed the phone number. Right underneath it was Dad.

Owner: Angelino Sophia

Address: 262 4th Street, Brooklyn, New York.

He was in Brooklyn, which made me wonder—was he there while we were there, too? Streets away from my school on Father–Daughter Day? Subway stops away, when he could have been lulling me to sleep with his latest theory or making me laugh with his newest invention? All those afternoons I spent crying, missing him, wishing he'd explain, was Dad on the other side of the borough doing the exact same thing? And if so, why didn't I ever see him?

"Sophie," Finny said, "are you sure you want to do this?"

"Yes," I said. I needed answers, and this was the only way to do it.

"But now we have an even bigger problem," I said. "It's New York. What are we going to wear?"

"Something fabulous!" he squealed, diving into his closet, which meant I had to go home and dive into mine.

When I got there, Mom's car was gone, so it was safe to go in. At least, I hoped it was. If she popped out of my closet or something, like in a horror movie, I was going to come unglued.

"MEOW!"

Balzac flew off the couch and landed at my feet instead.

"Crap!" I said, jumping back. "You scared me. Did you miss me?"

He meowed, which I took as a yes, even though we both knew he snuggled up with Mom in my absence. The first time I spent the night at a friend's house in New York, Mom said Balzac whined at my door all night. I think we all do some form of that when someone leaves unexpectedly. Meowing at the door, crying yourself to sleep, it's all the same. Which is why I was never going to do that to anyone. If I had to leave for some reason, any reason, I promised myself I'd always leave a note.

I ran up to my room, grabbed my Army Navy messenger bag from under my bed and stood in front of my closet. What did you wear to a reunion, especially when you hadn't seen the person in four years? And especially when that person was your father?

Balzac meowed and batted my elephant skirt, which was kind of the perfect choice, if I wanted to analyze it. Elephants had amazing memories, and that's what this entire trip was about: making a memory. No matter what happened, I wouldn't have to start every morning not knowing whether or not I would be okay. Instead of hiding from the craziness that was my life, I was doing something about it.

The skirt was blue with a gray elephant pocket and a trunk that wrapped around the bottom like it was coming to life. I paired it with my favorite black turtleneck, thin black V-neck sweater, black-and-white-striped tights and boots. I packed the rest of the bag with another skirt and a few T-shirts, a thin striped sweater and socks. Another scarf, a woolly hat, gloves, underwear, *Franny and Zooey*, a journal, some pens, lip gloss and dangly earrings. Just in case.

"See you soon," I said, giving Balzac a kiss. He rubbed against my knee, and I thought about taking him but took my wool pea-coat off the chair instead. I scrawled Mom a note on the back of a bill and left it propped up next to that psychiatrist's card on the kitchen counter, next to the phone. The note said that I'd borrowed the emergency money, that I'd pay it back and that I was taking the night train with Finny to New York. I promised to call her when I got there. I promised to be safe. But I didn't tell her when I was coming back. I needed proof that I wasn't crazy, and I'd stay gone however long it took to get it.

"Someone looks adorable," Finny said, sizing me up as I approached my locker. I had no idea how many costume changes he'd had, but I loved what he'd landed on: a *Life's Rich Pageant* R.E.M. T-shirt, vintage suit jacket, striped scarf and gray Levi's corduroys.

"Thanks," I said, twirling around. "As do you. Very New York."

If Dad had been in Dallas or Cincinnati, I'm not sure Finny would have gone, but New York was an easy one. Not only was he following his science project—me—he was also going to walk the same sidewalks as his idols, go to the Museum of Natural History and hopefully meet one of the greatest physicist minds of all times—my dad.

"So we'll meet at your locker after class?" Finny said, bouncing beside me. There was no way he was going to keep his mouth shut until after school.

"Yes," I said. "But you can't tell anyone."

"What makes you think I'm going to tell?" he said as we sat down in physics class.

I smiled. "You're especially enthusiastic about everything today," I said.

"Maybe that's because I drank too much coffee," he said. "At least, that's my party line."

"Got it," I said.

"Mr. Jackson? Ms. Sophia? Would you mind if we began?" Mr. Maxim stood in front of us, tapping his foot.

"Sorry," I said. "This one has a case of the caffeines."

Everyone laughed, including Finny, and Mr. Maxim lectured about kinetics or something, but I barely heard him. All I could think about was a certain train leading to a certain person until the bell rang and knocked me out of my reverie.

"Mum's the word?" I said, looking at Finny and zipping my lip. "Right?"

"Mum," he said, grinning. Bringing him to New York was like packing extra sunshine. We walked into the hall.

Finny turned left, and I took the stairs two at a time, not looking where I was going, which is probably why I ran into

Drew. Drew, who I hadn't seen since The Cure or the Massive Mom Fight or the Great Dad Finding Adventure. A lot can happen in a day.

"Oh!" I said. "Sorry." And then, like an idiot, I just stood there.

"Sorry for running into me or sorry for bailing on our date?" Drew said.

So it *was* a date.

"Both," I said. "I feel awful."

"I waited for almost an hour," he said. "I got that waitress friend of yours to knock on the bathroom door, but nobody answered. That's when I figured out that you'd left."

"I know this is going to sound weird, but I didn't mean to leave," I said. "I didn't want to."

The stairwell was small, and Drew leaned against the wall while I leaned against the railing. We were so close I could smell his citrus-rific hair again.

"So why did you?"

"I panicked," I said, which was true.

"Like a panic attack?"

Lie for the greater good.

"Yes," I said. "It happened while I was in the bathroom. I was too embarrassed to face you like that, so I left."

"Huh," he said, crossing his arms. He was wearing a black button-up shirt over a white T-shirt with flat-front khakis. I was tempted to tell him that Kerouac had called and wanted his pants back, but he mentioned him first.

"You know, Kerouac had anxiety."

"He did?"

"Yeah," he said. "It's in here." He held up a copy of *Big Sur*. "I was reading it while I was waiting for you."

"Well, at least your hero and I have something in common," I said, smiling, but he didn't smile back. My heart dropped and then I realized—not only did I leave, I never called. Strike two, Sophia.

"I should have called you last night," I said.

He didn't say it was okay or that I could make up for it the next time; he just looked at me. I'd thought I'd screwed it up, but now I *knew* I had. The second bell rang, and he squeezed my arm.

"Calling is good," he said, letting his arm linger on mine. I wouldn't wash that sweater again. Ever. "I was worried about you."

He let go, and I stood there taking it in. He didn't ask me out again or say he forgave me, but he was worried about me, which meant he was thinking about me.

"Maybe I'll see you at lunch?" I said as he walked away.

"Maybe," he said. I could tell he was trying to be tough, but he smiled. Just a little.

I understood if he was being aloof, if he thought it was safer to keep me at a distance. But he could have also been channeling Kerouac. It was hard to tell. All I knew was that he liked the me he thought I was, and I wanted to keep it that way. If there was a chance I could make my hallucinations go away—make it seem like none of it had happened in the first place—I wanted someone waiting for me on the other side. And I wanted it to be Drew.

Dad loved trains so much that he built one out of the things I gave him—pieces of a broken *Pop Goes the Weasel* record, a hairbrush, an apple key chain—and things he found around the house like spatulas and eggbeaters, paper clips and soup cans. Christmas tree lights covered the top, and they flashed while it moved around the basement floor.

"It works!" I said, so excited that I jumped up and down.

"I know!" Dad said, jumping up and down with me.

We held hands, bouncing and hollering at the train he'd built out of nothing. When Mom found us, she didn't even look at the train, she just whisked me up and away to the kitchen, where she sat me down and put a glass of milk in front of me.

"Drink," she said, turning away.

"But, Mommy," I said, "Daddy made a train out of nothing!"

I didn't know why she hated the train, but when Dad came upstairs, she threw a plastic colander at him. He ducked, and it hit the wall behind him instead.

"She missed school again," Mom said.

"And yet she still learned something," he said, winking at me.

"Angelino, I swear," Mom said, which was how she started a fight.

Dad stood there, waiting, and I hiccuped and squirted milk through my nose, a five-year-old's version of a protest. The only way I knew to say "stop."

The seats on the train were red like strawberries, like beating hearts, like stop. Stop the secrets and lies. Stop the hallucinations. Stop my life, I want to get off.

"Nervous?" Finny said. He gave me the window seat and then settled in beside me for the next twenty-something hours.

"Yes," I said, hugging my bag to my chest. "I can't tell if he likes me or not."

"Of course he likes you," Finny said. "He's your dad."

"Not Dad, Drew," I said. "We have twenty hours to fill. Can't we start with a little gossip?"

I knew Finny wanted to work on the Normalcy Project, also known as Me. He wanted to be prepared when he met my dad, and I didn't blame him, but I'd been up all night. I wasn't ready for string theory just yet.

"Yes!" Finny said. "Gossip. Spill it."

"He cornered me in the stairwell," I said.

"Dramatic! Go on."

"He was so close I could smell him," I said.

"Musk?" Finny asked. He knew as well as I did that a guy could be everything you ever wanted, but if he smelled like Old Spice, it was over.

"Citrus," I said. "Clementines, tangerines, mandarins."

"Swoon," Finny said. "What happened next?"

"He busted me for running out of the café and not calling him."

"Ouch," he said. "And then?"

I played with the frayed ends of the arm of my sweater. "He didn't ask me out again," I said. "And he didn't show up at lunch."

"Maybe he wasn't hungry?"

"I blew it," I said.

"Maybe not," Finny said. "He could be playing tough."

"Meaning?"

"Smart girls like you don't like being worshipped. You are feminist and punk rock. You'd rather be an equal."

"Where did you read that?"

Finny opened his bag and there, in between the physics books, was a copy of *Teen Vogue*. I laughed.

"You treated him like crap, so even if he agreed to go out with you, you wouldn't respect him. So he treats you like crap to even the playing field, and you'll be all into him again."

"But I'm into him now," I said.

"So you say," he said. "I'll bet you twenty bucks he texts you later today."

"Deal," I said. "But only if you agree games are ridiculous."

"Of course they are," Finny said. "But according to the magazine, they're necessary. Welcome to the big, bad world of dating. Leave everything you thought you knew at the door."

"I think I already did that with Walt," I said, yawning.

"Who's Walt?"

"My shaman panda," I said, drifting off. "He shows up when I need guidance."

And then I realized what I said. My eyes popped open, and

judging from the look on Finny's face, I could have used some guidance right then.

"You have a recurring hallucination?" Finny said.

I nodded.

"Who's a shaman?"

I nodded again.

"And a panda?"

"Yes," I said. My life was like a cartoon.

"Would it kill you to tell me everything all at once?"

"I told you that I hallucinate. Dad hallucinates. And we bring back souvenirs," I said. "Do you really think you'd be here if I added a shaman panda to the mix?"

Finny leaned back in his seat, sighing. "Of course," he said, crossing his arms in front of him. "Fan of the unexplained, remember?"

That's what I liked about Finny. He huffed and puffed for five minutes and then he was over it.

"It sounds crazy when I say it out loud," I said. That's why I hadn't wanted to say it. But if I was going to come out of the shadows and into the light, I might as well bring my panda with me.

"It doesn't sound any crazier than you looked at Café Haven," he said.

He was right. I hoped I never looked that way again. It was why I was going to New York—to prove that I wasn't the one thing I didn't want to be—my dad. I could only hope the trip came with an antidote.

"Walt, huh?" Finny said. "Is he a grumpy old man panda?"

I laughed. "Not exactly. He plays in bands—and not just marching bands."

"Now you're blowing my mind."

"You'd love him," I said. "He likes Audrey Hepburn and Chinese food and being snarky . . ."

"Go on," Finny said.

"He thinks I'm on some kind of path, which is why he's here. He's supposed to guide me or whatever."

Finny tapped his left foot. It's what he did when he knew there was more to tell.

"Basically, Walt's my guardian angel," I said. "Except he's a panda sent by the High Panda Council. And I don't disappear into his world, he pops into mine."

"Wait, have I seen him?" Finny said.

"Don't you think you'd remember seeing a giant panda?"

"Good point," he said, tapping. I put my hand on his knee to make sure his leg didn't fly off his body.

"I'm the only one who can see him," I said.

"But I'm your physics adviser," Finny said. "How can I possibly run a true experiment without all the data? Please tell your guardian panda healer that I need to meet him. Pronto."

"I would love for you to meet him," I said. He had no idea how much. "But that's not how it works. Walt can't appear to anyone but me, per the rules of the High Panda Council."

"Since when did hallucinations have rules?" His leg stopped moving, but a red flush crept up his neck.

"Since I'm doing more than hallucinating," I said.

"Right," he said. "I knew that."

I loved that Finny was just as open-minded as Dad was. I loved that he went from hearing that I hallucinate to trying to solve me with science in less than ten minutes. I loved that he cared about me enough to come to New York, even if it was partially to meet one of the greatest minds in physics. I knew part of it was about his future, but I also believed that part of it was about mine, which is why I had to give him something.

"Walt and I talk about you," I said.

"Walt knows about me?"

"Of course," I said. "Walt knows about everything. Not the future—I wish—but he's pretty intuitive for a panda."

"What does he think of me?" Finny said. "Does he like my outfits? The whole Normalcy Project name?"

"He thinks you're great," I said. "He's the one who convinced me to tell you everything."

"Walt!" Finny said, high-fiving the air. "My man."

"He's not here," I said.

"How should I know?" Finny said. "It's not like you tell me anything."

I'd told him plenty—it just took me a while. I was still getting used to having a best friend, especially one who kept my secrets. It was easier to be vulnerable with Walt because he wasn't real, but that wasn't fair. Not anymore.

"From here on out, I will tell you everything," I said, holding out my hand and extending my pinky. "I swear."

Finny linked his pinky around mine, and we squeezed.

"Me too," he said. "Which means I have to tell you something."

I stretched my arms over my head and yawned. "Can it wait until after my nap?

"Sure," he said, grinning. "But I doubt you'll be able to sleep knowing your dad wrote a book."

Finny got his iPad out of his bag and handed it to me. There, right on the screen, was a website that looked like a new age explosion. It was aqua and green with an animated GIF of some earth-moon-sky celestial thing and the name of the press across the banner: Possible Realms. I was about to hand the thing back to him when I saw their featured author, Angelino Sophia, and his book: *The Heart of Physics: The Role of Love in the Theory of Everything.*

"Whoa," I said, scrolling down, clicking, hoping for a photo. "Wait, I Googled all night and never found this."

"That's because you don't search like a scientist," Finny said. "I wasn't even looking for it, I was just making sure I was up to date on string theory. I was reading a blog post about it and parallel universes—it was so awesome—when I saw your dad's name in the list of references. I followed it until I ended up at this website."

"The book's out of print," I said, wanting to curse the cursor.

"That's why it's good we're headed to New York," Finny said. "Who needs a book when you can have the real thing?"

I do, I thought. Finny wasn't the only one who needed to prepare to meet my dad.

"Don't look so sad," he said. "There's an intro you can read online."

He took the tablet from me, pointing to a link, and clicked it. We leaned together, holding the iPad between us, the screen lighting up our corner of the train while Dad's words illuminated everything.

INTRODUCTION

Socrates said the unexamined life was not worth living. As scientists, we rise every day because of the search, no matter how often the answers elude us. As husbands, we leave those we love to fend for themselves because there are questions only we can answer. But as fathers, we're brought back to ourselves. Brought back to the reality that we search and rise, day after day, for someone else.

I wrote this book to prove that the thread between physics and emotion exists; that it's just as important to question as it is to answer; and that if you walk through the world with a different view, maybe it's not your world that you're walking in.

Sophie, may this book help you to know me—and therefore, know yourself.

"Where's the rest of it?" I said, my heart pounding. "Why isn't there more?"

"It's just a sample," Finny said. "But isn't it great? The whole *maybe it's not your world that you're walking in* thing?"

Part of it was my world, the part where Dad never called.

The part where I cried myself to sleep and then vowed never to cry again. But then there was the other part where hearts rolled off sleeves and rock stars serenaded me in grocery stores, things of a different world. Whichever world I was in, it made me realize I needed him. I needed my dad.

"And he mentioned you!" Finny said, pointing to my name. "You, my dear, have just become immortal."

My hand shook as I took it away, letting the iPad rest with Finny.

"Wait, are you okay?"

"I just need some air," I said, crawling over him and walking through rows of people like they weren't there, reaching the back door of our car.

I waved my arms in front of it, hyperventilating, until it finally whooshed and opened up. Standing in the space between one car and the next felt like limbo, like the place I'd been for the past four years. Bits of air rushed in, but even the deafening sound of wheels against tracks, steel against steel, couldn't drown out the message running through my head: Dad wrote me a book. Dad wrote me a book. Dad wrote me a book.

SIXTEEN

I walked back in, the door whooshing behind me, but something had changed, like chairs and armrests. Lamps and wallpaper. This wasn't the same train I'd been on, it was better. Bright green seats gave way to pink armrests. Green, pink and plaid curtains hung from the windows, and the walls were covered in hot-pink wallpaper with velvet blackbirds on it. Amtrak, brought to you by Jonathan Adler.

Finny would love this, I thought, feeling like I'd just walked into the most amazing party in progress, except most people were sleeping or reading, just like the train I'd been on before. I chose an empty row in the middle and plopped down beneath a delicate green wire lamp—a birdcage with a miniature bulb hanging from the center. The lamps floated above each seat like tiny, aviary chandeliers. I turned mine off as light seeped through the curtains. Night had turned to day and bright green hills rolled by, pink flowers scattered across them like stars.

"The interior design is crazy good," I said to no one in particular, admiring the cursive M embroidered on the seat back in front of me. M like moody, like mind over matter, like multiverse. Like M-theory.

M-theory was an extension of string theory, Mr. Maxim had said in class last week. We were studying velocity, but he couldn't stop skipping ahead, probably because parallel universes were way more intriguing than one toy car versus another. The idea of parallel universes had lost its appeal in popular media, but with the emergence of M-theory, the idea was plausible again.

He'd said that originally the M stood for *membrane* but it was such a big theory, scientists thought the letter should be open to interpretation. How do you name something that could be the answer to everything?

I didn't completely understand it, but I liked its fill-in-the-blank aspect. The Marvelous Theory, I thought. Magnificent Theory. Morose, how I sometimes felt. Miniature, mayonnaise, milliner. Miser, munchkin, meringue. I was on a roll when I saw something out of the corner of my eye. It was a blackbird, slowly peeling itself off the wallpaper and coming to life. First it was one, then two, then all of them, peeling away and hovering above my head like a hoodie, enveloping me in darkness.

The birds scattered and flew higher, waving their wings, flitting their bodies and flying full-fledged above my head on an Amtrak train.

Blackbirds used to gather on the electrical wires in front of our house and I was scared of them—their dark, beady eyes and big bodies—until Dad told me they were a good omen, not a bad one.

"Blackbirds are all about intuition," he said. "What you feel in your gut."

I'm afraid that I'm my dad.

"According to Native American tradition, they represent increased awareness," he said.

I'm pretty sure that I'm my dad.

"And the magic of worlds you can't see? It's now available to help ground you as you walk your path."

Parallel universes. Walt. The path.

I stood up and they flew in, out and around me like rain, reminding me it was time to do what Walt said. What Dad said. What they were saying. Wake up, Sophie. It's time to pay attention. And even though a magpie was different than a blackbird, it was close enough.

"Magpie," I said, smiling at myself. "It's the Magpie Theory!"

I ran up and down the aisles, arms held high, fingertips grazing the wings of blackbirds. They twisted and twirled, spun and soared through my arms and up to the ceiling, diving at seats and spreading their wings as I expanded my mind. My flock on the inside as the world went by outside, whichever world I was in. I spun and fell into one of the chairs, my laughter mixed with the cawing of blackbirds.

"Excuse me, miss?"

A piercing voice took me from Birdland back to Trainland.

"You're in my seat."

A woman in a hot-pink shirt towered above me, her flowered fanny pack in my face, the smell of coffee wafting over me.

"Sorry," I said, trying to get my bearings. "My mistake."

I stood up, felt the door whoosh and walked into the café car.

"One hot chocolate, one coffee, please," I said. "With room."

Room for books written by missing dads. Room for parallel universes. Room for blackbirds, which stood for intuition, something I was starting to discover within myself.

I walked through three automatic doors until I saw Finny's hair sticking up over the seat.

"Thanks," he said as I gave him his coffee and he gave me back the window seat. And then he pointed at my hair. I could feel it rising off my head like a bad bouffant.

"You weren't back there hanging out, were you?" he said.

"Not exactly," I said.

Finny smiled and pulled a chocolate bar out of the inside of his coat pocket. I guess birds of a feather did flock together. I smoothed my hair down, set my hot chocolate to the side and went for the chocolate bar.

"Can I ask what you saw?"

"Blackbirds," I said, pulling a feather out of my pocket. "One minute I was getting some air and the next I was on a train car like this one but prettier. Hot-pink seats, birdcage lights and wallpaper filled with velvet blackbirds."

"Chic," he said, his foot tapping.

"Yes, except the birds peeled off the wallpaper and flew around the car."

"Whoa," he said. "They attacked you?"

"Not exactly," I said, but when I looked down at my arms, they were full of little nicks, like from the beaks of birds. Had I been so into the magic that I hadn't noticed that part, or was that just the hazard of raising my arms in the middle of hundreds of birds?

"Sophie!" he said, grabbing my arm. "You look like a cutter."

It was scary now, but it didn't seem scary then. It felt good to be surrounded by them, soft, warm and aware. Being part of a flock was always better than going it alone.

"They didn't bite me—they embraced me," I said.

"If by embrace you mean rip into your skin, then yes," Finny said, pulling a packet of wipes out of his coat pocket. "They embraced you fully. This is going to sting, but after what you've been through, I doubt you'll feel it."

As he dabbed my arm with antiseptic, I let the stinging wake me up to my purpose. I was serious about finding my dad, but maybe it was time to be a little more serious about all of it. The fact that I had run away from home, leaving only a note. That Dad was alive and well and apparently still in Brooklyn. And that we were on a train, headed there without calling, without texting, nothing. Maybe my memories were wrong. Maybe we weren't as alike as I thought. Maybe his book was total trash, a theory that couldn't hold up, which was why we'd never heard of it. Why it was out of print. And why I was probably out of my mind for being on this train with my best friend, headed into I Didn't Know What.

"Just wave your arms," Finny said, putting the antiseptic pad in between our two seats. "The air makes it sting less."

I didn't want it to sting less—I wanted it to sting more. The way it would sting if Dad slammed the door in my face. I wanted to be prepared. I wanted Finny to be prepared, but instead we sat in silence for a while as the train propelled us forward. Maybe this was as far as Finny could go, should go, but it was farther than anyone had ever gone with me before.

"You need to sleep," he said, packing away his iPad and putting up the tray table. "You want to be awake for New York, right?"

I wanted to be awake to what was really happening to me, but for now, I'd settle for sleep. I drank the rest of my hot chocolate, put up my tray table and leaned against the window.

"It's more comfy over here," Finny said, patting his shoulder. "Come on."

I was too tired for pride, so I leaned over and nestled into the corner of his jacket like a bird seeking shelter from a storm. It was time to batten down the hatches. Fortify the heart. Make sure the mind was intact and don't forget to bring a friend. There could be rough skies ahead.

SEVENTEEN

As soon as the train stopped, I grabbed my bag and resisted doing my usual dart and dash. This was New York, and I was used to getting places, not playing tour guide, but I had to slow down for Finny. Penn Station could be overwhelming even if you'd been there hundreds of times before. I couldn't imagine what it felt like to a newbie.

"Are we underground?" Finny said as we walked off the train. "Like mole people?"

"You shouldn't believe everything you read," I said. And not because I didn't believe in mole people but because I didn't want *Finny* to believe in them. "We're not in underground tunnels, we're in the extremely well-planned urban subway system. Welcome to Penn Station."

Finny's mouth dropped open as I pulled him up the escalator and led him through commuter traffic to the 3 train.

"Here's the thing," I said, holding his hand tightly in mine. "You have to keep moving. And maybe close your mouth. The only gawker-approved places are things like the Empire State Building or the Statue of Liberty."

Finny closed his mouth, but his eyes remained big, eyes that had never been out of Havencrest. This kid *so* needed a proper introduction to New York.

"Hungry?" I asked.

"Starving," he said as I pulled him inside Bert's Bagels and took a deep breath. It was a smell that had been lost but not forgotten. Pumpernickel, rye, sesame, come to me.

"I'll have a whole wheat with blueberry cream cheese," Finny said.

"Uh, no," I said, butting in. "He'll have what I'm having—sesame with plain cream cheese, tomato, capers and black pepper."

Finny crossed his arms over his chest.

"Trust me," I said. "You're never going to look at bagels the same way again."

Minutes later, we were on the platform holding warm bags of bagels. Finny unwrapped the paper, took a bite and looked like he was going to pass out.

"Oh. My. God," he said, chewing.

"I bet you never thought a bagel could render you uncon-scious," I said, smiling. "Ooh! Here's our train."

I put Finny in front of me like a kid and pushed him through the doors before they closed. The train was packed, but I saw one seat and Finny saw another one. Too bad it was farther down and on the opposite side. There was no way I was going to be able to hold his hand.

"I'll be fine," he said, grabbing the seat while I took the one in front of me.

"Hey!" he said, yelling over the crowd. "I can still see you!"

"Great," I yelled back. "Just make sure to get off at Grand Army Plaza."

As we reached our stop, I'd stand by him, making sure he got off the train. But until then, he was on his own—and I think that was the way he wanted it. The train was full of something I hadn't realized I'd missed: people. All kinds, all languages, smashed together in one place. Two women arguing in Chinese, another man singing a soul song along with his iPod, and two girls my age with screen-printed T-shirts, one with a lion, one with a tiger. I loved how people didn't even blink at my elephant skirt in New York. I also loved how plastic orange seats, bizarre smells and a homeless guy playing the flute could feel like home. I bit into my bagel and a caper rolled off and into my lap as the person beside me got up and Walt appeared in her place.

"You gonna share that?"

"Wow," I said, putting my bag in Walt's lap so no one else would sit there. I kept my hand on it, making sure no one stole it, but I was sure they wouldn't. People didn't take bags from crazy girls who talked to said bags. Even though I was about to have a conversation with Walt, no one else would see it that way.

"You're the last guy I expected to see," I said, keeping my head down and talking into my lap.

"Why are you talking like that?"

"I don't want Finny to see me talking to myself," I said. "Why are you here again?"

"Where else am I going to get a good bagel?" he asked.

I handed him half of mine, and he shoved it into his mouth.

"That's worth traveling for," he said. "Is it the boiling process? Because I always wondered what made New York bagels better than, say, Seattle bagels."

"You're not just here for bagels," I said, popping the rest of mine in my mouth. "What gives?"

"Just a friend," he said, licking cream cheese off his paw, "being here for another friend."

"More like making sure a friend stays on her path," I said.

"Something like that," he said. "I support you finding your dad, but you know meeting him won't solve everything, right?"

"Of course it will," I said, shifting around in my seat. "Dad wrote this book that sounds like it's about us, our experiences. From the sample I read online, it seems like he wrote it just for me."

"So why not just order the book?"

"It's out of print," I said. And then I borrowed from Finny. "Besides, why rely on the book when I can have the real thing instead?"

"Let me rephrase myself," Walt said. "Nothing is a magic pill, not even your super-intelligent, amazingly perceptive dad. He may teach you something, but you can't just rely on him. You still have to use your intuition."

I knew about pandas from my animal totem book, the one Dad brought back from one of his trips. From what I remembered, the panda is the seer of the unseen. He brings you the focus and awareness you need to overcome a problem, which sounds good, but when it came to Walt, I had to wonder: why couldn't he just solve my problems for me? If he had all this power and knowledge, like he said he did, what would it hurt for him to make an exception? To give me some of the answers instead of making me work for them myself?

"I know I have to pay attention," I said, getting up and moving toward Finny. "If I don't, we'll miss our stop."

Before I entered the Dad Hating Years, I begged Mom to tell me where he was. I searched boxes under her bed, photo albums hidden in her underwear drawer, everywhere I could think of, but I always came up empty-handed. That's why I thought if I ever found him, I'd make the journey alone. But now, with a boy genius on one side and a shaman panda on the other, it seemed obvious. Not all journeys were meant to be made solo.

"This is Grand Army Plaza," I said, bumping Finny's knee with my knee. "This is our stop."

Finny stood up, and I looked back at Walt's seat, which was now filled with a kid bouncing a red ball.

The train stopped, and I guided Finny off the subway,

through the people and up onto the street. I sighed, happy to stop traveling for a moment. He rubbed his eyes.

"Where are we?"

"Prospect Park," I said. "It's just a short walk from here to Park Slope."

"Should we get a cab?" Finny said. "It's getting dark."

"No way," I said, keeping him out of the crowds and with me. I felt my phone vibrate in my pocket, so I pulled off to the side, outside a bodega. When I took it out, it practically blew up, message alerts and texts all over the place.

"Finn, you left your mom a note, right?"

"Of course," he said. "That's why I have twenty-seven messages on my phone. But at least she knows where I am."

"Me too," I said. "But that didn't stop my mom from leaving eighteen messages. I'm glad she's not good at texting."

"So no texts?" Finny said, leaning against the brick wall.

"There's one text," I said. "From Drew."

"Bam!" Finny said. "Twenty dollars, please. And text him back."

"What do I say?" I said. "Hi, I know I don't really know you, but I'm in New York trying to find my dad, who abandoned me, so he can help me stop hallucinating?"

"First? That's way too long," Finny said. "And second? Give me your phone."

He held it up to his face, reading.

DREW: Missed you at lunch. You okay?

"So he *did* show up at lunch," Finny said. "How long did you wait for him?"

"Ten minutes," I said. "Was that not enough?"

"Not even. Try this," Finny said, typing something.

SOPHIE: Sorry I missed you. Called out of town, family thing. All well. Will call soon.

"It's short but responsive," Finny said. "All you have to do is hit Send."

The text sat there on the screen like a lie.

"It's not a lie," Finny said, reading my mind. "You are out of town, you are dealing with a family thing, and you will call him soon."

"What about the all-is-well part?"

"You have a choice," Finny said. "You can either stand here and worry about it, or you can make a move."

Finny spun around and stopped, jazz hands extended. "I'm sure Fourth Street is around here somewhere. Are you ready?"

Thanks to a bagel, my best friend and a panda, I was as ready as I'd ever be, which wasn't very ready at all.

But I hit Send anyway.

How to Prepare to Meet Your Dad when You're Not Really Prepared at All by Sophie Sophia

---

1. Brush your hair. You just rode on a train for twenty hours, and you're a mess.
2. Think about all the food you can eat if it doesn't go well: shawarma, saag paneer, cannoli, mmmm.
3. Let Finny do most of the talking, at least at first.
4. Put your hands in your pockets or something! You're way too excited.

5. Take three deep breaths in, three deep breaths out. You've been fine without him for four years. And no matter what happens, you'll continue to be fine. Period.

We walked down Fourth Street, and everything looked like I remembered—lush maples, colorful brownstones and blue skies that went on for miles.

"That's the apartment," I said, looking at the slip of paper I'd tucked into my pocket. "Number two sixty-two."

"Is this the house you grew up in?"

"No, but our apartment wasn't far from here." I suddenly had an urge to go backward, back to a time when everything made sense.

"Hey, is this your dad's car?"

Finny pointed at a Volkswagen Beetle that was parked in front of the house. It matched the gingko leaves that fell around us.

"It's probably a neighbor's car," I said. "It's almost impossible to find parking in front of your own house."

Finny peeked in the back window.

"If this is your dad's car, cleanliness is definitely *not* next to genius."

I looked inside and saw physics books and Hershey wrappers, a picnic basket and empty wine bottles. It was definitely Dad's car, even though there was a stuffed elephant in the passenger seat. He must have had amazing parking karma.

"Maybe he has a dog," Finny said.

"He could have a completely new family," I said, hands shaking. "I never thought of that."

"True, but you're his original family," Finny said. "Plus he wrote a book for you, which totally trumps a tacky old elephant."

I appreciated what he was doing, but my brain had already left the station, bound for What-if-ville.

"What if he doesn't recognize me?"

"He will," Finny said.

"What if he has a beard or a mustache?" I said. "What if he lost his hair? What if he went corporate? Or gave up physics for the circus?"

Spinning mind, out of control.

"Finny, what if my dad is a professional clown?"

"Wow," he said, taking my hand and squeezing it hard. "In the history of forever, no world-class physicist has gone from string theory to wearing a flower that squirts water, okay?"

A flock of blackbirds flew by, squawking and scattering in the sky like pepper.

"Okay," I said. I cleared my throat and straightened my skirt. "Let's do this."

Finny led me up the stoop—around the purple flowerpots with ivy flowing out of them, around the pile of newspapers and straight to the buzzer, which we didn't have to use since a woman rushed out and we rushed in.

"That was easy," I said. "Maybe we won't even need our story."

In case Dad didn't answer the door, we had a story ready:

Finny and I were reporters from the *Erudite Reader*, a high school literary journal that celebrated science. We were there for a scheduled interview with Dr. Sophia. Was he in?

Finny knocked on the door while I took a deep breath. Calm, Sophie, calm. A tall woman with long blond hair answered the door. She had a Calvin-Klein-meets-hippie vibe going on: faded jeans, white button-up man's shirt, turquoise necklace and earrings. Sandals even though it was freezing outside. And she was standing there instead of my father.

"Hello," Finny said, staying with the plan. "We're from the *Erudite Reader* and have an appointment with Dr. Sophia."

Her eyes were red and puffy.

"Dr. Sophia only does phone interviews," she said. "And he's out of town at the moment. Are you sure you have the correct Dr. Sophia?"

"Is he the same one who wrote *The Heart of Physics: The Role of Love in the Theory of Everything?*"

She looked surprised. "Yes. How did you hear about it?"

"We're in AP physics," Finny said. "Dr. Sophia's thesis has been a great complement to our studies."

You go, Finny.

"Oh," she said. "That's wonderful. I'm Peyton Greeley, Dr. Sophia's assistant."

"And you live with him?" It flew out of my mouth before I could stop it.

She smiled. "I'm also his girlfriend."

It took everything I had not to lunge at her way-too-young-for-Dad body.

"Would you two like to come in for a minute?"

"We'd love to," Finny said, giving me a look. Begging me not to blow it.

"Excuse the mess," she said, opening the door wider and leading us through the house. "Every time there's a new theory, housework goes by the wayside."

When I lived with Dad, housework always went by the wayside. Mom said she couldn't work and clean up after two children, one of them being me, but the other one being Dad. I had no doubt that he lived here.

Stacks of books, models of atoms and dead houseplants covered every possible surface. The fireplace was filled with foil balls in progress, one of them pretty big. And the mantel was covered in shells, photos and astronomy charts, more like stuff a girlfriend would have. Why did he have a girlfriend when he could have had me and Mom?

"Can I get you two anything?" Peyton said, motioning toward the purple couch. She wanted us to sit down, but I wanted to spy on their lives.

"I'd love something to drink," Finny said. "If it's not too much trouble."

"No trouble at all," she said. "I'll be right back."

I wished Peyton and her white floaty shirt would never come back.

"Do you think something's off?" I said, walking over to the mantel.

"Kind of," Finny said. "Maybe they had a fight or something."

"Maybe," I said. I traced my finger along the wood.

There was a photo of the two of them at the ocean. Dad looked older, but at least he didn't have a beard or a clown nose. And then I saw it: me. Blowing out candles on my tenth birthday. The picture was sitting there in a gold frame like I was still a part of the family, like nothing had happened. Like that hadn't been the last birthday of mine he'd seen.

"Fresh ginger ale!" Peyton said, carrying in a tray. "I made it myself."

And I was ready to make her life miserable.

"Where's my dad?" I said, holding the photo.

She set down the tray and walked toward me.

"Wait," she said. "I'm confused."

"I know it's been four years, but I don't look that different," I said. "So where is he? Teaching a class? Out on an errand?"

I recognized a feeling in my stomach. I felt it right when we walked in the house. I'd felt it a dozen times before.

"Sophie?" She tried to touch my arm, but I pulled it away.

"Where is my dad, and when is he coming back?"

"Sophie," she said, her eyes welling with tears, "I am so sorry."

Fire built in my belly and spewed out of my mouth. "Are you sorry that he left me or sorry that he's shacking up with you?"

She looked away, toward the door, like he was about to walk through it. And then she looked back at me. "I'm sorry that he's gone," she said, her hands shaking. "Sophie, your dad has been missing for two weeks."

How to Survive Finding Your Dad After Four Years Only to Discover That He's Missing Again
by Sophie Sophia

1. Feel it. You kind of don't have a choice on that one.
2. Acknowledge that the feelings suck. A lot.
3. Cry if you need to.
4. Know you have a panda and a boy genius on your side.
5. And then, when it's out of your system, do what you have to do: find your dad.

"Let's get you some food," Peyton said, heading toward the kitchen.

Finny linked arms with me as we walked. He thought I was going to fall down from shock, but I wasn't. As soon as we'd entered the house, I had known Dad wasn't there, that he hadn't been there for a while. I hadn't said anything because sometimes I was wrong, but I also didn't want it to be true.

"Whoa," I said, falling back. "That's our table."

There, in the middle of the kitchen, was a big round table just like the one Dad and I had collaged one morning and regretted that evening when Mom yelled at us. That table had seen spilled milk and reheated lasagna, puddles of glue and piles of confetti, homemade birthday cards and roses tied together with a bow.

"Your dad made that," Peyton said, setting a plateful of banana bread in front of me. "He said he needed something that reminded him of you. If you look, there's a picture of you in there somewhere."

I couldn't believe he'd made a copy of our table. The original one—we gave it to our upstairs neighbor when we moved—had pictures of me everywhere, along with newspaper articles and construction paper hearts held down with glue. This one was more physics and less Sophie, probably because Mom had all the photos. All Dad had were memories, but it looked like he'd been busy making new ones. He could have been making one right now.

"I feel like I know you," Peyton said. "I've heard so much about you."

"And I've heard nothing about you," I said.

Peyton got up and stood over the sink. Finny shot me a look.

"Try the banana bread," she said, her voice all raspy.

I ran my finger over a photo of Dad and me that was collaged onto the table. It was taken on Halloween, the time he was Captain Hook and I was Peter Pan. All I needed was for Tinker Bell to sprinkle some fairy dust and make Dad appear. Peyton would have wanted that, too.

"This bread is really good," I said, remembering my puffy eyes, the ones that wouldn't go away because I cried too much. The same eyes Peyton had. "Does my dad like it?"

Peyton turned and smiled, sniffling. Finny grabbed my hand under the table and squeezed. I could hate her all I wanted, but I should at least wait until Dad was back.

"I like it," Finny said, grabbing another piece and stuffing it in his mouth. "But we have bigger things to do. Who's ready to get to work?"

"To work?" Peyton said. "On what?"

Finny and I looked at each other. We knew what we had to do, but we weren't sure we wanted to bring her in on it.

"Filling in the gaps," Finny said. "We didn't ride on a train for twenty-something hours to give up. Sophie hasn't seen her dad in four years and then we get here and he's gone? We'd like to know why. Or at least learn more about him."

"Of course," Peyton said. "Right. Let me make some tea, and I'll tell you everything you want to know."

I grinned and high-fived Finny across the table. We were a search party, a spy mission, a family tree who wanted its branches back. And together, we were going to find my dad.

EIGHTEEN

Dad and I used to play a game called Secret-Schmecret. The premise was simple: he thought of a secret, and I guessed what it was. The best part was the clues, which involved at least one of the five senses. Sometimes the clue was a mixture of nutmeg and cinnamon, and the secret would be that my oatmeal was ready. Another time he made stuffed animal pants and wore them around the house to indicate that we were going to the zoo. And once he had me close my eyes, open my mouth and chew whatever he put in there, which happened to be a carrot. This meant we were either going to build a snowman or make carrot soup. Both would have worked since it was snowing outside, but

I never knew which one was happening until it happened. With Secret-Schmecret, it was always a surprise. And that was kind of the point.

"It's no secret your father and I were having problems," Peyton said.

"I didn't even know about you, so it was a secret to me," I said. "But go on."

Peyton brought the kettle over from the stove and filled three teacups with hot water. They didn't have tea bags in them, but I didn't want to say anything.

"Maybe I should start at the beginning," she said.

"Fine," I said, looking around the kitchen for clues as she spoke.

Peyton and Dad had been together for two years. *Photos of them on the refrigerator.*

They met at NYU, in the physics department. *Chipped green sugar bowl on the counter with plastic babies in it.*

Dad started disappearing more often. *Pink elephant planter filled with tongue depressors.*

He got demoted to part time. *Broken radios everywhere.*

And then no time. *Blue dog painting in the corner.*

He had tenure, so he did guest lectures, but not classes. *Round gold mirror with dust on the surface.*

Peyton stayed on in the department in hopes of continuing his work, but it was hard with Dad disappearing all the time. *Paper lanterns spilling out of a trunk on the floor.*

"What happened before he disappeared this time?"

"We were fighting," Peyton said, sipping hot water. "Silly domestic stuff."

I knew Dad, which meant he could have brought home ten rabbits and gotten angry when she didn't want to care for them or encouraged her to make a five-course meal only to insist on eating ice cream sandwiches instead. There was nothing domestic about Dad.

"But he didn't take anything with him," she said.

"What do you mean?" I asked.

"Your dad didn't go anywhere without his books and journals," she said. "But they're here. Still. That bag."

You can tell how worried someone is by how they jumble their words or leave things out. Little words like *and* and *the* stay in, but more important ones like *unstable* or *danger to himself and others* fall away. The story comes to you in pieces because they, themselves, are in pieces.

"Did he ever tell you where he went?" I said.

Finny leaned so far forward in his chair he was practically lying on the table.

"Sometimes," she said. "I want to believe he went where he said he did, but once the police called me to come pick him up from a hostel in Manhattan, so I'm not sure. But you know this. He disappeared on you all the time."

Including the time he disappeared forever.

"Maybe the answer's in his book," Finny said, looking at Peyton. "Do you have a copy?"

"Of course," she said. She walked over to a desk right outside the kitchen. It was piled high with boxes, and there, on top of a real dictionary, was a book.

"Here you go," she said, handing it to me.

The cover was plain—white with black letters like something academic, no new age graphics from the publisher's website anywhere. I ran my fingers across the title, which was pressed into the cover: *The Heart of Physics: The Role of Love in the Theory of Everything*, by Angelino Sophia.

"We read the intro online," Finny said. "Did he write this book for Sophie?"

I ran my hand up and down the spine, leafing through the pages, breathing it in, hoping the book would smell familiar. I held it tightly to my chest, as if I could absorb Dad through close contact.

"In a way, yes," Peyton said. "Angelino wanted to marry his unique view of the world with the basic tenets of physics to create something extraordinary, a legacy of sorts, that he could leave for his daughter."

"I know I'm just in high school physics, but I'm having a hard time seeing how love has a place in any of this," Finny said.

I hugged the book even tighter.

"It's theoretical physics," she said. "When you're theorizing, there's room for everything."

"Even philosophy? Emotion? Psychology?"

Peyton sighed and leaned back in her chair. I liked how much she was challenged by Finny. How much she sounded like Dad. "Do you want to be a scientist?"

"More than anything," Finny said.

"Then you'll learn, very quickly, that the universe is massive, full of things we can't see, including other universes. It hasn't been proven, but we know they're out there. And then there's quantum and string theory and all of these branches of physics that are so much more than science. To work on these equations—some of them for a lifetime, never getting an answer—you have to take a leap of faith."

I wanted to hate her a little because she was a part of Dad's life and I wasn't, but I couldn't. She was too much like him.

"Is that what he does in his book?" Finny said. "Take a leap of faith?" He was good at this.

"Angelino leapt by adding emotion to the equation," Peyton said. "He believed that a certain kind of love had the power to transport people to parallel universes."

I bolted up out of my chair. Finny pulled on my arm.

"Sophie?" Peyton said, like she knew before she asked it. "Do you see things like your dad?"

"Of course not," I said. It flew out of my mouth like a protective mechanism, a lie that had slowly become my truth.

"I thought for sure that was why you were here," Peyton said. She was staring at me, and I could tell she wasn't convinced. I'd have to work on my lying skills. "Your father was always afraid you'd see things like he does."

Then maybe he should have called, I thought. Given me a warning. And if he was going to write a book about it, maybe he should have mailed me one. Made sure his instructions actually made it into my life.

"What did my father tell you about me?"

"Pretty much everything," she said. "Besides physics, you're all he talks about."

I found it hard to believe that someone so enamored with me wouldn't pick up the phone once in four years, which reminded me of something.

"Is there somewhere I can get some privacy?" I said. "I need to call my mom."

"Sure," Peyton said, taking our teacups and placing them in the sink. "I'm sure she'll want to know that you made it here okay."

The cups clanged. Ceramic on ceramic.

"Let me talk to your mom when you're finished, okay?" Peyton said.

"Okay," I said, lying. If Mom didn't want to talk about Dad, I doubted she wanted to talk to his new girlfriend. "Where can I get some privacy again?"

"Our bedroom," she said. "Go upstairs, the first door on your left."

I walked up the stairs, walking the same steps Dad had probably walked a thousand times. Wondering where his steps led him now. Was he still here, or was he somewhere else? Had he gotten stuck in an episode? That was one of my biggest fears—that something would happen and I'd be stuck forever in a world that was magical but wasn't completely mine. Just like vacation, some places were nice to visit, but that didn't mean you wanted to live there.

I turned the knob, and I was in their bedroom. It smelled

like jasmine, not tin can and tomatoes like Dad. Empty Kleenex boxes and candy wrappers covered the green bedspread, but I pushed them aside, ignoring the journal on the nightstand. I flopped on my back and stared at the collaged painting hanging above the bed. It was full of old gas pumps and globes, video cameras and sixties bathing beauties. In the middle was an oddly placed elephant.

I dialed Mom's number and she answered immediately.

"Sophie? Is that you?"

I was prepared to be tough. I wouldn't be in New York if she'd given me the answers I needed. Or hadn't threatened stupid psychiatry.

"Sophie Sophia, you do not do this," she said. "You do not go to school and then, instead of coming home, hop a twenty-hour train to New York with your best friend."

"But I left you a note," I said.

"A note does not make up for the fact that you're fourteen, alone and way too many states away from me."

"I have Finny," I said. "And Peyton."

"Is Peyton another panda?"

"No, she's Dad's girlfriend."

Awkward. Pause.

"How's your dad?"

One awkward paused deserved another.

"He's not here," I said. Voice shaking.

"Oh, Sophie."

"He'll probably be back soon. You know how he is."

"I know all too well," she said. "How long has he been gone this time?"

"Two weeks," I said. "Peyton said it was unusual."

"He wasn't usually gone that long with us," she said. "What else did she say?"

"Peyton works with Dad," I said. "She filled me in on a bunch of stuff."

"Like?" Mom's voice softened.

"Dad wrote a book," I said. "Did you know?"

"He was always working on a book," she said. "I didn't know he finished one."

"Do you know what it's about?"

"Not really," she said. "Physics, I'm guessing."

"It was about love," I said. "And he wrote it for me."

Mom sighed. Her voice sounded heavy, like a thousand blankets stacked on top of one another. "I'm coming to get you."

"You can't!" I said. "I have to find him."

"No one can find your father," Mom said. "He leaves when he wants and comes back when he wants."

But I knew Dad like I knew myself. And if there was one thing I was sure of, it was that hallucinations didn't let you choose. You were at their mercy. I just had to hold out hope that his book held a clue or the people who worked with him could give me some missing information. There was nothing for me in Havencrest, not if I didn't come back with answers.

"Finny's never even been to New York," I said. "Can we at

least stay an extra day? Peyton promised we could sleep here, and she'd feed us and take us around and everything."

"I need to talk to her," Mom said. "We don't even know her."

And I didn't believe that Dad slept in this room. I looked around, but there were no hammers or ripped-up plaid shirts. No brooms with the end missing or lightbulbs strung together like pearls. Only normal stuff, like piles of books and perfume, candles and a vase full of flowers. If Dad were there, that vase would have been full of pinwheels instead.

"Sophie?"

"So talk to her," I said.

"What about school?" Mom said. "You don't have an infinite number of sick days."

"And I haven't taken any," I said. And with any luck, I wasn't going to be sick anymore when I returned. Not sick in the head, anyway. "Please? It's for a good cause."

You know, the Sophie-Stay-Out-of-Psych-Ward cause.

"Finny had his first New York bagel," I said. "And tomorrow we were going to go to the Empire State Building, MoMA and Katz's."

Mom paused longer than usual, which meant she was actually thinking about it.

"Twenty-four hours," she said. "I want to talk to Peyton, and I want you to buy train tickets for tomorrow night. Do you need more money?"

"Always," I said. "But Finny has an emergency credit card."

"We'll work it out," she said. "We'll pay him back." And then she said something I didn't expect.

"Is she nice?"

"Who?"

"Peyton," Mom said.

"Mom . . . ," I said.

"What? I'm just curious who my daughter is spending time with."

"She's fine," I said. "A little hippie for my taste, not stylish and sophisticated like you."

Mom laughed. "You're still in trouble, but thank you."

"Anytime," I said. "Can I ask you something now?"

"No, you cannot stay two more days," she said.

"It's more important than that," I said, looking at the scratches on my arm. "No therapy."

"What?"

"Promise me you're not going to send me to therapy."

"Is that why you ran away?"

"Just promise," I said.

"Honey, I'm sorry I didn't tell you more about your father, but I didn't know a lot. I'm sorry that he's not there, that you're hurting, and I can't reach through the phone and hug you. But I can't promise that you won't ever go to therapy."

"Please," I said, my voice falling as I said it.

"Just come home," she said.

But since therapy was still on the table, I had to get off the phone. I had to figure things out. Now, more than ever, I had to find Dad.

"I'll have Peyton call you," I said. "I have to go."

"Sophie—"

"Mom," I said, the courage rising in my voice, "I'll come back tomorrow. But that doesn't mean I have to like it."

"I don't care if you're mad and never want to speak to me again, but listen to me," she said. "I love you. I have always loved you. And nothing in the world can change that. Do you hear me?"

"Yes," I said, wiping the tears as they came. Wishing she would leave me more options. "I'll talk to you soon."

I hung up the phone and sat on the stairs, the third one from the top. The smell of tomato sauce and onions wafted up, making my stomach growl. I guess you could be melancholy and hungry at the same time.

"Do you believe in the spirit world?" I heard Peyton ask. I almost laughed and blew my eavesdropping cover.

"In what way?"

"I think you two are a sign that Angelino's still out there."

"Him calling you would be a *better* sign," Finny said.

"Come on," she said. "Of all the times for you to show up— it has to be more than coincidence."

"Sounds like something Sophie's shaman panda would say," he said.

I wanted to run down and strangle him, but I also wanted to hear the rest of it.

"She has a shaman panda?"

"Maybe," Finny said. "I'm tired. I don't know what I'm saying."

"So she *does* hallucinate."

Silence. He knew he was in trouble. But I knew his silence just gave me away.

"You should ask Sophie all of this," he said. "But I assume if you wanted to know her, you would have called her."

"We couldn't," Peyton said. "Her mom put a restraining order on Angelino. No phone calls, no contact, nothing."

Wait. A. Minute.

"I met him not long after her mom kicked him out," Peyton said. "He was such a mess, I didn't think he'd ever get over it. But then he threw himself into researching that book, and since he was doing it for Sophie, it really helped."

"So he didn't leave," Finny said.

"Not of his own accord," Peyton said. "It was more like they left him."

All of this time I'd hated Dad for leaving, for making Mom cry, for making me think he never loved me at all. Because you don't leave the people you love. Or so I thought.

"We have to tell her," Finny said. "She thinks her dad doesn't love her."

"He worships her," Peyton said. "Everything he does, everything he's ever done has been for her. Some of it's in the book, and some of it's in the basement."

And there it was. The magic word. I practically ran down the stairs.

"Hi, guys," I said, waltzing into the kitchen. Playing it cool. "Making dinner?"

"I thought we needed to eat," Peyton said. "I hope you like spaghetti."

"I love it," I said. "But do you think I could look at some of Dad's old stuff while you guys make dinner?"

Finny looked panicked. The longer we knew each other, the harder it was to hide things from each other. And the whole "we left Dad" thing was written all over his face. I loved him for being so transparent, but at the moment I had other things to worry about.

"Sure," Peyton said. "Your dad's stuff is all over, so give me a second to find it."

We both looked around, but she was looking for a photo album, while I was looking for a clue. Looking for Dad. And then I found him.

"Does that door go to the basement?" I said, nodding toward the aqua-blue glass doorknob.

It was the kind of thing installed by someone who pulled frogs out of his beret. Strawberry ice cream cones out from behind his back. And flowers made of gum wrapper chains from his pocket. Life with Angelino Sophia was one surprise after another, which is why hallucinating didn't destroy me. And why knowing that Mom and I were the ones who left him wouldn't stop me. If anything, it was going to make me try harder. Go faster. I put my hand on the knob, and Peyton rushed the door like a tree hugger in the redwoods.

"Let me take you down there," she said.

"Let me go with you," Finny said, face flushed. Hands shaking.

"Finny, you need to help with dinner, and Peyton, my mom wants you to call her. Finny has the number," I said, brushing past them. "If it's okay with you guys, I'd rather do this alone."

I turned the knob, and twinkling white Christmas lights flicked on and lit my way; it was like walking through a constellation. Purple and yellow paper birds flew from the ceiling, and polka dots covered my shirt, showering me with confetti. But this wasn't a hallucination. This was paradise.

"Mai tai," I said as I floated down the stairs. "Mai tai, mai tai, mai tai . . ."

NINETEEN

Dad didn't mean to take me to a bar, but that's what he did. I was five, and we were in the middle of an art project when he decided we needed more supplies. And we couldn't just go to any art store; we had to go to his favorite one in the East Village. He wanted me to switch from watercolors to acrylics because the colors were better—cadmium lemon 86, cerulean blue 137, permanent sap green 503. Never mind that I'd be covered in paints that wouldn't wash off—it was all for the sake of art. At least, that's what he said when he paid for five tubes of paint and left. Then, to improve my chances of becoming the next Picasso, we stopped at Waikiki Wally's to pray to the art gods.

In addition to saints, Dad taught me there were gods for everything. When the kitchen trash overflowed, we prayed to the garbage gods, hoping they'd take it out. When we ran out of food, we prayed to the delivery gods to bring some. When Mom was in a bad mood, we prayed to the vacation gods for plane tickets and some new luggage. So when Dad said we were stopping off to pray to the art gods, it wasn't anything new.

"Welcome to paradise!" Dad said, swinging open a huge wooden door to reveal the closest thing to a tropical island I'd ever seen. Huge glass lanterns hung from the ceiling in all the colors from the art store. The one in the corner? Yellow ochre. That one above my head? Burnt sienna. And if the one by the bar wasn't phthalo green, I didn't know what was. There were masks, tropical flowers and totem poles. And except for the woman wearing the lei, we were the only ones there.

"Aloha," she said in a totally monotone voice. "Welcome to Waikiki Wally's."

She motioned toward the bar and clomped away, leaving us to island music. Dad ordered something called a "pu pu platter," which sounded gross. I looked around, and there in the corner was the reason we came: an Easter Island head surrounded by fading fake flowers. It was the art god. I went over and knelt in front of it.

"Hula-ha-ha," I said to the statue, bowing forward, but nothing happened. "Mekka-mekka-pukka!" I said, even louder. I thought the art gods might hear me better if I spoke up.

Dad knelt beside me.

"What are you doing, Sophie?" Each of his hands held a

ceramic coconut with a yellow umbrella and a pink straw sticking out of it.

"I'm praying to the art god," I said. "Am I saying the right thing?"

The coconut was full of pineapple juice. Foamy and delicious.

"Mai tai, Sophie," he said, raising his coconut. "The prayer is mai tai."

We chanted different variations of it in between sipping our drinks. He went high, I went low. He held his notes long, I kept mine short. At one point, I stole the umbrella from his drink, put it behind my ear and did the hula for a minute. When I finished, the guy behind the bar clapped. I followed Dad to the bar and had started to climb up on a stool when a bunch of other men came in.

"Why don't you go back to the art god, and I'll bring you the pu pu platter when it's ready, okay?"

"Sure, but I'm not eating that," I said. "And you can't make me." I was six going on eighteen, and he knew it.

"Make mine a double," Dad said to the waiter as I walked away. I wondered if he meant double umbrellas.

I wandered around, getting lost in the fake ferns and palm trees, creepy masks and puffed-up blowfish. I was looking for more hula girls when Mom walked in.

"Sophie!" She ran in and grabbed me, folding me into one of her patented suffocating hugs. "I was so worried."

I wriggled away. "We went the art store and then came here to pray to the art god, see?" I pointed to the Easter Island head.

"I see," she said. She had that tone in her voice, the one that happened before a fight. "Where's your father?"

I pointed in his direction. At the time I didn't wonder how she found us. It was only later, after I learned about his favorite places, that it made sense. He had three favorites, and Waikiki Wally's was one of them.

Dad perched on one of the bamboo barstools, drinking pineapple juice and chatting with a guy who stumbled. Mom stormed over and tapped Dad on the shoulder, which almost made him fall off his stool. They talked, and she used her hands a lot, I remember that. I also remember that I didn't want to be a part of it. I never wanted to be a part of it. So I started praying, again.

"Mai tai!" I said. "Maaaaaaaiiiiii taaaaaaiii!"

They both ran over to me.

"Honey," she said, "that's enough. I'm taking you home, and your dad's going to stay here and finish up some . . . business."

He leaned down, and I reached up and hugged his neck. "Bye, Daddy," I said.

"Bye, pumpkin," he said, raising his coconut. "See you soon."

On the way home, we picked up rocky road ice cream and ate it before the quiche that had to be reheated. It wasn't until years later that I realized I'd been in a bar. Once, when I asked to go back to Waikiki Wally's because I was feeling brave and wanted to try the pu pu platter, Dad said no, that place was inappropriate for someone my age. It made me think about that word, *inappropriate*, since I loved the big statues, flowered necklaces and the way I'd felt lost in there. Kind of like the way I felt on the inside all the time, but at least there it came with pineapple juice.

I walked down the basement stairs and grass grew beneath my feet. It was Astroturf, slippery but lush, like descending into a forest. Dad had never met a surface he didn't make better. Around him, pancakes became faces, doors became murals, and basements were turned into playgrounds that were almost too good to be true.

Paper lanterns bobbed from the ceiling like spaceships and gave the room an aqua and tangerine glow. Lime-green streamers ran from corner to corner in between stuffed clouds made from patchwork quilts. Every inch of every surface was covered in fabric or curly ribbon, patches of carpet or tinfoil. There was even a chair covered with bubble wrap that popped when you sat in it. Everything was old because Dad said found things were the best things. "Why bring home apples and orange juice when you could show up with tricycle wheels instead?" he'd say. Mom never agreed and made him go back to the store, but that didn't stop him from bringing home bricks instead of bagels anyway.

The back wall was painted plaid. And in front of it, Dad built a makeshift hitching post out of two broomsticks and a rope from which a team of eggbeater horses hung. I should have been amazed by his ability to make something out of nothing, but I was used to it.

On another wall was a bulletin board filled with sketches of inventions, numbers that didn't make sense and blueprints for contraptions that were probably never built. Quotes by famous physicists and authors hung everywhere next to photos of places he probably never went. And there, in the middle, was a picture of me during Christmas 2000, holding my Holiday Surprise Barbie. I ripped an article next to it off the wall, tore it into tiny pieces and threw them above my head, like confetti.

I heard the basement door creak open, and Finny's voice floated down.

"Sophie? You okay?" I heard footsteps.

"Don't come down here," I said.

"I just wanted to check on you," he said. "Need anything?"

"Just privacy," I said. "Keep Peyton out, too."

"No problem," Finny yelled down. "But if you need anything, scream. We'll hear you."

The door closed, like a vacuum, and the air suddenly smelled like peppermints. I grabbed the photo off the bulletin board and one of the sketches fell off, too. It was labeled "inter-dimensional travel machine." It looked more like a new version of a spaceship and didn't come with any instructions, but I loved it anyway. I stuck it in my pocket and walked on a path made of old oatmeal labels and jelly beans, packing peanuts and stickpins. I passed a collection of pogo sticks and stilts, a table of rubber bands and toothbrushes and a huge sculpture made out of tennis balls and putty. It sat on a card table with a sign next to it that read ATOM SMASHER. I was dying to touch it, but it looked fragile, like it had been there awhile. There were two towers, five tiers high, made of tennis balls on toilet paper rolls and connected with Silly Putty that had hardened. I wasn't sure what an atom smasher was, but I liked the idea of it, particles crashing into each other and forming something else. Like a horse with the body of an octopus. Or a bicycle spaceship. I had moved on to something made of marbles when I stepped on a squeaky hot dog. It let out a *wheeeeee*, and I kicked it to the side. That's when I saw a box with my name on it.

If Dad had been there, he would have insisted I wear an eye patch. "You can't find a treasure box if you're not properly attired," he would say. "Even the most amateur pirates have to look the part."

I lifted the box and would have shaken it like a Christmas present, but it was heavy. So I sat on the floor around it, legs in a V with the box between them. Maybe it was old baby clothes or papers from school. Art projects and poems and things not worth saving. I opened the lid, and dust flew out, making me cough. A homemade postcard sat on top, a Warhol head floating in the middle of a galaxy. Dad must have made it, but Warhol would have liked it. Especially if the galaxy contained celebrities. "It's better to be a head than a derriere, darling," he'd say, and then run off to film someone sleeping. I hoped the back of the postcard would say something. It didn't, but it was what was underneath that counted: hundreds of mixtapes. The ultimate treasure.

"Oh, wow," I said. "No way."

I checked the lid again. It still said FOR SOPHIE, so I took out the tapes and looked at them, one by one. Were they full of songs or conversations or both? Did he spend hours picking the right tracks or talking into a microphone? The tapes were titled everything from *Chai Tea Catastrophe* to *String Theory Orchestra*. If I hadn't left my Walkman upstairs, I would have popped them in and listened until I knew him better than I knew myself. Some of the tapes looked older, like he'd bought a pack at a garage sale or taped over ones he had, but some of them were brand-new—tapes made in a time when no one was making tapes anymore. Dad, always and forever the purist.

I grabbed a handful of cassettes and brought them to my face, drinking him in. I traced the cases with my finger, imagining what it would have been like to have been him making tapes for me. I picked one out of the bunch, hoping it was about something meaningful, something he wanted to share that he couldn't say in person. Instead I got a tape called *Gravitons and Gravy*. On the inside there was a list of tracks, plus a recipe for making the best gravy in the universe.

I read a few more, knowing I'd have time to listen to them and decode their secret messages later. At a glance, *Atomic Antics* was full of Adam and the Ants, which I loved, but hoped when I listened to it, it would be more about the atoms themselves. And even though *Equation Store* was full of songs with numbers in them, I was sure there was more to it. I kept digging around, hoping to find one that was less cryptic, which is when I saw it, stuck to the bottom. The case was cracked and dirty, but that didn't matter, especially since the word on the cover was one I'd been thinking about for years: *Love*.

My hands shook as I opened the case. It was stiff, like it was one of the first tapes he'd made. I went to remove the tape, but the entire thing flew out of my hand like a plastic bag in the wind. I chased it until I caught up with it in the corner, under-neath a bunch of deflated beach balls. I picked up *Love* and put it in my pocket. I didn't have my Walkman, but I wasn't prepared to hear it. When I thought about what could be on it—a missive or a miss—I wasn't ready to go there. Not yet. Just like I was never ready when Mom had pulled me out of bed in the middle of the night, even though she said we were doing it for love.

"You know I love you, don't you?" Mom would say, tossing the covers back and helping me put my coat on over my pajamas. Most nights I kicked the blankets off in my sleep, and Mom showed up and tucked me in tighter, building a cocoon to keep me in. But then, on other nights, she took me out of bed and put me in the car.

"Where are we going?" I asked as she drove away from our house.

"To find your father," she said.

"Isn't he in bed?"

"No," she said. "That's why we're going to find him."

"Why do we have to go and look for him?" I said. "He'll come back."

"Because," she said, giving me a little squeeze on my shoulders. "No one should be out alone in the middle of the night. Would you like to be out alone in the middle of the night?"

"I'd like it if I were alone in my bed."

"Smart girl," she said. "You'll be back there soon."

I sat in the backseat with my blanket and pillow. Some mornings I woke up still in the backseat, driving around the city. I felt a breeze or smelled food cooking, morning air blowing in, filling the car with the rest of the world. I liked it better when the windows were closed, when it was just the smell of my blanket and Mom's flowery lotion. One morning I woke up and the car was parked in the driveway. Mom was in the front seat, drinking coffee. She said she didn't want to wake me up because I was sleeping so well. Another time Dad was in the front seat, snoring. I guess she didn't want to wake him up, either. And still other times, he was already home when we got back, a box of doughnuts in his hands and a smile on his face. "My girls!" he'd say. "I've been waiting for you. I brought sprinkles!"

At the time, it never occurred to me that this wasn't normal—driving around looking for your father instead of just having him there, sleeping, making pancake faces when you woke up in the morning.

"You know I love you, don't you?" Mom would always say. Whether she was taking me out of bed and into the night or trying to make me feel good after Dad left, she always said it the same way, like a quiz. Like she was checking to make sure that even with the chaos in our lives, I knew the answer: *Yes.*

I added some confetti into my pocket and walked upstairs. My legs moved slowly, like sandbags. Step, step. Away from the past. Step, step, into the future. The weight of a thousand conversations in a box at the bottom of the stairs. I opened the door and the smell of tomato sauce hit me in the face. Peyton stood at the stove, stirring with a wooden spoon.

"Perfect timing," she said. "Dinner's ready."

"I'm not hungry," I said, my eyes glazing. "I think I have to go to bed now. Like, immediately."

"You're not going to tell us about the basement?" Finny said.

My right knee buckled.

"Can we talk tomorrow?"

Peyton put her arm around me, which I would have resisted if I hadn't been so tired.

"It's late," she said. "Head upstairs and take the second bedroom on the left. I'll be up to check on you soon."

"Me too," Finny said, his voice like an echo.

Hours later, I woke up, yawned and stretched my arms over my head. The room was dark, and the blanket was scratchy, like my throat. Finny came into focus, sitting in a chair in the corner.

"What time is it?" I asked.

"One o'clock," he said. "You've been asleep for a few hours."

"Why aren't you in bed?"

"I felt bad," he said. "You went down there by yourself, and I stayed upstairs and talked to Peyton, and when you came up, you looked really upset. I just wanted to be here in case you woke up."

"You're reading Dad's book, aren't you?" I said.

"Of course," he said, grinning. "Like you could keep me away from it."

I could tell he wanted to launch into a conversation about Dad and his amazing brain, but I wasn't up for it. I flopped a sleeve against my face. Flannel. Like Dad used to wear. I loved that even under extreme duress, my brain knew enough to put me in comfy clothes.

"What are you wearing?" I said, pointing to his jogging pants and sweatshirt.

"Whatever Peyton left out for me," he said. "Same as you. She's washing our clothes."

"Why?" I said. "We only wore them one day."

"I think she just wanted something to do," he said. "That or they had travel smell."

I laughed and sank into my pillows. "We should go to sleep. We have a big day tomorrow."

"A big day of what?"

"Seeing whatever you came to New York to see," I said. "I know you're here to meet my dad, but this is the greatest city in the world. Don't you want to go to the World Science Festival?"

"That was in June," he said. "But maybe I could go to the Museum of Natural History after we've done some Dad research."

"Perfect," I said, even though I was developing another plan that didn't include Finny. "But all work and no play makes Finny kind of a pain to be around. I'll talk to Dad's old coworkers while you hit the library. Then we'll meet, share intel, and you can go do something cool. Deal?"

"Deal," he said, yawning. "You know, your dad was kind of brilliant."

"Is kind of brilliant," I said. I felt shaky on the inside. "I overheard you, you know."

"Overheard what?"

"On the stairs," I said. "Before the basement."

"Sophie . . ."

"It's okay," I said. "It wasn't my fault. I didn't kick Dad out, Mom did."

"I was going to tell you," he said. "I wanted to wait until you had some sleep."

"It's not your job to tell me," I said. "That job belongs to Mom."

Finny sat on the edge of my bed, sinking in as I felt my heart do the same. "Can I ask you a question?"

I nodded as he moved even closer.

"Can I give you a hug?"

I wanted to say no. I wanted to be the girl of steel, the one who didn't need anyone or anything, but I knew we were past that. Finny knew my truths and hadn't told anyone. And no matter what amount of weirdness I threw at him, he was still there.

"I guess a hug wouldn't kill me," I said, sitting up off the pillows.

And even though he wasn't that much taller than me, Finny scooped me up like Walt, reaching around and right through to my heart. I coughed and tried to push back a sob.

"Let it go," he said into my hair. "Your secret's safe with me."

I leaned in, and the tears came. My whole body shook as I cried like I did when I was little, like when Dad left. But Finny stayed right where he was. He didn't bundle me up and put me in the car in the middle of the night or pretend he didn't hear me. He held on and didn't let go. All so that I could.

TWENTY

*Now I know how Joan of Arc felt—as the flames rose
to her Roman nose and her Walkman started to melt.*
—The Smiths, "Bigmouth Strikes Again"

"Finny says you have a boyfriend," Peyton said, standing in the doorway.

I opened my eyes and looked around like I did every time we moved to a new town.

"Not exactly," I said, realizing I was in New York. I sat up and threw a heavy quilt off me.

"I thought Finny was your boyfriend," she said, handing me a glass of orange juice.

"He's gay," I said, sipping it, citrus washing over my tongue.

"Oh," she said. "He's really cute."

"True," I said. "He's going to make some boy extremely happy one day."

She stood by the bed like she wanted to sit on it, but we weren't there yet. "Did you sleep okay? That quilt can be kind of hot."

I held a piece of it in my hand. Maybe it was her quilt, made by someone who loved her, pieces of her childhood in one place instead of scattered, like mine. Maybe the red patch with the bright green apples was from a dress she wore on the first day of kindergarten, which she hated because she was taller than everyone else. Maybe the dress that had seen her through a horrible day had just seen me through a rough night.

"I slept fine," I said, leaning back into the pillows. "Is this your quilt?"

"My grandmother made it," she said. "It's nice to have someone you love make you something."

"I'd rather have the person," I said, thinking about the way Dad tucked me in at night if he was home, or surprised me with breakfast in the morning when he returned.

"So would I," she said.

She leaned over and patted my hand. I knew I should respond, but my body wouldn't move. My hand stayed stiff like something out of the morgue, which made her remove hers.

"I talked to your mom this morning," she said. "Since you have to go back tonight, would you like to go into the city with me? I have to work for a few hours, but I can hang out with you guys after that."

I got out of bed and walked to the window. Gray clouds marched in like robots, defending the sky.

"There isn't something more important you have to do today?"

I was planning on lying to her about my search for Dad—that wasn't the point. The point was that she was thinking about the Statue of Liberty and Central Park while I was focused on uncovering answers. Securing sanity. Finding my father.

"I haven't given up on him," she said, joining me at the window. She'd abandoned the whole turquoise motif for black pants, a black sweater and an orange wooden necklace. "But there's nothing to do at this point but wait. You might as well enjoy the city while you're here."

Adults had this insane ability to compartmentalize. I'd watched my mom do it and tried to copy her because it seemed so convenient. Emotions? On. Emotions? Off. It was the kind of thing that could come in handy, post-episode, but I never made it work. Maybe I needed more practice, but when something was going on with me, it was *really going on*. At least in my brain. Even if my feet kept walking, my mind was still there, fully obsessed with the problem. But maybe it would work. Just this once.

"You're right," I said, turning away from the window. Lying for the greater good. "We'd love to meet up with you, but I want to take Finny to my favorite breakfast place before we hit Chinatown."

"I don't know," she said. "I promised your mom I'd look after you. What would she think if I let you run around New York by yourself?"

"She wouldn't think twice about it," I said. "I lived here for years and took the subway to school with her and everywhere else, for that matter. I know my way around."

She looked worried, but then she looked at her watch. It was delicate and small.

"I don't love this idea, but I have to get to a meeting," she said. "I'll leave a MetroCard and an extra key for you on the hall table. Finny gave me both of your cell numbers, and he has mine, so just call me after Chinatown. At the very least, I want to take you to dinner tonight. Anywhere you want."

"Anywhere?" I said, thinking about all the things I missed, from pizza to pierogi. "I'd love Italian. If we're lucky, maybe Dad will even show up."

It left my mouth before I had a chance to catch it. Peyton leaned back against the wall.

"I'm sorry," I said. "I'm horrible until I've had coffee."

"I'll remember that," she said. "But considering you traveled for twenty hours to see your dad and ended up with me, I'll let it slide. That is, if you promise to meet me for dinner."

"Deal," I said, knowing it wasn't. I had no idea where the day would take me.

She smiled, walked out of my room and then turned back around. "I want to find him as much as you do," she said. "I just wanted you to know that."

When I heard the lock click, I thought about what I'd do if I were her. If she cared as much as I did, I'd think she'd use every single second—especially ones with his daughter—to find him. No farewell dinner, not even if it consisted entirely of chocolate, could change the fact that she'd given up.

I got my phone out of my bag and turned it on. I'd turned it off after talking to Mom last night, afraid she'd call. I wasn't ready to talk to her yet, not now, knowing what I knew about us leaving Dad instead of the other way around. I clicked on Drew's name, thinking I might text him, but the phone started ringing instead. I'd accidentally called him. And before I had the chance to hang up—

"Hello?"

His voice had the same effect on me that his hand did when it brushed my sweater.

"Hi," I said.

"Hey," he said. "Are you back?"

"Nope," I said. "Still in New York."

"Wait, you're in New York?"

I had to be careful—Drew only knew part of the story—but his voice made careful go out the window.

"Yeah," I said. "I'm visiting my dad."

"Are you going to Strand? The book mecca of the East?"

"Of course," I said, wishing I had time for anything but the search. "You've been?"

"Only once," he said. "But I'd live there if I could."

Swooooon.

"Sophie!" Finny's voice floated through the door. "Are you up?"

"Is that your dad?" Drew asked. If only.

"Cousin," I said. "I hate to do this, but I called you on

accident. I mean, I was going to call you later, but I didn't mean to call you now, and people are waiting for me."

I opened the door, pointed to my phone and mouthed "Drew." Finny hopped up and down, which was annoying but at least it didn't make noise.

"And I have to go to school," Drew said. "But I like hearing you."

"Hearing me what?"

"Your voice," he said.

"Oh." I collapsed back onto the bed. I knew I was supposed to say something witty, but I was stunned. He liked my voice.

"Hey, do you want to have lunch this weekend? Will you be back?" he said.

"Maybe lunch or real lunch?"

"Real lunch," he said. "If you promise not to run away, I promise to have lunch."

"I'm not going to run away," I said. Not after I found Dad. Not after I found some answers.

"Cool," he said. "It will be like our own secret rule. No running allowed."

"Maybe I should wear heels," I said. "You know, to hinder my bolting instinct."

"I like your shoes," he said. I looked over and saw my Docs standing in a corner by themselves. I liked *him.*

"Me too," I said.

"Sophie!" Finny shouted through the door. "We need to go."

"Okay, I have to go," I said, even though I could have stayed on that phone forever.

"Yeah," Drew said. "Me too. So I'll see you soon?"

"You will," I said, wondering if I'd be a different person. Hoping I'd come home better—and saner—than when I left. I hung up quickly before I said something stupid. It was inevitable, but my awkwardness would have to wait. Today was going to be tough enough.

"Anytime today would be nice," Finny yelled through the door.

I was hungry and definitely needed coffee, but this might be the last time I saw this house, the last known place Dad had been. Maybe there was a clue I had missed, or maybe I just wanted a moment here. Another peek at the basement. Good thing Finny could fend for himself.

"Why don't you go ahead?" I said. "You know how long it takes a girl to get ready."

"Almost as long as me!" Finny said.

I opened the door a crack and stuck my head out.

"Yes, you need a shower," he said. "And yes, I'm dying to hear about your little love chat with Drew."

"All in good time," I said. "Which will be about thirty minutes."

"I'll be one coffee ahead of you," Finny said, bounding down the stairs. "Come any later and I'll be jittery."

"I'll be there!" I shouted, meaning it. I was definitely a little wacky on two cups of coffee, but Finny was beyond. It was like the caffeine tapped into the part of his brain that loved physics and opened a secret door, the one that made connections to everything. Maybe that was what had happened to Dad. Maybe if he'd switched to herbal tea, he'd be here right now.

I had packed another skirt and could have worn something else, but I saw my clothes, clean and stacked on the dresser. The elephant skirt seemed lucky, like the time Dad told me he walked home with elephants. Two of them lumbered on either side of him like a wall, protecting him from the outside, but gentle creatures, protecting him from his insides. Each step thumped, like the echo of a thousand friends. Elephants carried you when you couldn't go the distance, he said. They made you feel less alone.

I threw on the skirt, a long-sleeved T-shirt and my short-sleeved tape tree shirt in honor of Dad. Mixtapes hung from its branches instead of fruit. There had to be something promising about that.

"Perfection," I said, packing the rest of my bag and heading to the kitchen. I wrote Peyton a note, asking her to send the box of tapes to my address in Havencrest, and then I leaned it next to the phone. The phone I should have used to check in with Mom, but I wasn't going to do that. Not yet. Then I turned to the basement, its aqua doorknob gleaming in the morning light.

As soon as I opened the door, I wished I hadn't. Without the romance of the evening or the twinkling lights, the basement looked dirty, like the contents of a crazy brain spread out in the sunlight. Since I didn't know when—or if—I was ever coming back, I took a mental picture of it. And then, because it was depressing, I erased it.

I closed the basement door, blew a kiss to the kitchen table and waved good-bye to my photo on the mantel. As I stepped out onto the stoop, I felt a drop on my head. Then two drops. Then rain fell like little tennis balls, pounding my back. I ran toward the diner, dodging raindrops, but bumped into a green umbrella with white polka dots instead. And the panda who was holding it.

"Nice timing," I said, slipping underneath.

"Isn't it always?" The rain hit the top of the umbrella, making a nice *plop* and then a *swoosh* as it slid off the side.

"Where are you headed?" he said.

"To meet Finny," I said. "Breakfast."

"Yum," he said. "I could destroy a Greek omelet about now. How'd it go with your dad?"

I started to tell him the whole thing—Dad's car and the kitchen table, Peyton and the basement—when I realized that Walt was omniscient. He knew where I was and when I needed help, which could only mean one thing.

"You *knew*," I said, backing out from under the umbrella.

"Knew what?"

"That Dad was missing."

"Come back, you're going to get soaked," he said. "And I didn't know for sure. I hoped he'd show up by the time you got here."

"God!" I said, stomping my boots in a puddle, sending rain up onto my knees. "I can't believe you! You're all *Sophie, watch for signs. Sophie, pay attention. Sophie, stay on the path.* And all this time, you knew my path would lead me to nothing?"

"I wouldn't say nothing," he said. "What about the book? The basement? The tapes?"

"A mixtape is not a substitute for a person," I said, and I knew. I'd been trying that for years. "I need my dad."

Tears ran down my face, mixing with raindrops. Before New York, I thought that letters or phone calls would be enough, but they weren't. I wanted more.

"I helped you the only way I could," he said. "I can't predict the future."

Walt walked closer and extended the umbrella over me so that he was left out in the rain, unprotected.

"Tell me where he is," I said.

"You know I can't do that," Walt said. "First, I don't know where he is, and second, that's not how it works."

"So you know where he's *not*, but you don't know where he *is*?" I said. "As far as magical powers go, you got gypped."

"I'm not a genie," he said. "I don't grant you wishes or consult an eight ball—I protect you. And guide you toward the truth."

"And what is the truth, exactly?" I said. "You know, for someone who tells me so little, you hold an awful lot of power over me."

"You have free will," he said. "You act as you please."

"Yeah, but I take your advice," I said. "And I don't know anything about you except that your boss is a council, and their rules run your life. I don't know why you're here and why you're even bothering with me. Are you giving guidance or messing with me? Why do I even listen to you?"

"Because we have a connection," he said.

"Not anymore," I said, walking toward the diner.

"Wait," Walt said, following me. "Let's talk."

I turned, rain dripping from my hair into my face.

"I don't want to talk," I said. "I want to eat breakfast with my best friend, someone who is actually trying to help me. And then I want to go to NYU and look for clues. I would ask you to help, but we both know where that got me."

"Sophie, please," he said. "I don't make the rules."

"Oh, yeah?" I felt anger rising, with a vengeance. "Well, then I don't follow them."

Drizzle started up again as I walked away, Walt's voice fading in the background. He could show up again, right in front of me, but I didn't think he would. He may have been a lot of things, but the panda who blocked my path wasn't one of them.

"Whoa," Finny said as I slid into the booth across from him. "Good thing these booths are vinyl."

"I know," I said, wiping my face with a napkin as water dripped from my hair. "But Walt had the umbrella, and he made me mad, so I wouldn't stand under it. Hence the wet-dog look."

"Use this," Finny said, handing me his jacket. I squeezed most of the water out of my hair into it and I would have felt bad, but I was with him when he bought it. And it was only three dollars.

"What did you fight about?" Finny pushed his orange juice to the side and flipped his phone over.

"Who were you talking to?"

"No one," Finny said, grinning like Cupid. Wait.

"Finny . . ."

"Like I can help it if your super-hunky boy crush called me."

"Drew called you?"

"I might have slipped him my number when I slipped him yours."

"Finny!"

"What? If you two get together, we'll all be friends and he'll be calling me, anyway," Finny said.

"What did he want?"

"My lips are sealed," he said. "He's doing something special for you, and I don't care what you threaten me with, I'm not telling you."

I leaned back in the booth. When it came to love, Finny was horrible at keeping secrets, which meant all I had to do was wait it out.

"That's fine," I said. "I'll see Drew this weekend if I'm not eternally grounded. I think I can wait."

"You're not even going to grill me?" he said, picking up the notebook sitting on top of Dad's book.

"It's not important," I said. "Well, not as important as that."

I pointed to Dad's book.

"And this," I said as a mug of coffee appeared in front of me. Finny stared as I held the sugar pourer over it, counted to five and then added half of the silver cream container.

"What?" I said. "I call it Comfort Coffee. It only appears in times of crisis."

"Buckwheat blueberry pancakes with fruit?" the waitress said, holding two plates over our table.

"You ordered me breakfast?" I said, scooting my coffee over.

"Yup," Finny said. "You said those were your favorite."

"Hearts," I said, cutting into the stack with my knife. Not finding Dad was making me ravenous. "But Dad's book is my new favorite. Can you tell me about the first part?"

"I can do better than that," he said, clearing his throat. "I can read it to you."

CHAPTER ONE:
THE LAW OF TRAVELING

. . . *People often talk about traveling, from Bangkok to Brussels, from Taiwan to Timbuktu. Yet no one talks about traveling to parallel universes. And that's what the Law of Traveling is all about.*

String theory is very much a work in progress. But if we take it at its word, we know that everything is composed of tiny, vibrating strings that split and reconnect. There is evidence to support the idea that in between all these strings are spaces—gaps, if you will. Some are large, some are small, and some are just the right size for energy, gravity and matter to pass through.

The Law of Traveling contends that if those things can travel to parallel universes, so can soccer balls and

raindrops, bicycles and balloons. And if we take it a
step further, this principle asks you to imagine: if those
things can travel, why can't we?

I leaned back against the vinyl seat like I did another time
I'd had my mind blown. The time I saw the heart roll off the
sleeve.

"Is he saying what I think he's saying?"

"That depends," Finny said. "What do you think he's
saying?"

"That traveling to other universes is possible?"

"Yes!" Finny said. He was so excited he bumped the table
with his knee and spilled coffee everywhere. "And that's just
the beginning. You won't believe what's in this book."

I mopped up the coffee with napkins, hands shaking.

"Sophie, he talks about souvenirs," Finny said. And then he
opened the book and pointed to a diagram that connected different parts of the brain to various atomic structures. "I think he
was using physics to prove he wasn't crazy."

And there it was—another marker along the path. Just like
Walt had said.

"I haven't read the whole thing, but if your dad proves his
theory, it's not mental illness he's dealing with," he said. "Which
means you're not dealing with it, either."

I wondered if there was a limit to the number of times your
brain could be blown in an hour. Walt knew my dad wasn't
there, Dad believed in dimensional travel, and he mentioned souvenirs in his book for anyone—everyone—to read. I came here

hoping physics would explain everything, but I never actually thought that it would.

"It's an amazing idea," I said softly, tucking my hands under my legs so they wouldn't shake.

"You choose now to start being skeptical?" Finny said.

"Not skeptical, careful," I said.

Maybe it came from being abandoned by Dad or having to move a bunch of times, but I'd had my heart broken enough to be cautious. At least when it came to believing that there truly was one answer for everything.

"There are people who know Dad and who know more than we do," I said. "They're all at NYU. Hopefully they can fill in the blanks left by the book."

We ate in silence for a while, grounding ourselves for what was to come. Finny had a third cup of coffee and I had a second, full of more comfort than the first. I looked at Dad's book sitting on the table, wondering where it would lead us. Wondering if anyone believed him and, if they did, hoping they'd talk to me.

Finny pushed his plate back and his mug away.

"I'm cutting myself off," he said.

"And I'm full," I said, eating the last syrup-soaked blueberry. "Want to get out of here?"

"Yes," Finny said, bounding out of the booth like a super-hero. "Take me to your teacher!"

"They're called professors," I said, giggling.

"I know, but that didn't rhyme with leader," Finny said, leaving money on the table. "Take me anywhere that's not Haven-crest, and I'll be happy."

"Then you are about to bliss out," I said, linking arms with him and heading for the subway.

On the way to the Q train, we passed a guy playing kazoo, a woman selling god's eyes and an old man with no teeth and a coffee cup full of coins.

"Happy yet?" I said.

"You have no idea," he said. "You weren't kidding."

"You get used to it," I said. And then you learn to love it, I thought.

The train was packed until a guy in a bathrobe got up and an orange seat appeared. Finny nodded at me, and I took it, squeezing in between a man wearing a suit and a woman wearing a purple jacket with shoulder pads. Papers went up, and Finny disappeared.

"Finny," I said over a *Wall Street Journal*. "If you see a seat, take it. Just get off at Canal Street and wait under the sign. I'll find you."

"Okay," his muffled voice said. "Canal Street. Got it."

I read headlines ranging from "Big Polluters Told to Report Emissions" to "White House Considers Economic Strategy Shift." But the best one was on the paper right in front of me: "Study Assesses Women and Responses to Love." According to the article, a recent study showed that 84 percent of women weren't emotionally satisfied with their romantic lives. I wasn't even sure what that meant, but it didn't sound good. It also mentioned that we didn't trust men, even though we wanted to. I wondered what the numbers said about pandas.

I took my Walkman out of my bag and felt around in my pocket for the *Love* mixtape, but it wasn't there. My logical mind knew that Peyton had washed my skirt and that she probably put the tape somewhere else, but my emotional brain panicked. What if it got washed? Or fell out and someone stepped on it? What if *Love* was gone like it had never existed? I felt in my other pockets and dug through my bag, but it wasn't there, either. No *Love* anywhere. Nada.

"No," I said. I had come too far for this. "No, no, no, no."

Gray Suit stared straight ahead, but Puffy Shoulders turned.

"Can I help you with something, honey?"

"I lost something important," I said, looking through my bag again.

"Maybe it can be replaced," she said, closing the book she was reading—*Women Who Love Too Much*. "Unless it's a photo. Once I lost the only photo I had of Mr. Murphy, and that was sad."

She had curly hair, and bright orange balls hung from her ears, the same color as her lipstick. "I'm from Montana," she said, as if that explained why she was talking to me, since no one talked to anyone on the subway. "Mr. Murphy was from Oklahoma, but he was a great tabby."

A cat. She'd lost a photo of her cat. And I'd lost the closest thing I'd had to a conversation with my dad in four years.

"It was a love letter," I said, thinking that was the best way to explain it.

"Oh, that's awful," she said. "According to this book I'm

reading, though, we shouldn't depend on others. We can get all the love we need by loving ourselves."

I think Puffy Shoulders forgot that I was a kid, and kids weren't supposed to *have* to do all the loving themselves, but whatever. The train slowed as we approached Canal Street, and I squeezed through the door as it was closing, hoping Finny had made it.

"Ta-da!" he said when I found him standing under the sign. "What's wrong?"

"I lost the *Love* tape," I said.

Finny grabbed my hand and pulled me up the stairs, for a change. "Not lost, just misplaced," he said. "Like your dad."

I punched his arm, and we walked through neon signs and chickens hanging from the ceilings, colored lanterns and tables of herbs and teapots. I'd have to compartmentalize again, or at least try. I had to put lost *Love* away for a minute and focus on what I could find instead.

"This is where you used to hang out after school?" Finny said.

"Only sometimes," I said. Dad and I went there on the way home a few times, trying on slippers and doing origami. That's what happened when your dad was a professor. Afternoons weren't spent at home, they were spent on campus at another school or in the neighborhoods around it.

I grabbed a wok and tried it on as a hat. "Who could resist this?"

"Not me," Finny said, hanging two bundles of herbs from his ears like earrings.

For a minute we forgot about the book and just had fun, like we did in school. We faked fights with chopsticks, tried on masks like that scene in *Breakfast at Tiffany's* and put slippers on our hands and made them talk like puppets. I picked up a red dragon mask, which reminded me of the time Dad took me to a Chinese New Year parade. Huge dragons lined the streets, and even though I knew that the floats and masks were fake, I was terrified they were going to eat me. Dad picked me up and put me on his shoulders, but instead of walking away, he walked right out into the middle of the parade, putting me at eye level with the dragons. Their eyes bulged and their teeth flashed, but when I saw the seams—and the people inside them—I knew I was safe. As the music played and the lights glowed, as I sat on Dad's shoulders eating cookies, I thought I'd always be safe.

"How about this one?"

Finny spun around in a kimono, which he dubbed the Chinese Smoking Jacket.

"Debonair, right? Or whatever the Chinese word for debo-nair is?"

"You look fabulous," I said. "Buy it, and let's get out of here."

"What's the rush?" he said, taking it off.

"There's more to see where this came from," I said. I could only hope Dad would be one of them. "Plus I'm hungry again. Let's hit the hum bao stand."

By the time we arrived at Washington Square Park, it was almost noon. And since the rain had stopped, the park was full of jugglers and chess players, acrobats and a guy playing a baby grand piano. Parts of a shiny orange and purple dress flew by me as cards appeared in my face.

"Future?" the purple-dress lady asked. "Want to know your future?"

I did, but I didn't want to know it from her.

"No thanks," I said, pushing Finny along. "We're good."

We walked past a group of guys playing jazz, and I had the urge to ask the flute player or cardboard box drummer if they remembered Angelino Sophia. He ate lunch there every day and was the kind of guy who'd borrow an upright bass and try to fit in, even though the only stringed instrument he knew how to play was a banjo he'd made out of rubber bands. But things like that never stopped him.

"I want to go with you," Finny said. "On your interviews."

I'd stopped to look at the Matchstick Man's boxes. You'd never see something like that in Havencrest.

"Would you be offended if we divided and conquered?" I said.

"What do you mean?"

"I mean we only have a day," I said. "What if I took the interviews and you researched? Since I know some of the professors, it kind of makes sense. Plus you've read all of Dad's book, so you know what to look for."

"Like more copies?"

"That, and other books or articles that support his ideas," I said. "Maybe other grad students wrote papers on his work, and this would be the best place to find that stuff."

"True," Finny said. "You know I'd do anything to help, but I was really looking forward to meeting a few professors."

"And you will," I said. "But can you spend a few hours at the greatest library on Earth? For me?"

Finny's eyes followed my hand as it pointed to a tall, red building that resembled a Lego from the outside but looked like the future on the inside. Twelve stories of glass and miles of words. I always thought if brains were square and could be categorized like the Dewey decimal system, they would look like the Elmer Holmes Bobst Library.

"Wow," he said. Then he shook his head and faced me. "If you need me to make the ultimate sacrifice and go in there, I will. For *you*."

"You really are the world's best friend, did you know that?"

"I did," he said, spinning around. "Which means you owe me."

"I always owe you," I said, thinking about all the times he'd helped me in the short time I'd known him. "Let's hope I can deliver in the form of a famous physicist."

"Maybe the librarians knew him," Finny said.

"Now your Sherlock Holmes is showing," I said. "Anything you can find will help."

"Even stuff on the whole parallel-universe-and-panda thing?"

I laughed. "If you can find a book on that, we'll have a slumber party at the New York Hall of Science."

"That's what I call motivation," he said grinning. And then he took Dad's book out of his bag and handed it to me.

"You'll need this more where you're going," he said.

I held it in my hands like a promise. And then I put it in my bag so I wouldn't lose it.

"Thanks," I said. Then I pointed to a bench up ahead, right outside of Bobst. "Let's meet here at three. And good luck."

Finny laughed. "Who needs luck when you have over three million volumes?"

He walked away, waving, and I reviewed my plan: if Dad wouldn't come to me, I'd go to him, retracing his last-known steps and making them mine, like when we used to play Copy Me. It was a game that involved me doing whatever Dad did. And even though that sometimes meant wearing suits to sell tubes of toothpaste to our neighbors, it was fun. Most of them thought he was an actor. None of them knew he was a scientist trying to change the world.

Dad modeled dimensions using whipped cream and balloons. He made punching robots named Energy and Matter. On good days, he shared his loftiest thoughts with me, and on bad ones, he acted like I didn't exist. I wondered if he was always like that or if I made him that way. When I left, did he get worse? Because I know I did. It was why I had to find him. It was also why I was there, dealing with energy and matter. The matter being my father, the energy being myself, propelled toward him. Step by New York City step.

TWENTY-ONE

I found Dad's old office without even thinking, my legs walking through the Meyer Hall of Physics, my brain forgetting that he didn't work there anymore. Someone was in the office, though, so I kept walking, three doors down, to Dr. Perratto.

"Office hours are on Thursday," Dr. Perratto said when I knocked on his door.

He looked like I remembered—gold wire-framed glasses, bushy gray hair and a light blue shirt with a brown tweed vest. His desk was covered with coffee cups and papers, and behind him, bookshelves were overflowing, crammed with everything I'd ever wanted to know about theoretical particle physics.

"I read the sign," I said, "but I'm not a student here. Not yet."

Dr. Perratto looked up from his papers and pushed his glasses up on his nose.

"Sophie Sophia?" He hopped up and shook my hand. "Sit down, sit down!"

He pushed a pile of papers off a chair.

"It's been a long time, dear," he said. "You look wonderful. What brings you to New York?"

"I came to see Dad," I said, taking a picture frame off his desk. He and Dad were standing in front of a lake with fishing poles, but no fish.

"That was taken at a retreat," he said. "Your father was even more inspiring away from the office. He liked to prove his theories out in the world, not just on paper."

"Do you think that's what he's doing now?" I said, handing him the photo.

"I'm not sure," he said. "But I'm sure he'll come around. He always comes back."

"So I've heard," I said. If I was tired of people telling me that, I could only imagine how Peyton felt.

Dr. Perratto cleared his throat. "Yes, well, I'm sorry to repeat it. Would you like some coffee?" he said, pointing to his mug. It said *Physicists take matter(s) into their own hands.* "I call it nature's sweet elixir."

"I'm good," I said. And even though Peyton mentioned it last night, I wanted to hear it from the source. "Can you tell me why Dad doesn't work here anymore?"

Dr. Perratto squinted at me like he was looking at the same person he'd kicked out of his office for being volatile on more than one occasion. The colleague who'd been suspended but was kept on because of his innovative work. The friend whose scholarship surpassed his tendency to disappear without warning. I was me, but I was also part Angelino Sophia.

"Teaching assistants do a lot of the work, but at the end of the day, we needed a professor who could lecture on more than lollipops," he said. He leaned back in his chair. "You look like him, you know."

"It's the nose," I said. And my tendency to believe things no one else did.

"It's also the eyes," he said. "They're intense, like your father's eyes, like everything means something."

His voice drifted off. Everything *did* mean something, especially when you were trying to find your dad. I reached in my bag, took out Dad's book and set it on the desk.

"Since Dad isn't here, what I'd really like to talk about is this."

Dr. Perratto shook his head as if he were coming back to the present.

"The beginning of the end of his career," he said. "Have you read it?"

"Only the first few chapters," I said. "What do you think of it?"

"Your father is a brilliant physicist, but this book reads like a cross between poetry, philosophy and science fiction," he said. "It's not an academic work. When you read it all, you'll understand."

"What exactly am I going to understand?" I said.

"That you can't bend string theory to make it fit some strange idea," Dr. Perratto said. "Physics and emotion don't mix."

I hadn't gotten to that part of the book yet, but I wasn't surprised. Dad's brain was like a blender. He thought everything belonged together.

"Just because you don't believe in traveling doesn't mean it's not possible," I said.

"We believe there are parallel universes," he said, leaning forward. "But we don't believe you can slip through the gaps from one universe to the next. Or that those universes contain giant pandas. No one believes that."

A WORD ON PARALLEL UNIVERSES

Thanks to the multiverse theory—the concept that asserts that there are multiple universes within the greater cosmos—the potential for parallel universes has become more widely accepted. One idea that resonates more than the rest is that parallel universes are like our universe but with one noticeable difference.

For example, things could look exactly the same, except the people are half of their original size or the universe is run by large, intelligent pandas. Perhaps you could end up in a universe where unexpected objects animate or where everything's a music video. Each one has its own rules, and since the number of universes is undetermined, so are the possibilities for what happens within them.

Dr. Perratto took off his glasses and polished them as I completely freaked out on the inside. Dad visited the same places I went, places where chairs flew around or great bands serenaded you or pandas walked around like people. Were there other universes, or were those the only ones? And was there a chance we could meet one day, maybe in the panda-verse?

"Are you all right, dear?" he said, blinking through his glasses.

"Yes," I said, even though I wasn't. Overwhelmed couldn't even begin to describe it. This was why I should have brought Finny.

"It's shocking, I know," Dr. Perratto said. "A universe run by pandas? Please." Dad's book created more questions, and if I was going to find him—and save myself—I had to get answers. I had to keep going.

And then I remembered something Mr. Maxim had said.

"I thought physics was the one part of science that ran on possibility," I said.

"Possibility within reason," he said.

Was it reason that made them drop Dad as soon as they disagreed with him? Or was it reason that explained why everyone was sitting around instead of looking for him?

"But he proved his theory," I said. And if panda, music video and animating universes were any indication, I was proving it, too. "Doesn't proving something make it true?"

"Normally, yes," he said. "But proving a theory usually involves a test group larger than one."

Dr. Perratto came out from behind his desk and sat in the chair beside me.

"Keep reading the book," he said. "I don't know if it's any consolation, but your father believed the answer to everything—even complex scientific problems—was love. And you were the inspiration for that."

Love in my pocket, which was now gone. Dad, who I'd found, but was missing.

"Someone had to believe him," I said, wishing, hoping. "Is there anyone else I can talk to?"

Dr. Perratto wrote a name and an office number on a slip of paper and tucked it into my hand.

"Betty Russo," he said. "She worked with your dad for years. She can talk to you about all of it, especially souvenirs."

My breath got stuck in my chest.

"Sophie, are you okay?"

I coughed, trying to make it move, but it didn't budge. I needed water. I needed air. I needed to get out of there.

"Sure," I said. "I just need to take a break. Thanks for seeing me."

"It was my pleasure," he said. "I may not have believed in your father scientifically, but I did believe in him as a person. Make sure you finish his book. I think he was trying to tell you something."

Someone was always trying to tell me something, and I wished they'd just come right out and say it. Enough with the blackbirds and the souvenirs, the Walt wisdom and Dad's thesis. Would it kill a person to have a normal conversation with me for a change?

"Thanks," I said, sticking the book in my bag. And instead of heading upstairs, I went for the door.

I needed blue skies—something bigger than that man's office—if I was going to talk about souvenirs. Plus, my head was pounding. Nothing a few minutes in Washington Square Park wouldn't fix. When I got there, it was sprinkling. Not enough for an umbrella, but plenty of people had them, like the little girl twirling a pink and green plaid one above her head and spinning, like she was performing for the clouds.

The rain came down harder, like my headache. I walked over to the fountain, put my hand in the water and patted my face, hoping it would revive me, but I felt strange. Dizzy. There were too many people, and the sky was too bright, even with the rain. As I looked up, little black balls fell from the sky. As they got closer, I saw they weren't balls, they were bears—baby black bears falling everywhere.

They rained down, like miniatures, and bounced off the ground as if they were made of rubber. Bounce, bounce, bear to the right. Bounce, bounce, bear to the left. They were furry and cuddly, and soon they covered all of Washington Square Park.

People studied, ate and danced as little bears fell into the open spaces between them. Hundreds of baby black bears, raining from the sky. One of them bounced into my lap and I gave it a hug as I watched others crawl between the striped pant legs of a sax player. Around the juggling pins of a woman in a pink feather boa. Bears peeked over the shoulders of chess players and people eating noodles from cartons. They didn't cry or growl; they just giggled, crawled and explored the park like babies. The one in my lap licked my hand.

I remembered that my animal book said bears showed up when you needed to pay attention. They were a sign to listen to your heart, feel your power and make choices from that place. I'd always thought about getting a bear necklace, but I guessed a hundred bears falling from the sky would do the trick. Dad would have loved this, I thought. And then I realized—he already did. One summer night, in our backyard. Except it was probably an alternate version of our backyard in a parallel universe. And Dad had been there, baby black bears falling everywhere. At least, that's what he told me. I never saw it myself, until now.

"I have to get out of here," I said to the little bear beside me, to bears all over the park.

I picked up the one in my lap, sat her by the side of the fountain and stumbled. I saw double bears and triple bears, and the trees swirled around me. The backs of my eyes felt like fire and then there was nothing. The darn sky actually fell.

"Sophie!" I thought I heard someone say as my body moved through space.

My head felt dark and muddy like the inside of one of those caves I always saw advertised on the highway but never actually got to visit. Mom drove fast the few times we moved and she didn't stop for anything but bathroom breaks and snack attacks.

"The basics," she said. "If you really need to pee, tell me, and we'll stop. But we're not pulling over for a new *Greatest Hits of the '80s* tape or magnet that says 'The Cheese State.'" I wanted to tell her to stop forever, to quit leaving one town and hitting the highway toward the next. I wanted her to know there wasn't enough chocolate in the world to make up for the fact that, since New York, I hadn't been anywhere long enough to want to be somewhere else. So far, I always left my heart a few cities behind.

I opened my eyes. The bears were gone, replaced by strangers, crowded around me.

"She's awake!" the lady holding lavender under my nose said.

"You fainted," another woman said, shoving Vitaminwater in my face.

"Oh," I said, taking the water and sipping. Gulping.

"Do we need to call someone?" Vitaminwater Woman said.

"I'm fine," I said, even though I let them help me up and over to a bench. "I think it was just low blood sugar."

"Take this," Lavender Lady said. "I never eat the whole thing anyway." She handed me a turkey on rye.

"Thanks," I said, unwrapping it and taking a bite. I knew she wouldn't leave until she saw me eat. Since when did New Yorkers have so much time to waste?

"We're visiting from California," Lavender Lady said. That explained it.

"I appreciate your help," I said, eating more of the sandwich. "But I have an appointment. I have to go."

"Can we walk you?"

"No," I said. I had to get away from these women. "I'm fine, really. Go enjoy the city. Besides, if I need help, my dad works in that building." I pointed. "I'll just go see him."

They nodded, the dad answer appeasing them, and walked over to another bench. I grabbed my bag, threw the rest of the sandwich in the trash and waved good-bye. As I walked, I thought about how rain turned into bears, like the blackbirds had peeled off the wallpaper. Objects animating. Dad was in that world, just like he said. I picked pieces of black fur off my shirt, proving that I'd been there, too.

I needed to talk to Dr. Russo, but that would have to wait. Too much was happening for me to keep it to myself. So I walked to a place where Dad and I used to go. A place full of books and promise and a friend named Finny.

TWENTY-TWO

Saturdays were research days, and sometimes Dad took me to Bobst, also known as the Big Library. We started with slings and strollers, but eventually advanced to hand holding and lower-shelf book gathering. I got older, but not old enough, because everything still loomed above me—people and purses, books and tables. Luckily, Dad's hand was always there, guiding me through it, except for that one day. I was five years old, and he was frantic, running from table to stacks, returning with huge volumes whose titles I couldn't yet read. I sat at his feet instead of the table, coloring in my notebook, my tiny Mary Jane leaning against his black loafer.

"Ten more minutes," he said every ten minutes for the next two hours. But I got bored and wandered, following a girl with shiny red shoes. Her shoes were made of sequins, and Dad had said only good people wore sequins, so I ran after her even though she went far away from our table. I trailed behind as she pulled book after book from the stacks. Some of them even had pictures on the front. Dad's books never had pictures.

"Hi, there," she said, finally turning around. "Are you lost?"

I shook my head no and pointed to some stranger at another table.

"Ah, okay," she said, and then she left, her glittering shoes disappearing around another corner. I walked the opposite way, trying to retrace our steps, but everything looked the same— tables, books and people who were all strangers to me. I started to cry.

"Daddy," I said. I hated being alone. "I want my daddy," I said louder, and people started to notice. A man walked up to me, but I ran the other way. I didn't know him, and his shoes were dull and flat.

"Sophie?" Dad's voice came from far away.

"Daddy!" I said as loudly as I could, wanting him to find me. Hoping he wouldn't leave me alone in the world of books forever.

"Stand up and sing," he shouted, coming closer. "Sing your favorite song so I can find you."

I wiped my tears on my sleeve. I didn't want to sing. I didn't want to spend another Saturday at the Big Library. I just wanted to go home.

"Sophie, sing," he said.

I gulped and let the words float out of my mouth, softly.

"Happy birthday to me," I said.

"Bigger!" he shouted.

"Happy birthday to me," I sang, less timid.

"Louder!" he said.

"Happy birthday, dear Sophie," I sang with all my heart.

"Happy birthday to you," Dad bellowed as he appeared at the end of my aisle. The man moved away, and Dad picked me up, hugging me tightly.

"My girl," he said, kissing the top of my head. "My cream puff. I don't know what I'd do without you."

I hated that he'd had to find out.

Revolving doors spit me out into the Big Library—twelve levels of glass and steel with an atrium in the middle. People scurried like ants up and down stairs, across floors and in between the stacks of this massive metropolis. Adding to the science-fiction vibe was the floor, which looked like an optical illusion—gray, black and white cube-shaped interlocking tiles. Dad once said it reminded him of Q*bert, his favorite video game from the eighties. Now that I was back—and knew about the game—I totally saw the resemblance.

I sent Finny a text and then switched my phone to vibrate, hoping that he'd done the same thing so he'd feel it when I called him. I could look for him—he probably started on the second floor—but no telling where that led him. Who knew where anything led anyone? Two weeks earlier, Dad was on Fourth

Street with Peyton, a photo of me on the mantel. And now he was lost.

I was halfway across the lobby when the floor blurred. I rubbed my eyes, hoping it would go away, but instead my body moved up even though I was standing still. Like I was riding an elevator.

"Hey!" I said, looking down, half expecting to discover I was sitting on the shoulders of a giant who'd decided to stand, but it was just the floor, rising beneath my feet and taking me with it.

I dug my boots into the square I stood on, struggling to keep my balance. The rest of the library fell away as I went up, up, up, teetering on a tiny square. It was like surfing, only we were going up instead of out. And there was no water to catch me if I fell.

My mind hopped into survival mode, which turned out to be the voice of my PE teacher, who taught yoga last week. "Find your inner calm," she had said. "Let your balance come from the core, the middle of your body." I tried to focus on the middle of my body, but that was impossible, considering that I was now five floors up at the top of a pyramid.

"At least we're not moving," I said, looking down. Way down. How the heck was I going to get back to the ground? It was too high to slide. I didn't have climbing gear lying around, and as far as I knew, I hadn't yet developed the ability to fly. And then the whole thing shook like an earthquake. I had to find my way to solid ground.

I looked at the square diagonally down from me, held my breath and jumped.

"Yes!" I said as my feet planted into it and the square turned green. It was like being in another world, like gravity was different here or something. My feet stuck to the square like Spider-Man on the side of a building. I jumped diagonally and down to the next square, and it turned green, too, and made a noise. *BOINK*. All roads led to the floor, so I kept hopping, turning squares green. Sending sounds into the lobby, like cartoons. Like a video game.

"No way," I said as familiar fireballs and curly snakes appeared.

This was Q*bert. And I was Player One.

I dodged snakes and fireballs like a pro until I was halfway down, face-to-face with the purple guy. He tried to knock me off my square, but I was in the zone. Nothing was going to stop me, not even this super-pesky little guy. No wonder people knocked him off the side. I thought about doing it, but it seemed mean, like cheating or something. That was probably why I wasn't normally very good at video games. Empathy wasn't required, just survival skills, all the time. Kind of like my life.

I hopped down and to the left, outsmarting the snake. Down and to the right, fireballs bouncing off my head, wondering if Dad ever visited this universe, and if he did, did he get the high score? If this were a video game, I'd probably be dead by now, but the real-life version was easier, letting me experiment, explore and hop my way to the floor and, ultimately, to victory.

"High score!" I said as I got to the bottom. The pyramid collapsed, and I raised my arms in triumph, but no one was there to see it, not the snake, not the purple guy, no one except my calves, which were burning. If I had to be a video game, I'd much rather have been Ms. Pac-Man. All she had to have was a big mouth.

A few people milled around the lobby, unfazed by what had just happened, but for the most part, it was empty. Everyone must have been entrenched in the stacks. I heard a fluttering sound like papers falling but didn't see anything. There was one swoosh and then another, like tiny planes flying across the atrium. I looked up and I was partially right—things were flying. Only instead of jets zooming back and forth, it was books. Objects animating, just like Dad said.

The Plexiglas barriers were gone, and one by one, books flew off the shelves and into the middle of the atrium, swirling like birds, their pages carrying them like wings. They soared together like a flock, synchronized, creating intricate formations. I imagined *The Great Gatsby* working with *War and Peace*; Emily Post's *Etiquette* in rhythm with *Fahrenheit 451*. Big and small, their covers and pages carrying them, flapping. It was the most beautiful thing I'd ever seen, knowledge and wisdom floating above me, hypnotizing me with their grace.

I looked down at the floor, checking to make sure it wasn't rising below me, and when I looked back up, the books came together forming an *S*, an *O* and then the rest of the letters to spell my name.

Okay, universe, I thought. You have my attention, which made me think about what I'd seen since I'd been in Havencrest. Since I'd hooked up with Walt.

Mosh pit, tribe, band.

Flock, pack, Player One.

"I get it," I said. "Someone wants to make sure I don't feel alone. Wouldn't it have been easier just to reunite me with my dad?"

A huge *SNAP* echoed throughout the atrium.

"No," I said. "No, no, no, no, no."

The *SNAP*s continued, books slamming shut, closing their wings, hovering for a moment, skydivers without parachutes. They had nowhere to go but down.

I checked my souvenir pocket and there it was—the small plaid umbrella from Washington Square Park. I popped it open just as the books fell like rain. At first it was a drizzle, children's stories and sheet music, barely grazing my umbrella. But then the others joined in—poetry with plays, science with sewing manuals, geographies and biographies bouncing off my umbrella, covering the floor with knowledge. Thudding like thunder. A few came at me from the sides, knocking into my arms. I had to do something before I was literally beaten up by words.

"Take that," I said, swinging my umbrella like a sword at research tomes and outsider art books, volumes on socialism and the collected works of every philosopher ever known to man. There were over three million volumes in this library, and I didn't see an end in sight, so I dodged and ducked, running head down and umbrella first toward the front of the library. I felt the revolving door suck me in, but instead of ending up outside, I found myself back in the lobby, skirt turned around, my umbrella in someone's back, both of us on the floor. Surrounded by a crowd of people and two security guards.

"What's going on here?" one of the guards said.

I reached into my elephant pocket and felt a slim book, proof that I was back, which was good. But it would have been better if I'd been unscathed. I'd been battered by Byron, smacked by Salinger, bruised by Brontë. And once I rolled up my sleeves, I'd have the marks to prove it.

"She totally attacked that dude," a student with a large blue backpack said. "I saw everything."

By "everything" did he mean watching me survive the Q*bert floor and flying books? Or was he talking about just now, when I'd maybe popped from one universe back into another, umbrella in some guy's back? I was starting to see how that could have worked. And it terrified me.

"You're going to pay for this," the guy underneath me said as I got up. He adjusted his red sweater. "You knocked the breath out of me."

"I barely touched you," I said. Unlike the books that spelled my name and then pummeled me. "You're fine."

But I wasn't. My breath came fast and short, like it had other things to do. Like I was finally realizing the implication of my dad's book. I came to New York looking for answers. But traveling to parallel universes? I needed more than a moment to come to terms with that. I drank a bottle of water that appeared and felt the oxygen returning, glad my brain was taking over, doing the compartmentalizing thing. Panic was valid. But I was not about to let panic land me in the psych ward.

"Are we finished here?" I said, standing up and turning my skirt back around, attempting to appear normal.

"We haven't even started," the tall guard said. I could tell he was itching to use handcuffs, if he even had them. "Assault was involved, so we have to hold you for questioning."

"But I didn't do anything," I said.

"You call this nothing?" Red Sweater lifted up his shirt to reveal a tiny circle-shaped bruise in the middle of his back, like the tip of an umbrella. "Now I'm going to have to go to the chiropractor."

"You're hauling me away for that?" I said, feeling like Dad, being taken behind closed doors. This was probably how it started. They question you, don't believe your story, label you as crazy and then—boom—aqua gowns and little cups of pills at your service.

"Let's keep it calm over here," the short guard said, as if I were a member of the Umbrella Militia. He was obviously the pacifist of the two.

"Look, I was just trying to open this umbrella, it got stuck, and I tripped and fell into him. That's all that happened," I said. "I didn't mean to hurt anyone."

"She's lying!" the backpack guy said. "She came out of nowhere, umbrella blazing."

The crowd murmured, like the guy was right. Fellow book lovers on a witch hunt.

"Miss, you need to come with us," the tall security guard said, taking my arm. "You knowingly and willingly . . ."

"Willfully," the short guard said. "I think it's willfully."

"Don't correct me," the tall guard said, whipping his head around. "You attacked a man with an umbrella. I'm taking you to a secure location until the police arrive."

Police, then psych ward. I had to get out of there.

"We'll be back in a second," the short guard said as he dumped me into a small room with no windows.

The lock clicked, and I fell into one of the chairs. If Red Sweater decided to press charges, it was all over. Not only would I not be able to find Dad, I'd barely be able to find myself if I ended up in a mental hospital. I took out my phone, but there were only a few bars, horrible reception. I texted Finny anyway:

SOPHIE: Trapped in small room in library.

Police coming. Help!

That was weird, so I texted again:

SOPHIE: Lobby. Turn right at the front.

Conference room down hall. Find me.

And, in case he didn't get the first one:

SOPHIE: Police coming. Assault charge. Help me!

The phone looked like it was trying to send the texts and wasn't having any luck. I looked around the room, but it was empty. No rulers, no crowbars, nothing to pry the door open. I reached into my wallet, took out my Havencrest High School identification card, walked over to the door and slid it between the door and the frame. I jiggled it and turned the handle, hoping it would give way. It didn't, so I pulled it out and started again. And again. I didn't know what I was doing, but I had to do something.

"Starting a life of crime?"

Walt appeared behind me.

"I already have one, in case you hadn't noticed," I said. "Apparently I attack people with umbrellas."

"How rogue," he said. "And your side of the story?"

My eyes welled up. I wanted to speak, but my emotions spoke for me instead.

"It's okay," Walt said, putting his arm around me. "You're okay."

He knew. I didn't have to tell him how scared I'd been that I wouldn't make it off Q*bert mountain or escape from books bent on destruction. I didn't have to explain that the whole traveling thing was starting to make sense to me but that it terrified me. He knew. He also knew three travels in less than three hours was too much for anyone. I leaned against his large, furry body, letting the rhythm of his breath guide mine.

"Sometimes you can stop them," Walt said, smoothing my hair with his paw.

"The police?"

"The panic," he said. "Sometimes the episodes, but mostly the panic."

"What do you mean?" I said, sniffling. "Like yoga?"

"Like the more grounded you are, the less likely you are to float away."

I smiled. I hadn't realized how much I'd missed his fortune cookie wisdom.

He squeezed me. I hoped he'd never let go, that even though it wasn't how things worked, he'd take me with him to the panda-verse anyway. We'd hang out in trees, and he'd chew on bamboo, and I'd learn how to relax. How to do that breathing thing.

"Clock's ticking, princess," he said, releasing me. He took my ID and headed for the door. "So you forgive me?"

"Yes," I said. "Especially if you get me out of here."

He jiggled the credit card in the door. "They don't call me sticky fingers for nothing."

I laughed. "I think that's what they call shoplifters."

"Whatever," he said. "I can bust you out of here like a bad tomato."

"That doesn't make sense either," I said. "But I'm rooting for you. Have any advice for me once I get out?"

"Read the rest of your dad's book," Walt said. "The good part is coming up. And then believe it."

"No, I mean, how to actually get out of the *building*."

"Oh!" he said. "That's easy. Blend in like you belong."

Belonging wasn't one of my things, and neither was blending, so I'd have to fake it.

"Tell me this—are the answers starting to come?" Walt asked.

"Some of them," I said.

"That's good! You're definitely on the right path. The world is making space for your voyage."

"Like Columbus?" I said, grabbing my bag, preparing to push off.

"Exactly," Walt said, popping the lock and handing me my card. "Maiden voyages are the best voyages. Now, get out of here."

I blew him a kiss, opened the door and blended in with the crowd, squeezing my way through name tags and fanny packs, camera bags and maps, a group tour that happened at the perfect time. I was a salmon, swimming upstream. And then I was outside, breathing fresh air, jogging. Which turned into running, because I was officially on the run. Which then turned into Where the Heck Was I Going Next?

TWENTY-THREE

How to Survive Becoming a Fugitive
by Sophie Sophia

1. Try not to become a fugitive in the first place.
2. If you do, wear comfortable shoes.
3. Realize that running has become a way of life now, as has sneaking, crouching, freezing and hiding. Embrace them.
4. Get a tattoo of your future inmate numbers to remind yourself why you're running.
5. Actually, don't get a tattoo. And don't become a fugitive in the first place. (It's overrated.)

I found myself in front of a frosted glass door at the other end of Meyer Hall.

"Come in," Dr. Russo replied when I knocked.

Her voice was deep, and she looked like a younger Sophia Loren. Mom said Sophia Loren was the epitome of glamour and that having a little curve was a good thing. I remembered looking down at my stick body and thinking I would never have any curves, not that it mattered, boys didn't like me, anyway. But that had changed. Not the curves so much, but the boys. One boy, at least.

Dr. Russo looked up from her papers and eyed me over her bifocals. Either her eyelashes were fake, or she wore tons of mascara.

"And you would be?"

"Sophie Sophia, Angelino Sophia's daughter," I said. "Dr. Perratto sent me."

"Sophie of the Sophie Effect," she said, taking off her glasses. "My day just got a lot more interesting."

I wasn't sure what the Sophie Effect was, but I was about to find out. After the library, my first instinct was to run, but then I realized no one knew me there. I wasn't a registered student. And once the security guards opened that door and discovered I was gone, they'd probably be too embarrassed to pursue me, anyway. So why not continue down to the path toward Dad?

"Have a seat," Dr. Russo said, motioning to the yellow velvet chair in front of her. "Sparkling soda water?"

She got up, picked up a vintage red siphon and shook it.

Then she squeezed the trigger—just like in the movies—and shot fizzy water into two glasses, finishing each one off with a slice of lemon.

I took out my phone, which was vibrating all over the place, and texted Finny that I was okay, I'd escaped the police, I was with another physicist and would text him when I was finished. At the moment, though, I was about to enjoy a mocktail.

"Everything okay?" she said, handing me a glass.

"Yes," I said. "Thank you, Dr. Russo."

"You're welcome," she said. "And call me Betty."

I sipped my super-fancy drink and Betty leaned back in her chair and adjusted her long, mustard scarf. I looked around at her office: shelves brimming with books, an Oriental rug, a vase filled with maroon dahlias and a framed black-and-white photo of the cosmos covering one wall. I wasn't sure if I was going to learn about theoretical physics or engage in talk therapy.

"How's your father? I haven't seen him in ages."

"He's missing," I said.

"Yes, well, he'll come back," she said. "He always does. Chances are, he's in the same time frame as we are, only in a parallel universe."

I loved how the phrase "parallel universe" rolled off her tongue.

"Dr. Perratto said there's no way to prove that," I said.

"That's where the good doctor is wrong," she said. "It sounds like you two discussed your father's book."

"We did," I said. "I've only read the first few chapters, but it was enough to talk with him about it. And find out he thought Dad was crazy."

"What's crazy?" she said, waving her hand in the air. "The idea that a theoretical physicist might stumble upon and then pursue an idea so challenging that it threatens everyone else?"

She was passionate, just like Dad.

"But Dr. Perratto said you can't mix physics and emotion," I said, leaning back in the chair.

She laughed. "Dr. Perratto has a lot of rules. Did he also say that traveling's not possible?"

"Yes," I said, grinning. "But I think he's wrong."

"Because?"

"This is theoretical physics," I said. And then I quoted Mr. Maxim. "Anything is possible."

"Bravo," she said, raising her glass, which made me raise mine.

"Here's to your father, who believes in the impossible," she said. "And to you, who are pursuing it."

We clinked glasses like the first day of school. Like poker with pandas.

"Now, on to the business of traveling," she said. "What do you know about souvenirs?"

I reached up and felt the whistle around my neck.

"Less from Dad's book and more from life," I said. "I have souvenirs, too."

CHAPTER THREE:
THE LAW OF SOUVENIRS

In order to prove a theory, one needs physical, measurable proof. And in the case of traveling, that proof is souvenirs. A souvenir is an object a traveler brings back from his or her travels. It can be anything—a key, a rock, a piece of clothing—but it is undeniably from another place. Most likely another universe.

Logistically, the traveler doesn't acquire the souvenir. It simply shows up, usually in a pocket, once traveling has concluded. This gives souvenirs a dual purpose. On the one hand, they help you remember where you've been. And on the other, they act as a cue, letting you know that you've returned.

Betty walked over to a large red chest that was next to her credenza.

"One of the benefits of being one of your father's research assistants was the actual research," she said. She opened the chest and objects spilled onto the floor—jars and bowling pins, animal masks and a disco ball. There was a tin of drawing pencils and a tuxedo, reel-to-reel tapes and what looked like a magnifying glass.

"Whoa," I said, kneeling in front of the disco ball. "Can I touch them?"

"Of course," she said. "They've traveled through many dimensions. I think they can handle your fingers."

I picked up a blue glass jar and saw a ticket stub in it. Depeche Mode.

"Isn't the shade of blue lovely?" she said.

It was more than lovely, it was validation. Proof. A weight off my shoulders but a bigger weight in my heart. I had to find Dad.

"What's the Sophie Effect?" I said.

Betty walked over to her desk, picked up Dad's book, opened it to the middle and gave it to me.

"It's the theory that explains traveling," she said. "And it was inspired by you."

CHAPTER FOUR: THE SOPHIE EFFECT

The brain is composed of billions of neurons. But those neurons are no match for the emotion of love. Think of how strongly a parent feels about a child, how powerful a first love is and how the love between a husband and wife feels like a bond that cannot be broken. These types of love fill the heart, making it feel complete.

The Sophie Effect proposes that when you lose that type of love, the effect is so strong it creates minuscule holes in the heart, like gaps. These gaps connect you to the gaps between the strings, the fabric of the universes. When triggered by loneliness, the enemy of the heart, this connection allows you to slip through the strings to parallel universes. Often without even knowing it.

I fell back in my chair, dizzy.

"Sophie?" Betty said, refilling my glass. "Are you okay?"

"So you're telling me that breakups cause actual holes in the heart?" I said.

She laughed. "That's what your father is telling you," she said.

"No wonder people write so many songs about being

dumped." I sank deeper into the chair. "When it ends, it actually damages you."

"It's just a theory," Betty said, gently taking the book from my hands and placing it on her desk. "I know it's a lot to take in."

It was more than a lot. It could be everything: the answer I'd been looking for. The key that would keep me out of a mental hospital forever.

"Do you think it's true?"

"I think it was true for your father," she said. "And I think it might be true for you."

I didn't know why I felt so angry, but I did. I wanted to be solved. I wanted my episodes to make sense, and so far, this was the best explanation. It wasn't schizophrenia or lucid dreaming, it was travel to parallel universes.

What I didn't like was that love made it happen, like the love between a father and a child. Like the kind that inspired you to write a book or name a principle after someone. Dad might have disappeared because of Mom, but I wondered if he stayed gone because of me. Not science, not protons and neutrons, but a bundle of matter, squeezed into an elephant skirt.

When Mom and Dad fought, Dad disappeared. And the more they argued, the more he faded away, only to pop back in out of nowhere. When the house was angry, Dad was angry, too, leaving on adventures or hiding in the basement, emerging only when he had a new idea to share. Usually it was something that didn't make sense, which made Mom yell at him all over again, continuing the cycle: yell, disappear, apologize, repeat.

"That's it," I said, hopping up from my chair. "Repeat."

"What?" Betty was sitting in the other yellow velvet chair beside me.

"Dad was the only test subject, right?"

"Correct," she said. "That's one of the reasons the scientific community negated his efforts."

"So I'll be a test subject," I said, getting excited. "Maybe I can't find Dad, but the one thing I *can* do is prove his theory. He's not crazy. I'm not crazy, either, but the only way to know that for sure is to prove that the Sophie Effect is true with another test subject: me. And if I can prove that—"

"Then you can prove you're traveling," Betty said. "Brilliant." And then it hit me.

"Why wouldn't Dad prove the opposite?" I said.

"What do you mean?" Betty said, leaning forward.

"If the Sophie Effect explains traveling, it should also explain *not* traveling," I said. "You create holes, you travel. You plug up the holes, you stay put like everyone else."

Betty smiled. "You think just like your father."

I thought about the panda-verse, the music-video-verse and the one where objects animated. Traveling.

And then I thought about eating in the cafeteria with no episodes, coffee dates without disappearing, seeing Mom enjoy me again instead of worrying about what I was going to do next. Not traveling.

"Dad must have known," I said, sitting up. "So why wasn't it in the book? Why didn't he try to stop traveling?"

Betty walked over to her credenza and picked up a zebra mask. "Maybe he did," she said, bringing the mask in front of her face. "Maybe he is."

I thought about Dad hanging with The Cure, getting hair tips from Robert Smith. Or Dad with a panda friend, like Walt, on a string of continuous slumber parties. Maybe he was enjoying it, or maybe he wanted to come back but couldn't. Maybe the holes were too large or too many for him to fill on his own.

"He needs me," I said, standing up. Finally getting it. This wasn't about me, it was about him. "Dad needs my help."

Betty put the mask aside and stood next to me. "I'm sure he'd never say no to that," she said. "He spoke very highly of you."

And I hadn't spoken very highly of him, not in a while. But as it turned out, he was thinking about me the whole time, making tapes and trying to devise a theory that would save us both. Now it was my turn, which meant it was time to do what I did best: make a list.

How to Prove the Sophie Effect
(a.k.a. How to Close the Gaps in Your Heart) by Sophie Sophia

---

1. Fall madly, deeply in love with someone.
2. Go to a yoga class and fall in love with the world.
3. If number one doesn't work, develop a crush.
   And then write him a poem.
4. Do something nice for someone else.
5. And if all else fails, draw little hearts on things.
   It can't hurt.

Betty looked at my list.

"Remember, I'm fourteen," I said. "My experience with love is limited."

"This is a great start," Betty said, smiling. "My advice? Be open to all kinds of love. There are many ways to love a person."

I thought about Drew. I didn't love him yet, but I loved the idea of him. It was different than the way I loved my shoes, which was different than the way I loved the idea of proving Dad's theory. All of which were different than the way I loved Finny—I had to find him. If anyone could help me brainstorm and cover off on all of the love bases, it was Finn.

"I like that idea," I said. "Thank you."

"Of course. And call me anytime with questions," she said, handing me her card. "I'm a big fan of your father's."

I wanted to high-five her, but that didn't seem very scientific.

"Me too," I said, shaking her hand instead, happy not to be the only member of Dad's fan club.

I had just texted Finny and was headed south when I heard his voice.

"Sophie?"

"Finny!" I screamed, turning and throwing my arms around him. If I had to fill the gaps, why not start immediately?

"What the heck?" he said, backing up. "You can't text me like that and just disappear."

"Wait, what? I sent you a text that I was okay."

"And meeting with a physicist," he said. "The *one* thing I wanted to do while I was here, but instead I was looking for you at the library, hoping I hadn't missed you. Hoping you hadn't been hauled off to the police station."

"But I sent you a note," I said. "I told you I was okay."

"Like an hour later! Just because you see things and your dad's missing doesn't mean you can act like you're the only person on the planet," he said. "There are other people. And we have feelings, too."

He stood in the middle of the sidewalk, arms crossed. This love thing was going to be harder than I thought. And if I couldn't do it with Finny, I didn't have a chance of doing it with anyone else.

"I'm sorry," I said, taking a step toward him. Trying. "But things are about to get really exciting, and I'd hate to do them without you."

"I'm sure you would," he said, pouting.

I wished I could hold my breath, like I did with Mom, and eventually it would be okay.

"It sucks to get dumped," I said.

He stood there, giving me the silent treatment I deserved.

"What if we made a deal?" I said.

"Go on," Finny said, arms still crossed.

"What if you got unmad at me now, and then as soon as we got on the train, you could ignore me for, like, ever?"

"You know I like to talk on the train," he said.

I grinned.

"There's no way I'll be able to keep that deal!"

"That's what I'm counting on," I said.

"Just admit it," Finny said.

"Admit what?"

Finny uncrossed his arms, fully aware that he had the power.

"That you need me," he said.

I wanted to shout it out to him, to Dad, to Mom, to all of them, but I paused for dramatic effect.

"Are you kidding?" I said. "I need you like Jack White needs Meg."

"He's doing solo stuff now."

"Whatever!" I said. "I need you."

"Uh-huh, uh-huh, uh-huh-huh-huh," he said, dancing around, waving his arms.

"What is *that*?"

"Victory dance," Finny said. "I knew I was needed. I just wanted to hear you say it."

"Hearts?" I said, stepping closer.

"Hearts," he said as I wrapped my arms around him, the way Walt did with me.

And then I whispered in his ear, "Dad wrote a theory about me."

"I know!" Finny said, backing up and unwrapping himself from the hug. "The Sophie Effect. I've been waiting for you to get to it. I didn't want to spoil the surprise."

"Surprise!" I said. "It's better that you already know about it since I'm going to prove it and everything."

"How?" Finny laughed. "It's one of the most scientifically impossible things I've ever read."

And there, like the old friend I'd never liked in the first place, it showed up. Doubt.

"Wait, you don't believe it?"

"It's a theory," Finny said. "I believe it has theoretical applications."

"Exactly," I said. "And I'm about to apply them to my life."

It was one of the first times I'd witnessed his skeptical face. I wanted to tell him about Dad, about how I wasn't just doing this for me, I was doing it for him, but I didn't want to add guilt to doubt.

"Dr. Russo thinks I can do it," I said.

Finny straightened up. "She does?"

"Yeah!" I said. "I even made a list at her office."

I took out my Moleskine notebook and handed it to Finny.

"What are we trying to prove, exactly?"

"We!" I said. "You said we."

"As if I could stay away," he said. "You know I love a puzzle."

"You love me!"

"I do, kooky as you are," he said. "So what's next?"

"Since there's no scientific way to measure travel, the best way to prove the Sophie Effect is to prove its opposite, which is what I've wanted to do all along."

"Oh!" Finny said, excited again. "You want to stop traveling."

"Exactly," I said. "And according to Dad's book, the only way to do that is repair my heart, love style."

Finny looked at my list. "I think we should start with the cookie one."

"Which cookie one?" I said, looking at my Moleskine.

"Number four," he said. "Do something nice for someone

else. Since you've pretty much put me through hell a million times, I think that someone should be me. And I request cookies."

He handed me my notebook—the one I was supposed to use to track data for the Normalcy Project and never did—and I put it in my bag.

"There used to be an amazing bakery around the corner," I said, walking toward West Fifth Street. "Can you hear the chocolate chips calling?"

Finny put his hand to his ear and craned his neck, like he was listening. "I can!" he said. "Too bad I'm going to eat them." He walked to catch up with me and then grabbed my arm so I'd stop. "If I come with you, you have to promise me one thing," Finny said.

"Yes, I'm buying," I said.

"That's great, but that's not it," he said. "You have to promise me you won't run away."

His voice sounded all crackly when he said it, the way Mom's did, the way mine did after an episode. It never occurred to me that my stress wasn't just mine, it also applied to Finny.

"Got it," I said, squeezing his shoulder, but I didn't promise. The night was young, the city was big, and I had a theory to prove.

TWENTY-FOUR

She's running to stand still.

—U2, "Running to Stand Still"

"Order up," the barista said, putting two hot chocolates with whipped cream on the bar.

Finny and I were at Chocolate Chocolat, where I'd just eaten the best chocolate chip cookie ever to inhabit my mouth.

"Want more?" I said, getting back in line. "No telling when we'll eat again."

"We're eating at six with Peyton," Finny said. "At some Italian place on Broadway, remember?"

"I remember," I said, even though I fully expected to miss it. I was going to be busy being a test subject, trying to prove the Sophie Effect and save myself before I hopped on a train.

I walked back to the table with our hot chocolates and half a dozen cookies. I opened the box and handed Finny another one.

"Mmmm," he said, munching. "I think you can cross number four off your list."

"Great," I said, even though I didn't feel any different. Too bad this filling-your-heart thing wasn't more like a video game. My life would have been a lot easier if I heard a *ding* every time a hole was filled. "What's next, poetry?"

"I have something better," Finny said, taking an orange Sharpie out of his bag. "Give me your arm."

He flipped it over, revealing my forearm, and drew a heart with an arrow running through it. On the inside he wrote "SS + FJ 4EVR."

"Cute," I said. "And the purpose of this is?"

"We're madly, deeply in love!" he said, grinning like he'd just solved all my problems.

"Fake love," I said, running my finger over his design. "Don't you think our hearts can tell the difference?"

"Maybe," he said, his face falling. "Why? Don't you feel anything?"

"Not yet," I said. No dings. But since I didn't want to disappoint him, I said something else. "It's not your fault, though. My heart probably has so many gaps it's going to take more than a fake-lationship to repair it."

"True," he said, opening the box and taking another cookie. "But as far as fake-lationships go, this is a pretty good one."

"It's amazing," I said, finishing off my hot chocolate. It was the best friendship of my life, but not because he was with me then. It was because he was always there—after I got suspended, after my freak-out at Café Haven, after Mom admitted she thought I was crazy. My chaos continued, but so did his loyalty.

"Ready to get out of here?"

"Sure," he said, wiping cookie crumbs off his mouth. "I'm feeling rather poetic. And walking is great for the creative process."

Walking also connected me to Dad, my feet taking me places he'd been. Dad loved walking so much that he used to pick a street and take it as far as it would go. Broadway was one of his favorites because it ended up at the top of Manhattan, his problem solved by the time he got there. I could only hope it did the same for me.

"Your current crush is Drew, right?" Finny said, following me down the sidewalk.

"As far as I know," I said. "Do you have a crush on him, too?"

"I am completely crushing on his style, but not his person. It's possible to fall in love with clothing, you know."

I knew. It was probably easier to love my Army Navy jacket than an actual person.

"I've got it!" Finny said, stopping in front of the Strand bookstore. "Check this out: Roses are red, hearts have holes, too. If you'll plug mine up, I'll give it to you."

I laughed. "I christen you the rhyming scientist."

"What would you do—something more esoteric? Like a haiku?"

"Of course," I said, leaning against the wall next to him. I counted syllables on my fingers as I recited. "You are my coffee, waking me up to myself. Pour another cup."

Finny laughed so hard people stared.

"That's how we met!" I said. "Coffee is a pivotal part of our relationship."

"But it's not very romantic. Should we go inside?" he said, motioning to the store. "For inspiration?"

And then I remembered what I had in my pocket: *The Pocket Emily Dickinson*. I took it out.

"Ooooh," Finny said, practically drooling. "Is that—"

"A souvenir? Yes," I said. "I'll tell you about it later, but right now I need to study the greats."

I turned to a poem called "Wild Nights" and held the book open between us. It was definitely passionate, but what struck me most about it was the word *moor*. I loved it. It sounded like *more* but actually meant "anchored." Secured. Emily wanted to secure herself to another person. Maybe that's what love was all about—safety—like how I felt the first time I saw Drew. It was like he filled one of the holes in my heart I didn't even know was there. And even though I hadn't said it out loud or written it down, I think that was poetry enough.

"Let's come back to this one," I said, even though I knew I was finished. "What's next? Yoga?"

"Sure!" he said, the optimistic partner in crime. "I'm sure there's one down the street."

This time I followed Finny, thinking about love. There was romantic love, which I'd just attempted. There was friend love, which I was attempting all over the place with Finny. And then there was unconditional love. The kind where people loved you exactly as you were, no matter how you showed up. Could yoga possibly help with that?

"I smell incense!" Finny said, opening the door to Yoga Love.

We walked into a class already in session, took off our shoes and coats and grabbed mats from the shelves lining one wall. I felt out of place in my skirt and tights, but since yoga was all about self-acceptance, it was probably okay. Finny and I set up our mats in the back in case we needed to make a speedy exit.

"Arms over your head and inhale," the teacher said. "Exhale, dive forward."

My hair flopped in my face.

"Inhale, rise up halfway and exhale, bow forward."

Finny looked seasick.

"Inhale, float back to plank and exhale, go through *Chaturanga Dandasana* to Downward Facing Dog."

Finny collapsed on his mat, and I got into Down Dog, the only pose I really knew. I tried to think about peace. About loving the world. But it was hard to open my heart when all the blood was rushing to my head. She took us through the sequence four more times, which was really three times too many.

"Arms out to the side like wings and inhale, rise toward the sky, exhale, hands to your heart."

Good thing she'd guided my hands there, I thought. My heart was beating so fast it would have popped out of my chest if my fingers hadn't been there to block it.

"Nice work, everyone," she said. "Let's move on to *Surya Namaskara* B."

"The *B* stands for let's bail," Finny said, his face red and sweating. He made it through two sequences before he fell on his mat, which he now rolled up and returned to the wall. I did the same, and we both headed for the door.

"*Namaste*," she said as we were leaving.

"*Namaste*," I said quickly, pushing Finny out the door before he could laugh. I knew it was a special word, but it always made me laugh, too. It sounded like "my nasty." And there was nothing sacred about that.

Finny put his hand in front of my heart, hovering a few inches away from my shirt.

"Oh, heart of hearts, are you filling? Do you feel the love, or do you just feel tired?"

"Tired," I said. Like bone tired. And not just from the yoga. It was exhausting trying to make something work that clearly was *not*. It was like Finny said. The Sophie Effect was impossible to prove.

"Don't give up yet," Finny said. "We have one more thing on your list."

He popped inside the dollar store and came out with a box of sidewalk chalk.

"What did your list say? It can't hurt, right?"

I tried to crack a smile, but my lips stayed small, horizontal.

"So forget about the list," Finny said, handing me a piece of purple chalk. "Let's just have fun."

He took a piece of pink chalk and together we drew little hearts and big ones, wide ones and skinny ones all over the sidewalk, up the buildings, down the curbs and into the street.

Hearts to catch people's attention, reminding them to put more love in the world. Reminding me to let love in. One guy high-fived me, and a little girl smiled as I drew hearts around her feet. I looked over and saw Finny connecting his hearts with swirls and getting smiles from strangers, right and left. We drew hearts around dogs, bicycles and fire hydrants, leaving little signs, messages to my heart, letting it know I understood. Messages to Dad, letting him know it was okay to come home. I knew the chalk would fade, but it didn't matter. I was connecting. Leaping. And I wasn't alone. Except when I looked up from doodling, I was. And I was at 34th Street.

"Finny?" I said.

His bird's nest hair wasn't anywhere, but Walt was. And he was standing in front of me wearing a pink tutu.

"Care to dance?"

I took his paw and he led me into Herald Square. Pandas sat at tables and on benches and still others wore tutus, which is when I realized: Walt hadn't come to me. I went to him. I traveled.

"Crap!" I said, flopping down next to Larry, who had one leg up on the bench.

"Are your muscles tight, too?" he said, attempting a hamstring stretch.

"Something like that," I said. Except it was nothing like that.

"What's going on?" I said to Merv, who was kicking. It looked less like dance and more like karate.

"Rockettes tryouts are today," he said. "We're all auditioning."

"Why?" I said.

"Dancing improves marching skills," Walt said. "You should try it sometime."

"Yeah," I said. "Because if poetry and yoga won't help me prove the Sophie Effect, high kicks will."

Walt stood up and balanced on his tiptoes. "You want my advice?"

"Yes," I said. "Generic as it may be."

"You're thinking about love in the general sense," he said. "Maybe the real work is closer to home."

"Like Havencrest?"

"Even closer than that," he said. The rest of the pandas had formed a line in the middle of the square and were waiting.

"You have a choice," he said, adjusting his tutu. "You could sit here with a sad face, or you could realize you're doing all you can. Forgive yourself a little. And then celebrate how far you've come."

He held out his paw, and I took it, joining my tribe in tutus.

The pandas linked arms, shoulder to shoulder, while I stretched mine as far as they would go around Walt and Larry's waists. Walt counted off, and before I knew it, we were kicking, blurs of black, white and Doc Marten flashing in the sun.

"You'll have to kick higher than that," Walt said, sending his leg up to eye level. Grinning.

"If the shaman thing doesn't work out, you definitely have a backup job," I said.

We kicked together, one perfect unit, as Merv busted out his own enthusiastic, acoustic version of "New York, New York."

As my legs stretched longer, I forgot about the Sophie Effect.

As my limbs went higher, I forgot about being lonely. Being angry. Being me.

I was finally getting the hang of it when Merv's chorus ended and it was over. The pandas and I took a bow and then we unlinked, tutus running for water, me wondering where I'd run to next.

"Drink up, doll," Walt said, handing me a bottle of water. "Hydrate that beautiful brain of yours."

"And my heart?"

"You're closer than you know," he said. And then he pointed to the Broadway street sign. "Just keep going. You're headed in the right direction."

The pandas disappeared, and the old Broadway reappeared. I didn't see Finny, just an old guy sitting inside a doorway holding out a tattered hat. I think it was a fedora.

"Lady, spare a dollar?"

"Enjoy," I said, putting one of my five-dollar bills in his hat.

SOPHIE: Where are you?

I texted Finny as I continued up Broadway, shadowed by tall buildings and tailed by taxis. I passed a theater, which was showing *Mamma Mia*, but remembered Dad talking about when everything was all *Cats*, all the time. It made me miss Balzac. I found him when he was a kitten, sitting on our stoop, all blue eyes and fur, no collar. When I asked if I could keep him, Mom said no, he was too hairy, but Dad said yes, and that I should bestow a regal name upon him. I ran inside to the bookshelf, closed my eyes and spun. When I opened them, I was pointing at *The Quest of the Absolute*, by Honoré de Balzac.

"I christen you Balzac," I said to the tiny fur ball who would turn out to be my best friend. He didn't care that I saw things that weren't there or that we moved a lot, just that I let him climb all over me when I was reading in bed, snuck him tuna from my sandwiches and talked to him every morning. His mom might have been Siamese, which gave him blue eyes, but his dad was definitely Maine Coon. Balzac was a talker who responded to anything that would respond, which Mom described once as manic.

"You know the real Balzac suffered from fits of mania and depression, right?" Mom said.

Apparently I'd invited mania into my house without knowing it was already there. It made me wonder what else I'd let in by accident.

Broadway curved and got busier with people, stores and clubs. Maybe one of them was a jazz club where Dad liked to go. Maybe he was in a jazz universe right then, showing horn players the connection between dissonance and mustard, accelerando and roller skates. How everything was linked, like the lines that ran between us. Some of those lines were really close, especially the one between science and sanity.

Buildings blocked my view as I ran into a crowd filled with babies and briefcases, my feet trying to keep up with my mind.

As the smells grew stronger, the avenue grew wider and the sky opened up, a big circle of dusk surrounded by TV screens and headlines. NASDAQ and neon. Pepsi, TDK, Toshiba. Toys "Я" Us, Bank of America, Target. Drink our soda, watch our sports channel, see our movie. Commercials played right, left and center, creating a constant circle of babble, while real life Statues of Liberty—people wearing green face paint and dresses—posed for photos with tourists who ignored everything else going on around them in their quest to get the perfect shot. People from all over the world came here, to the center of everything, where the apple dropped.

Nine-to-fivers ran by me to catch the train. Suit wearers and purse swingers rushed over me, headed for the first act. It was all bike messengers and bedlam, traffic and travesty, all that was and would always be Times Square.

Finny hadn't texted me back. My heart felt the same as before, and I sensed the dark place in my stomach darkening. The air left, the sky closed in, and a shopping bag hit me in the head. It was hard to think about love while chaos swirled around me, but maybe that was the point. A bike raced by and knocked me onto a bench, so I sat there, absorbing the neon.

"Are you crazy or traveling?" Panasonic asked.

"You think if you prove the Sophie Effect, things will go back to normal?" Sony wanted to know. Sony had a point. My version of normal was different from everyone else's, even before I started seeing things.

A woman in an American flag sweatshirt wheeled a double stroller past me, yelling at her kids. I would have yelled at Dad if he had been there. What if the last time I saw him was the last time I'd *ever* see him?

People poured past me and into theaters, trying to make the evening shows. As quickly as they filled, the streets were now clear. I hugged my knees to my chest and planted my feet on the bench. I was walking the streets he'd walked, trying to fill my heart. Hoping it would fill his. But Dad never tried to find me. Even though Mom kicked him out, he never came after me. He let me drift.

I could have sworn I felt the holes in my heart get even bigger.

And then I remembered something I hadn't been able to remember until now: the night Dad left.

"But she didn't drink any," I heard Dad say. I was sitting in the living room doodling while Balzac sat beside me, quiet for the moment.

"No one got hurt," he said.

"You put a bottle of rat poison in the kitchen cabinet. What were you thinking?" Mom asked.

"It was an accident, fruit pie," he said. Dad's pet names were always desserts, which I thought was funny. "I was using it, came up to make a snack and left it in the cabinet, I guess."

"This is a house, not a laboratory," Mom said. "Our closet is no place for chemistry sets, and samurai swords don't belong next to the toothpaste."

"I was going to put those away, too," he said. "I just forgot because—"

"You always forget," Mom said. "I understand that your brain doesn't work in a linear fashion, but you're not the only one who lives here. I can take care of myself, but what about Sophie? She could have been distracted and spooned rat poison into her milk instead of Ovaltine."

Balzac meowed. Exactly, I thought. I hated Ovaltine.

"No more mixing work and play," Dad said. "Next time I'll leave everything in the basement."

"That shouldn't be a problem," she said. "Since there won't be a next time."

Mom poked her head out of the kitchen.

"Sophie, it's past your bedtime," she said. "Go on up, and I'll tuck you in later."

I went to my room and buried myself under the covers but couldn't sleep. There was too much yelling. I put on my headphones, but I could still hear them in between songs, crying, yelling and more crying. It was too late to go anywhere else, so I got my sewing supplies, climbed back into bed and turned up the volume to R.E.M.'s *Reckoning*.

"It's a Dream Pocket," I told Balzac, who sniffed my scraps to see if they were edible, which they weren't unless you were a fan of felt. "I hope it works."

I heard a crash, and Balzac jumped.

"Sophie?" Dad said, knocking on the door. "Can I come in?"

"Sure," I said. Balzac flew off the bed and over to Dad. "Are you guys okay?" I asked.

"Of course," he said, but I knew he was lying. "I was dancing with your mom, and a vase fell."

You and Mom were fighting, and a vase broke, I thought. I wasn't stupid.

"You're supposed to be asleep," he said, nodding at my supplies. "What are you making?"

"Dream Pockets," I said, holding up a cloud-shaped piece of felt that was blue on one side, lemon yellow on the other and sewn together with a small opening at the top like a pocket. "You write down a dream, put it inside and put the whole thing under your pillow. When you wake up, your dream comes true."

"Impressive, my little genius," he said. "Does it work?"

"Not yet," I said. "I still have to sew on the buttons and test my theory. It's probably not an exact science, anyway, not like your stuff. Like things might come true, but not right away. Or maybe not in the way you thought."

"It's beautiful," he said. "You know, my science isn't an exact science, either."

"It's not?"

"Far from it," he said. "There are many things we don't know about our world, but that's okay. That means the possibilities are endless."

"Here," I said, handing him a Dream Pocket. "It's not finished, but I want you to have it."

"Thank you," he said. "I'll take it with me on my trip."

"But you just got back . . ."

I wanted him to stay so we could have toast with jam faces in the morning. I promised to be extra quiet so he could sleep late.

"And I will 'just get back' again," he said. "Can someone else write the dream for you?"

"Sure," I said, getting a piece of notebook paper and a red pen off my desk.

"Would you write it?"

"Yes!" I said. And there, in small, cramped letters, I wrote my dream for him. "Travel safely and come back soon."

I folded it up and put it in the front pocket of his jacket, along with a few other strips of paper.

"Those are so you can write your own dreams on other nights," I said.

"But I like this one," he said, looking like he was about to cry. "Daddy?"

"I'm just tired," he said. "I better get going, lemon drop."

Balzac rubbed up against his leg and meowed.

"Even the cat wants you to stay," I said. "When will you be back?"

I never really cared where he went, only when he would come home.

"Soon," he said. "I'll see you soon."

"I'd rather see you sooner," I said, patting Balzac's head. "We miss you when you're gone."

"I miss you, too, Sophie," he said. "No matter what you hear or what anyone tells you, know this: I will always love you. Come here."

Dad wrapped his arms around me and gave me the biggest hug ever, the kind that smashes your heart into the rest of your organs.

"I love you, too," I said. "But I can't breathe."

He laughed, releasing me.

"Be good while I'm gone," he said. "Listen to your mom, listen to yourself and don't be scared of things you don't understand. Remember—they're just possibilities."

"Okay," I said, wondering why he was acting so weird.

I picked up Balzac, and we walked Dad downstairs and to the front door. Mom stood off to the side, arms crossed, lips in a little ball. She'd been crying, you could tell, but she cried a lot lately. She needed a Dream Pocket, too, one that came with a Kleenex inside. Dad put on his captain's hat and opened the door.

"Bon voyage, ladies," he said. And then he did his good-bye dance and walked down the steps. Just like he always did.

"Bon voyage, Captain!" I said, leaning out the door and blowing him a kiss. Balzac meowed, and Mom went to the kitchen, but I stood in the doorway and watched Dad until he was out of sight, which didn't take long since it was dark outside. It was always sad to see him leave, but it wasn't that big of a deal. He'd be back before I knew it. He always was.

Tears ran down my cheeks and mixed with the smell of hot dogs and pretzels, the conversations of cabbies and people on cell phones.

Dad didn't come back, but other people came in. And they stayed.

I had Finny, master of best-friend-dom. Even though I hadn't been a stellar friend myself, he was there. Sidewalk chalk and all.

I had Mom, queen of trying to make things better, even

when it seemed like she made them worse. Dad was just being himself. And she was just trying to protect me from it.

I had Drew. And even though he was just the tiniest possibility of something, it was something.

And Betty, the other member of the fan club.

Morrissey, who wrote songs about what I was feeling. He made pain sound good.

Einstein, because he belonged to all of us. Without him, the Sophie Effect wouldn't exist. And science might have stayed small instead of what it was now: infinite.

I had Balzac, the cat with the biggest mouth and the even bigger heart.

Peyton, my closest link to Dad. Maybe we'd find our way.

And Walt. Everyone deserved a shaman panda. Guardian angel, sans the wings.

And Dad.

Let them in.

Let them in.

Let them in.

Armor off, heart exposed, holes and all. I wasn't sure I was ready for that.

My phone vibrated in my pocket. Finny. It had been vibrating continuously, but I'd ignored it. Just like I ignored what was right in front of me. Love wasn't about just one part—that happy ending you saw in movies and read in books—it was about all of it. Messy, disappointing, imperfect. But you needed it if you were ever going to be whole.

How to Close the Gaps in Your Heart, Part 2
by Sophie Sophia

1. Realize you have awesome people around
   you who want to love you.
2. Let them.
3. Show them you love them back. (Actions
   trump words.)
4. Do the forgiveness thing.
5. If necessary—and it almost always is—do the
   forgiveness thing on yourself.

Out of nowhere, I wanted to be at that dinner, splashing Finny
with red sauce and dangling noodles at Peyton. I wanted to be
Sophie minus the Sophie Effect, except that part where I show
up. I pressed 1 on my speed dial. Finny.

"Sophie? Where are you! I've been calling and texting and—"

"I know," I said. "I got stuck in the panda-verse."

"Oh," Finny said, his voice expressing how I'd felt when I
was in it.

"It's okay," I said, feeling inside my pocket. A ballet shoe.
"Really, it's better than okay. I think I figured it out."

"Let me come get you," he said. "I don't have to finish this
lasagna."

"You do," I said. "And I have to finish it with you."

"Huh?"

"Are you still on Twenty-third and Broadway?"

"We are, but—"

"But nothing," I said, hoisting my bag on my shoulder and standing up. "I'm about twenty blocks away. Order me spaghetti pomodoro? I'll be there as soon as I can."

"Take a cab," I heard Peyton say. "I'll pay for it when you get here."

I hailed one and collapsed into the backseat. I said I was tired before, but this topped it. This was like exhaustion. La grippe.

"East Twenty-third and Broadway," I said, taking out my phone again. Mom would hate shorthand, but I was going to text her, anyway.

SOPHIE: See you soon.

MOM: Are you on the train?

SOPHIE: Not yet.

Now that I'd been inside Dad's world, I understood why she didn't want me there. She loved Dad but was afraid of him. Like she'd started to be with me. But I wasn't Dad. And pretty soon she'd know that. My hands shook as I typed.

SOPHIE: I love you, Mom.

And then my phone lit up like Christmas.

MOM: I love you, too.

We never said it to each other, which is probably why it felt so good, like a warm bubble bath after trudging home in the cold. Like finally, I wasn't so alone. And when the cab pulled up in front of the restaurant, I saw Peyton and Finny through the window, waving. Confirming it.

TWENTY-FIVE

I am human and I need to be loved, just like everybody else does.
—The Smiths, "How Soon Is Now?"

"I don't know why people like tiramisu so much," I said, passing the plate over to Peyton. "I guess I'm not a pudding person."

"It's cake," Peyton said, taking a bite.

"With pudding in it," Finny said. "Maybe the whole pudding thing comes with age."

Peyton looked up from her fork.

"Not that you're old," Finny said. "You're a lot younger than Sophie's mom."

She laughed. You knew you'd broken through some barriers when honesty emerged and it was okay.

"The inside part is mascarpone," the waitress said, bring us our check. "It's a type of cheese."

"Even worse!" Finny shrieked.

My New York palate was more sophisticated than his, but even I thought the whole tiramisu thing was overdone—unlike Finny's reaction when I gave him one of my souvenirs. That was totally justified.

"For me?" Finny said, clutching the pink ballet slipper to his chest. "It seems kind of small for a panda."

"Merv has delicate feet," I said. "It probably belonged to him."

It was fun to talk openly about souvenirs and what I'd experienced at Bobst with someone other than Walt or Finny. Peyton made it all seem legitimate, which made me feel more normal than I had in a long time.

When I first got to the restaurant, Peyton was furious about how many times I'd lied to her that day. (A lot.) How was she supposed to look after me if I lied? What would my mom have thought? But we worked through it. I forgave her for, well, being there instead of Dad, and she forgave me for being a total nightmare houseguest. But we were there. We made it. And I was closer to my dad—and farther down the path—than I'd ever imagined.

"I have a present, too," she said, taking a rectangle out of her purse and pressing it into my palm. I knew the weight of it, the feel of hard plastic on my skin.

"You made me a tape?" I said.

"Not exactly," she said as I turned it over. It was *Love*.

"*Love!*" Finny said.

"*Love!*" I said. "Where did you find it?"

I ran over to her side of the table and threw my arms around her.

"I had it all along," she said into my hair. "It fell out when I washed your skirt," she added, smiling. "I meant to give it to you this morning, but I forgot. So I threw it in my purse to give to you tonight."

"Thank you, thank you, thank you," I said, hugging the tape to my chest like Finny's ballet shoe. "Does Dad make you tapes, too?"

"Nope," she said, pushing an empty dessert plate away. "He's too busy making those for you."

I imagined Dad staying up all night with records spread across the floor, picking out the perfect songs, using trial and error to find the right order. The same way I was using trial and error to prove the Sophie Effect. Dad had taught me that a mixtape was the perfect place to plant hidden messages and that the order of the songs meant everything. Start with something upbeat, he said, even if the tape was serious. And end on something emotional so that your efforts leave a mark.

"I'll send the rest of the tapes to Havencrest," she said, almost reading my mind.

"I left my address in the kitchen," I said. And then I said something I never expected to say. "We should keep in touch."

Peyton grabbed my hand and Finny's, making a chain. Linking us together.

"We will," she said. "This is just the beginning."

Half an hour later, I was looking up at the departure board at Amtrak. Everyone standing beneath it wanted to go somewhere: conference in Connecticut, reunion in Baltimore, boyfriend weekend in Boston. I wanted to go wherever Dad went and ask him questions. Why him? Why me? Why parallel universes? Couldn't our brains think of anything else to do? Why didn't our hearts pick another hobby instead?

Peyton bought our tickets, Finny went to grab magazines, and I walked around, passing the pay phones, which stood out against the wall like the ocean—waves of bright blue and white against a sea of silver. They looked lonely, empty and unused in the cell phone era. I patted the Walkman in my bag as if comforting one old piece of technology could reassure another. And then my phone rang, another person reaching out to me. Waiting for me to let them in. Drew.

"Shouldn't you be doing homework or something productive?" I said, glad he couldn't see the goofy look on my face.

"Shouldn't you be on a train headed my direction?"

I laughed. "Are you checking up on me?"

"I'm just confirming our lunch on Saturday," Drew said. "I have an insanely busy social calendar."

"Kerouac and coffee?"

"I have other interests," he said.

"Like?"

Pause. A pause could mean anything, like maybe he didn't have anything else to say, which meant we had no future. Or maybe he had other interests but was filing through them in his mind, figuring out which ones were cool enough to share with me.

"If I say what I'm thinking, you'll never let me live it down."

"Why?"

"It's way too teen movie," he said. "So let's just say I'm interested in hearing about your trip when you get back."

A pause could have also meant he was thinking about me.

"It's a date then," I said, wishing I could make the train move faster, partially to match my beating heart, partially because I wanted to be in Havencrest. Pronto.

"Peyton's coming with our tickets, so I have to go."

"Well then, bon voyage, Sophie," he said, chipping away at my armor.

"Au revoir, Nancy Drew," I said, hanging up the phone even though it was the last thing I wanted to do.

"Tickets," Peyton said, handing me two of them. She and Mom had decided to pay for them and give Finny's credit card a break.

"Thanks," I said, slipping my phone into my bag.

"Drew?" she said, nodding at the phone.

"The one and only," I said. "How do you know if a guy really likes you?"

"You just know," Peyton said. "You look like *you* know."

"Maybe," I said.

"And if that's not enough? Sometimes you just have to trust," she said.

"That they won't break your heart?"

She smiled. "That even if they do, you'll survive. You've made it this far, haven't you?"

"True," I said. I put my hands in my pocket, feeling the tape. She'd given me a lot since I'd been there. I wanted to leave her with something, too.

"I think I'm close," I said.

"To what?"

"Proving the Sophie Effect," I said. "Only time—and episodes—will tell."

"That's great, honey," she said, like she didn't really believe me. Like she didn't believe Dad was ever coming home. I had to convince her.

"The cool thing is, I think proving it for me might prove it for Dad, too," I said. "If I can stay in one universe, maybe he could do the same."

She looked as tired as I felt.

"Of course, you're smarter about this stuff than me," I said. An apology hidden inside a compliment. "What do you think? Do you think Dad's coming back?"

She looked defeated, like the weight of a thousand episodes.

"I think your father put toothpaste on his toothbrush in the shape of a smile because he was happy; he loved Mondays because he knew they were a fresh start; he loved physics because it was a way to talk about things bigger than ourselves. And I think, wherever he is, he wants to come back. On some level, I think he knows you want him back, too."

I wanted to pack her heartache in a box and ship it off to someone else.

"So, would another hug be totally out of the question?" I said.

Peyton pulled me in like Finny, like Walt, like Mom on a good day. We stayed there awhile, long enough for me to put my head on her shoulder. Long enough for her shoulders to shake.

"He's coming back," I said, whispering my new mantra in her ear.

She pulled out of the hug and patted her heart. "He never left."

Check, I thought, hoping my own heart took notice.

They called for boarding, and Finny ran up to us with a stack of magazines.

"Mindless entertainment, ready for your consumption," he said, fanning them out. "*Dwell, Elle* and *Physics Today.*"

"And I have *Physics Tomorrow,*" I said, patting my bag. Feeling Dad's book. I also had *Love.*

"Okay, you two," Peyton said, putting one arm around each of us and squeezing. "Be safe. I'm going to miss you."

"You want a photo?" Finny said. "It's almost like being there."

"Of course!" she said, taking out her phone and aiming it at us. "Strike a pose."

Finny and I linked arms and waved, Jackie-O style, for the camera.

"Bye!" we shouted as we boarded Amtrak, bound for home.

Finny found our row and gave me the window seat, as usual. The train pulled away, and outside the window I saw

Peyton waving, frantically, like a parent letting her kid go for the first time. Finny leaned over me, and we waved back and forth, hands moving sideways like spiders. Letting her know she wasn't alone, either.

For the first few hundred miles, Finny and I filled each other in, him versus me: Bobst Research versus Raining Books, Cute Guy Spotting versus My Daring Escape, Waiting Forever versus Betty, Heart Drawing versus Walt and the Rockettes—and my personal favorite, Being Stuck at the Restaurant with Peyton versus My Breakdown in Times Square.

"Wow," Finny said. "That's a lot for one day."

"Yeah," I said. "I prefer to limit my number of daily travels to one."

"And you had two," he said.

"Three, actually," I said. "While you were busy with chalk, I was in the panda-verse."

"Right," Finny said. "So that's one universe. What are all the other ones?

"The Ramones," I said, remembering the cafeteria. It felt like a million years ago. "The Cure."

"Everything's a music video," Finny said, leaning back in his chair. It sounded cool when he said it out loud. "What else?"

"Hearts rolling off sleeves," I said. "Blackbirds peeling off wallpaper. Rain turning into baby black bears. Flying books."

"Objects animate," Finny said, sitting back up. "That's—"

"Just like Dad said," I said. "I know."

It was also like Mr. Maxim predicted. And Walt told me. Sometimes we just know things. I wondered if I'd ever go to the panda-verse again or if it was over. If I was actually proving the Sophie Effect. For the past two years, I came in and out of my reality without even knowing it, which made me wonder: what would it be like to stay in my own universe for a change? The one that included Havencrest and Mom, Drew and high school and Café Haven. The one with manicured lawns and big, sprawling houses but nicer people than anywhere I'd ever lived. Not every person but most of them, like Mr. Rutherford, who brought us Jesus Bars when we moved in, even though they were just brownies with cream cheese crosses on top; Callie, the girl from the diner who would probably end up being a friend; and Mr. Maxim.

"Finny?"

His head was back against the headrest and his eyes were closed. It was late. And since it had been the longest day ever of the two longest days ever, I decided to join him.

I woke up while the rest of the train was still asleep, including Finny. It reminded me of the times I woke up early, on accident. Everyone was still snoozing and it was like the world was on pause, only I got to hit Play for a while. Just me. I took *Love* out of my bag and looked at it. Dad had decorated the case with an illustration of a man riding one of those old-timey bikes— the kind with the big wheel in front. There was a word bubble coming out of the guy's mouth with a heart in it.

I opened the case to look at the song list, and a note fell out. A note with Dad's telltale writing on the front that said *read after listening*. I didn't how long I could wait, but I was going to try. You know, to give the music a chance.

I popped in the tape, put in my earbuds and pressed Play. The opening guitar riffs of "Message of Love" by the Pretenders filled my ears, and I felt like Mom must have felt. Like someone Dad loved, listening to one of his tapes for the first time.

LOVE, BY ANGELINO SOPHIA

MESSAGE OF LOVE	The Pretenders
CLOSE TO ME	The Cure
HAVE LOVE, WILL TRAVEL	Thee Headcoatees
LOVE WILL TEAR US APART	Joy Division
THE PASSENGER	Iggy Pop
TWO HEARTS BEAT AS ONE	U2
THE VILLAGE	New Order
HOW SOON IS NOW?	The Smiths

Music was memory. I think that's why Dad liked making tapes and I liked listening to them. Without leaving my seat or traveling to another universe, I could go somewhere else as often as I wanted, a little world that existed for Dad and me alone. The tape started off happy, like I knew it would. I listened to the lyrics, decoding messages that weren't so secret, but ones I hadn't heard in a long time, if ever.

Dad loved me and wanted to be with me. He stayed away to protect me. He believed all worlds belonged to us and that when he felt something, I felt it, too. Because we were a part of each other. Tears rolled down my face, partially because of the messages but also because I missed him. I paused the tape and opened the letter.

Sophie,

If you're reading this letter, you're looking for answers. It's good to have questions, because life would be boring without them, so I'll attempt to answer a few.

On your mother: She made me leave, but she was right. She couldn't protect you from what I couldn't control, and it was her job to keep you safe. She's suffered enough. Forgive her.

On traveling: I was afraid what was happening to me could happen to you. So instead of wallowing, I went to work to find a connection between physics and what I was experiencing. When I came upon my inspiration—you— everything fell into place. Love was the answer. Because love is everything.

The words poured over me and into me, filling holes I didn't know were there.

Traveling can be difficult, but it's also a beautiful reminder that we're never alone, that

*there are people, places and pandas beyond our
imaginations. Especially your assigned panda.
Know that it's okay to be your own person and
follow your own path, no matter where it
takes you.*

I bent my knees and hugged them to my chest. Keep going,
Dad. Keep going.

*When you're ready to stop traveling—probably
when you're old enough to have a boyfriend or just
tired of being gone all the time—employ the Sophie
Effect. It's what makes you travel, but it's also what
could make it stop. It hasn't worked for me yet, but
maybe, with enough love, it will work for you. Until
we meet again, put your hand over your heart . . .*

I pressed my palm to my heart like the national anthem was
playing.

*. . . and I'll do the same. That way we'll
always be together, whichever universe we're in.*

*Love,
Dad*

I pressed Play and listened to the rest of the tape, letting it
wash over me.

The Cure sang about having a moment and never wanting it to end.

Thee Headcoatees should have sung "have love, won't travel."

Joy Division knew what they were talking about. Love will tear you apart, literally.

"The Passenger" by Iggy Pop was perfect for train listening but also a great metaphor for life. *La, la, la, la, la-la-la-la.*

People can say whatever they want about U2, but their early stuff was amazing, like this song. I think it was written for Dad and me.

New Order was also there, the sound of science, comparing love to nature, to longevity.

It was the perfect mix. And in true Dad fashion, the last song left a mark, especially the chorus. It said something I needed to hear, like a song that had always been with me whether I knew it or not. Like he'd always been with me, whether I knew it or not. Thanks for letting Morrissey deliver the message, Dad.

"*I am human and I need to be loved. Just like everybody else does.*"

Tears rolled down my face and dropped in my lap. I wiped them away, but they kept coming, so I let them. And then I closed my eyes, leaned back and put my hand over my heart, feeling it move with the oscillating guitar, pounding in sync with the drumbeat.

"Evening, night owl."

I opened my eyes and saw Walt sitting in the row across from me, legs stretched out, leaning against the window. That row had always been empty. And since everyone else was asleep, no one else noticed. I climbed over Finny, and Walt moved his legs so I could sit next to him.

"What's new?" he said.

"As if you didn't know," I said, taking off my headphones and wiping my eyes on my sleeve. And then I took the tape out of the Walkman and waved it at him.

"Aw, you heart me! You made me a mixtape."

"Dad made *me* a mixtape," I said. "It's called *Love*."

"How is it? Is Walt and the Pandas on it?"

"No," I said, but I would have loved that. "It came with a letter, though."

"How many stars would you give it, like two or like five with a chocolate mint under your pillow?"

"I'd give it a hundred stars," I said, looking out the window. "This is what I came for."

"I know," he said, patting my hand.

"He mentioned you," I said.

"Little ol' me?"

"Not by name, but he said my assigned panda. I assume that's you?"

"Correct. I couldn't tell you until you knew for sure, but everyone who travels gets a panda," Walt said. "It's part of the deal—protection, guidance and all that."

"So other people travel, too?"

"Sure," Walt said. "But not just anyone can travel. You know that. And if you don't, keep reading your dad's book."

"Were you my dad's panda?"

"Oh, no," he said. "But I've heard about your dad. He sounds like an amazing guy."

"He is," I said, feeling *Love* in my pocket.

I pushed a button to lean my seat back but forgot we weren't on a plane.

"Is there any way I can stop traveling but hang on to you?"

Walt smiled. "I'm flattered, but you know I have to leave at some point anyway."

"So is this a preemptive breakup?"

"Not at all," he said. "But no matter what you do, my work here will be done, eventually. Probably sooner than we think."

The night was dark, and the train was quiet except for the two of us.

"I like having you around," I said, remembering when I didn't. Remembering how I asked him not to sneak up on me or do bad football victory dances.

"I like being around," Walt said. "Chances are, my next client won't be half as fun as you are. But, hey—we'll always have Havencrest."

"Maybe I should put *that* on a T-shirt," I said.

He munched on a packet of peanut butter crackers he found in the seat in front of him.

"I still haven't proven the Sophie Effect, you know," I said.

"But you're closer," Walt said. "Would you like another hint?"

"Always," I said. "I'm going to miss your advice. You eating my egg rolls. Pointing out markers along the way."

"You're starting to see the markers yourself," Walt said.

I sat up in my chair. "I am?"

"You're graduating," he said. "Get the robe ready."

I saw the fur on his face glisten, like it was wet.

"Wait, are those tears?" I said.

"No way," he said. "Pandas don't get emotional. Emo, maybe, but never emotional."

Walt put his arm around me and kissed the top of my head.

"Be at home here," he said, pointing to his heart. "Especially when you get a glimpse of another world."

"So what, I travel when I'm nervous?"

Walt smiled. He liked to make me figure everything out myself, so I thought about it. I never traveled when I was hanging out with Finny, laughing. Or curled up on my bed, reading a book. I didn't travel when Mom and I made dinner together or when I went for a walk. That had to mean something. It was well documented that stress caused rational people to do crazy things. Was it insane to think it caused me to pop between universes?

"No matter what happens, don't be a stranger, okay?" I said.

I felt the tears coming, but Walt slayed them with his sarcasm.

"Always strange, but never a stranger," he said, hopping up and wiggling his butt in the aisle. And then he blew me a kiss.

"See you soon, princess," he said. And then he disappeared.

"See you soon," I said to the lunch ladies and baby black bears, to The Cure, the flying books, to all of them. They weren't gone yet, but I had a feeling they would be soon. And then I picked up my phone and said hello to my new world, texting Drew. Counting down the hours, letting him know I'd be there soon.

I crawled across Finny again, but this time it woke him up.

"Whoa!" he said, startled. "Did you travel? Are you okay?"

"I'm fine," I said. I wasn't in the mood to talk about Walt. "Go back to sleep."

And then I noticed Dad's book open across his chest.

"Dad's tape came with a letter."

Finny sat up, stretched his arms and turned on the overhead light.

"I can sleep when I'm dead," he said. And then he reached in his bag and pulled two chocolate bars out of it. "Spill it."

I handed him the letter so he could read it himself. It was better to let Dad do the talking.

And I distracted myself with grooming, running a comb through my bangs, making them as straight as Cleopatra's. I found my Strike-A-Rose lip gloss and a piece of gum, both of which totally improved my mouth. My clothes were wrinkled, but I was saved by a tiny deodorant and a sample of pineapple hand lotion, both of which made me feel better.

"Wow," Finny said, folding the letter back up and handing it to me. "My dad has never said anything this nice to me."

"Maybe leaving gives you perspective," I said, even though I would have given anything to have traded a letter for an actual father.

"So does staying," Finny said. "I hope he's right about the gaps."

"Me too," I said, remembering I still had work to do. And then Finny did part of the work for me.

"You know how you're always listening to those tapes?" he asked.

"Yeah . . ."

"Someone thought you might want to move into a new century."

"I told you," I said. "I love analog."

"Just think about a playlist as the modern version of the mix-tape," he said, handing me his iPod. It was already open to a playlist called *Welcome to Today.*

"You made this for me?" I said.

"I put it together, but someone else named it and dictated the songs," he said.

"Peyton?" I said, since she was the only other person who had been with him.

"Way better than that," he said. "Drew."

My heart beat faster, the thought of him, thinking of me.

"That was the secret," Finny said. "While you were off with Walt, we were planning a total Sophie Get Happy attack."

"But how—"

"Drew has good taste," Finny said. "I just read off some of the bands I had, and he instantly knew which songs he wanted to use. He likes those old bands you like, but he's also into the new stuff. And we both thought you might like the sound of the future."

I looked at the playlist. It was full of bands I didn't know, like Noah and the Whale and The Shins, but there was also a song by Sonic Youth. Kim Gordon, bringing me home.

"He's a keeper," Finny said.

"Drew wasn't mad that I didn't tell him you were with me?"

"He was at first," Finny said. "But I explained it to him."

I laughed. "I would have loved to have heard that," I said, and then it hit me. "Wait, what *did* you tell him?"

"Nothing you don't already know," Finny said. "I didn't tell him about your dad or anything. I also didn't tell him I was gay—I'm hoping he figured that out—but I let him know that you and I are best friends."

"That's all you said?"

"That, and that I will always know you better than he will," Finny said, grinning. "I told him I'm the guy you'll call in the middle of the night when some other guy decides he doesn't like you anymore. I'm the guy who buys you chocolate to make you feel better, the one your mom calls when she's worried, and the one you call when you have nightmares."

"I've never done that," I said, but he was on a roll.

"I'm the guy who picks up the pieces, keeps you going and inspires you. Because you inspire me," Finny said, grabbing my hand. "Look, I'm not worried about you liking anyone more than me because we're friends. Best friends. And you will always like me as much as you like yourself."

Friendship, summed up in a monologue.

"I adore you, you know that?" I said, not a bit surprised at the words coming out of my mouth.

"I know," he said. "I adore you, too, which is why I helped him. If anything's going to start closing those gaps, this should do it."

"You're already doing it," I said, giving him the biggest hug imaginable. "Thanks, Finn."

I took out my headphones to listen, but then I decided instead of being in my own little world, I wanted to bring Finny into it.

"Do you have your dual-headphone adapter?"

"Sure," he said, getting it out of his bag. "You want to share?"

"Of course!" I said. "But only if you'll dance with me."

Our car was relatively empty, so Finny and I spread out in the aisle, headphones reaching, iPod between us. Finny hit Play and the first song came on. It sounded like it came from the eighties but was new. I moved my head from side to side as Finny tapped his toes. As the music continued, we bounced up and down, arms flying as much as they could in the aisle. Outside it was pitch-black, like we were driving through the middle of the earth, but inside I felt bright, like light was bursting out of every cell.

When the chorus came, Finny grabbed my hand and tried to spin me. Headphone cords tangling, we fell down in the aisle, laughing, probably waking everyone else up, but I didn't care. One boy had made me a playlist. And the other one was dancing with me, just like he had from the beginning. No judgment, no fear. If that wasn't love, I didn't know what was. Which made me realize: I needed to make someone else a tape.

How to Make a Mixtape
by Sophie Sophia, as inspired by Angelino Sophia

---

1. Spread all of your albums out in front of you.

2. Think about what you want to say. Are you proving a point? Saying thanks? Or do you just have a theme?

3. Include *only* songs that remind you of your theme and person. (If your heart beats a little faster when you hear it, that's the song.)

4. Ordering is an art. Make sure it's perfect it before you press Record.

5. Be creative with the name of the tape. The world really doesn't need another *Randy's Favorites #3*.

6. Give without expecting anything in return.

7. Into digital? You should try analog. There's nothing like spending a day making a mixtape. (You can do the same thing with a playlist, just don't tell me about it.)

TWENTY-SIX

I feel so extraordinary, something's got a hold on me.
I get this feeling I'm in motion, a sudden sense of liberty.
—New Order, "True Faith"

"Have you ever seen a sky like that?" I said, pressing my face against the window, making wet spots on the glass with my breath. "I don't remember it being so blue before."

"Someone's happy to be home," Finny said.

"That would be me," I said, looking around as we got outside.

"Should I call my mom, or you want to call yours?"

"Neither," I said. "We're going to play it New York style and walk. Besides, I need to decompress."

Finny snickered. "Since when have you ever decompressed?"

"Since I realized that stress contributes to traveling," I said. "Apparently it's easier to feel love when you're calm."

"Yeah, because nobody loves a spaz," he said, smiling. "You want to do some yoga along the way, too? Or chanting?"

"Make fun of me all you want," I said. "I just want to breathe."

The station was twenty blocks from my house, which, before we left, felt like an eternity. But now we had New York feet. They came in handy, since the blocks here were twice as long as the ones in New York.

"I think my New York feet wore off," Finny said, slowing after several blocks. "Have you decompressed yet?"

"I'm getting there," I said.

My lungs took in air—I could feel it—instead of the panicked breathing I was used to. Something about my body was more relaxed. Maybe that was what happened when the gaps filled—you became whole. And when your body sensed that, it relaxed.

"I had my first authentic bagel," Finny said, trudging down the sidewalk.

"You got a glimpse of a famous physicist's basement," I said.

"I have an in with the physics department at NYU!"

"And an adviser for your science project," I said. "Oh, crap, we need to text Peyton."

I reached for my phone, but Finny was already on it.

"And . . . done," he said. "I also gave the boys at Bobst a run for their money."

"We need to go back," I said. "You totally have a future in New York."

"You do, too," he said. "With your dad."

I looked up and down Mapleberry, the street we were on. It was flat, like all the streets in Havencrest, and contained the same style of houses and trees, all in a row. Like someone had hit the Repeat button. I was strangely comforted by the monotony, which reminded me of my new possible life. Instead of hills and high-rises, my inner landscape could be more predictable, like suburbia instead of Manhattan.

"We're almost home," I said. "It's time for me to face the music."

Finny dropped his bag, regained his energy and tapped, doing his best Gene Kelly impression on the sidewalk.

"Facing the music's not so bad," he said, flashing jazz hands. "Unless, of course, it's disco."

New York was amazing, but it didn't have Finny. Which meant it had nothing on Havencrest.

We got closer to the house, and I saw Mom standing with her back to the picture window. According to her, that window was classic sixties architecture. It was designed to make the inhabitants feel closer with nature, which was funny since Mom's body language—arms crossed, hands digging into her back—was more hostile than Zen.

"Are you going to be okay?" Finny said, nearing the house with me.

"Yeah," I said. "I can't thank you enough for going with me."

"What are best friends for?" he said, grinning. "Besides,

it will be nice to have you owe me. Maybe I need a cool pocket or to hang out with you and your hot new boyfriend or something."

"He's not my boyfriend!"

"Not yet," Finny said. And then we saw my mom turn around.

"And I'll leave you to it," he said. "Good luck!"

Finny headed for his house, and Mom ran out the front door, hair in a ponytail. Mom never wore a ponytail.

"Sophie?" she said, arms outstretched.

"Sophie," she said, pulling me into her. We clung to each other like magnetic dolls and then hobbled over to the magnolia tree in our yard. Mom sat and leaned against the trunk, and I sat and leaned against her, leaves above us fanning out like millions of umbrellas. Shading us from everything but ourselves.

"You are very, *very* grounded," Mom said, stroking my hair. I knew she meant it, but I also knew she was happy to see me.

"Just put a GPS tracking device in my brain until I graduate," I said. And then I got brave.

"I wish *you* could be grounded," I said. "I know about Dad."

"What about Dad?"

"That you made him leave."

Mom turned to look at me.

"Peyton didn't tell me," I said. "I overheard her telling Finny."

"I was going to tell you," she said. "When you were older."

"I'm fourteen," I said. "How much older do I have to be?"

"I don't know," she said. "The timing never felt right."

"Mom, you lied," I said. I had stopped being mad at her. Now I just wanted to understand.

"Yes," she said, straightening her shoulders. "I lied. Because I'm your mother. And I will do whatever it takes to protect you, whether you like it or not."

Dad was right. She saved me from him.

"I just want to understand," I said quietly.

"You don't know how many times I went to work terrified you might not be there when I got back," she said.

I picked leaves off my tights.

"Never knowing what your father was going to do or when."

"I know we had to leave," I said. "I get that now. I just wish you hadn't lied to me. All this time I thought Dad didn't love me."

"Sophie," she said, grabbing my hands. "How could you think that?"

"He left one night and never came back," I said. "He didn't call me, and you said you didn't know where he was."

"I didn't," she said. "We agreed to stop all contact."

"But knowing we left him, it makes a difference," I said. "He was so devastated he disappeared almost continuously until he met Peyton."

"She sounded nice."

"She helped him write the book," I said.

Mom looked down.

"Mom, the book is about episodes. It's about me."

"Sophie—"

"I know you think he's crazy," I said. "And maybe he is. But he did that—research, writing, all of it—for me."

"That's because he loves you." Her eyes sparkled.

"I know," I said, taking the *Love* tape out of my bag and handing it to her.

"I found a box of these in the basement," I said. "There were hundreds of them, all addressed to me, and this one came with a letter."

Mom turned the tape over in her hands, looking at Dad's slanted writing.

"You can read it if you want," I said.

"That's okay," she said, handing the tape back. "It's between you and your dad."

I liked the way she said it, like she was okay with me finally having a relationship with him, even if it was only through a cassette tape.

"I know you're not your father," she said, running her hand down the leg of her black pants, removing leaves. Then she put her hand to my side.

"It's just that bipolar shows up around your age," she said. "Your dad left and we moved to San Francisco and then all of these things started happening . . . the suspension . . . and then we moved here and it was the same thing all over again. I had to call someone. I had to make sure the thing that destroyed him didn't destroy you, too."

I couldn't tell her what I was yet—a traveler. I didn't think she'd understand, but I could tell her what I wasn't.

"I'm not bipolar," I said. "And Dad may be sick, but that's not all he is. I have proof."

"I never said he was bipolar," she said. "I just said he had problems. What proof are you talking about?"

I took Dad's book and handed it to her.

"I think you should hear it from him."

By the time she read about the Sophie Effect, I hoped to have already proven it. To have stopped traveling, so it wouldn't be an issue. So she could love me again without fear. We were both quiet for a moment. Mom held the book in her hands, not opening it. That's when the new Sophie Sophia showed up.

"Thanks for protecting me," I said, laying my head on her shoulder.

"Thanks for coming back," she said.

"When Dad gets back, he can explain it even better," I said. "In person."

"Just don't spend your time waiting," Mom said. "He always comes back, but you never know when."

Leaves blew around and blackbirds flew in from wherever they were before, squawking at each other. I leaned over and hugged her so tight, I hoped Dad felt it. She squeezed me back, and this time, instead of wondering if she loved me, I knew she did.

"Here," I said, taking Finny's iPod out of my bag and handing it to her. "I made you something. I know you've always wanted me to go more modern, so I did. Welcome to today's version of the mixtape."

"You made me a playlist?"

"It's called *Love 2.0*," I said.

"You made me a playlist," she said, her face softening as she put the earbuds in her ears.

LOVE 2.0, BY SOPHIE SOPHIA, Courtesy of Finny's iPod	
TAKE CARE OF BUSINESS	Nina Simone
THE ONE I LOVE	R.E.M.
LA LA LOVE YOU	The Pixies
WITHOUT YOU HERE	Holly Golightly
THE SUN IS SHINING	The Dirtbombs
LOOK TO TOMORROW	The Now Time Delegation

Mom listened for a while, skimming through the songs. I'd had to use what was on Finny's iPod, but he had plenty of stuff I knew Mom would like, including some older songs. But since I was putting one foot forward, I included some newer music, too.

"I love it," she said. "I'll listen to the whole thing later."

"Great," I said. "Because I'm starving. And I need a shower."

She stood up and held out her hands, and I actually took them, letting her lift me up. I'd spent so many years being defensive and pushing her away that I didn't know what I'd been missing.

"On the bright side, Finny's mom brought over seven-layer dip for your homecoming," she said. "You know you want some . . ."

"Eeew, like that Jell-O thing she brought us when we moved in?"

"That dessert was indestructible," Mom said. "Kind of like you."

We walked in silence for a few seconds.

"I'm glad you're back," she said.

I saw Balzac sitting in the window.

"Me too," I said. And I actually meant it.

After Mom and I had a snack, I took a quick shower, changed and headed to The Lab. I wanted to be alone for a minute, and that was the best place to do it, even though I caught my green tights on the ladder, ripping them at the knee.

"Shoot," I said, rubbing a hole where fabric had been.

The tights were the same color as the green heart pocket on the front of my gray cheerleader-like skirt, which was a little matchy-matchy, but I was too tired to care. The hole probably improved the outfit, anyway. Like a punk rock revision.

The Lab looked just like we left it—charts on the wall, candy wrappers on the desk, supplies scattered everywhere. I borrowed a piece of Finny's paper and a marker and made a list. Soon I wouldn't need it anymore. I could feel it. But someone might. And if they were anything like me, they'd need all the help they could get.

How to Survive Traveling
by Sophie Sophia

---

1. Enjoy it. It's pretty amazing, when you think about it.

2. Have good friends, family and a cat named Balzac to come home to.

3. Practice coming in and out of universes so it's not so jarring.

4. Be careful with your souvenirs. They're kind of sacred.

5. When you've had enough of the above, employ the Sophie Effect to say good-bye to one set of worlds and hello to another.

I tacked the list on the wall for Finny, next to the owl. And then I took out Dad's letter and read it one more time.

Love is the answer.

We're never alone.

He's always with me.

"Thanks, Dad," I said, putting the letter in the fake fireplace, like a ritual.

Except I had no desire to burn it or watch it fly away, so I grabbed it back and put it in my pocket. I wanted to keep it forever or until I saw him, whichever came first.

I walked over to Finny's desk, took Walt's whistle off and left it in the top drawer like a thank-you note. I wouldn't be where I was without Finn. I thought about Finny's name again, which meant "oracle," a person who delivered a message from the divine. A message that you're okay just the way you are. If that didn't make you believe people came into your life for a reason, nothing would.

"Sophie?"

I heard Drew's voice at the bottom of the ladder. "Can I come up?"

How did he know I was there? *Finny. Of course.*

"I'm coming down," I said, feeling weird about being up there with anyone else. I popped a piece of gum in my mouth, took a deep breath for courage and left The Lab.

"Hi," Drew said, making me melt. His voice was one thing, but seeing him? It was like another universe unto itself, an entire set of emotions that were as new as seeing a panda for the first time.

"Let me help," he said, offering me his hand as I jumped off the ladder.

"I loved the tape," I said, almost falling into him. He brought out my inner clumsiness. "I mean, playlist. I really, really loved it."

"I'm glad," he said. "When Finny told me your family was in trouble, I wanted to do something, you know?"

I knew. It was hard, knowing someone was hurting and not being able to do anything about it.

"My family was in trouble," I said. "So was I."

I grabbed his hand, and as we walked, I told him why I really went to see my dad. I told him what he'd heard about me in the cafeteria was true and that it was the same thing that had happened on our date. I didn't have a panic attack, I had an episode, something similar to a hallucination. Episodes happened at school, at the store and sometimes on dates. If I was lucky, they often included a very charming panda.

For some people, hearing that a friend was crazy was the same thing as hearing they were dead. It suddenly catapulted them into the five stages of grief.

"*So you see a panda. That's not a hallucination, right?*"

Denial.

"*I can't believe you didn't tell me. I wish it was me instead of you.*"

Anger. Bargaining.

"*So you're sick. We can't date. What's the point of dating, anyway, if one day we're all going to die?*"

Depression.

Drew stopped and looked down for a moment. And then he popped his head back up.

"Kerouac hallucinated," he said.

"He did?" I said, surprised that this was nothing like the conversation in my head, but grateful that Keourac was saving me once again.

"Yeah. It's in *Big Sur*, too. He was in this cabin and had a nervous breakdown and hallucinated. Just like you."

And even though it wasn't just like me, even though I hadn't even told him the good news—that my hallucinations were actually travel to parallel universes—he completed the final stage of grief, ending with the luckiest one: acceptance.

"If it's good enough for Kerouac, it's good enough for me," Drew said.

And that's when I decided to tell him.

"I'm glad," I said. "Because that's not the entire truth."

"There's more?"

"It's a *new* more," I said. "As in two days new. According to this theory that my dad came up with—the Sophie Effect—I'm not hallucinating. He wasn't, either. We're traveling to parallel universes."

It was the kind of thing you couldn't tell just anyone, but I had to tell him. I didn't want to leave him with the idea that I was mentally ill. I'd rather start the conversation with parallel universes and move on. Just like I was moving on.

"Wow," he said. "That's what your dad's book is about?"

"Basically," I said. "It explains everything."

Drew stopped. "But does it change anything?"

"I hope so," I said. "I've been trying to prove his theory for a few days now, and I think it's working. If I prove it, I won't travel anymore."

Drew stopped next to a lavender bush, its purple tops filling the air with sweetness.

"If you're getting better, why did you tell me?"

"Because you talked to me even after I disappeared," I said. And then, because I was feeling brave, I said something else. "And because I want you to know all of me."

"I like that," he said as I felt anxiety leave and something else come in.

CHAPTER FIVE: THE PHYSICS
OF SAYING GOOD-BYE

Most physicists would agree that time is an illusion—there is no past, present or future. But whether it's

*leaving a universe or a person, people will still place
importance on good-byes. They'll sob at airports, feel
heartache when a child leaves for college and experience
profound loss when a loved one moves on. If you sub-
scribe to the idea that time is irrelevant, though, it takes
the bittersweet out of leaving. If we'll all meet again or if
we've already met before, there's no such thing as good-
bye. It's just a different way of saying hello.*

Walking toward my house, I thought I heard drums in the
distance. Uh-oh.

"Would you mind if I met you back at my house?" I said, standing
in the middle of the sidewalk. "I need to drop something off
with Finny."

"Sure," Drew said. He let go of my hand but stood right in
front of me, close, like there was only enough air in the world for
one of us and we had to share it.

"I'll be right back," I said quietly. "Promise."

"I know you will," he said, grinning.

And then he did something no boy had ever done to me
before: he kissed me.

Electricity, fireworks, butterflies.

Flying on a plane for the first time, riding a roller coaster for
the tenth time, diving off the high dive.

Timeless.

I wanted to save how his lips felt, how his breath moved,

how one minute we were two and then we were one. I wanted to replay it in my mind forever.

"You'll be back soon?" Drew said as the kiss ended.

"As soon as possible," I said.

I waved and floated down the street, wondering if kisses were like traveling, because I felt transported. Until a furry tail on my leg brought me back to reality.

"Balzac!" I said, scooping him up. Mom let him out, and I guess he'd followed me.

"Did you see that?" I said. "Were you jealous?"

He meowed, head-butting my nose. I hugged him as tightly as he'd let me until he squirmed out of my arms and ran away. Probably back to the house.

The drums grew louder, and I finally saw the pandas—xylophones and snares, mallets and plumes—marching down the other side of the street. Walt was up front as usual, twirling something that looked like a baton, but he didn't look at me. He was also really blurry. They sounded good, like a real band. I guess in between hanging out with me and eating, Walt had made them practice.

"Walt!" I yelled over the drums, but he didn't respond. They were playing "True Faith" by New Order, the band that sounded like science. The song that was about second chances.

"I'm over here!" I said, waving my arms wildly, but the pandas marched down the other side of the street like I didn't exist. Their bodies were so translucent they almost didn't exist, either. Like I wasn't fully in the panda-verse. I was just getting a glimpse.

I made a bullhorn with my hands and screamed even louder.

"Merv! I had my first kiss!" I said.

"Walt, I made up with Mom!" I screamed.

"Guys, I'm going to be okay!" I said, spinning around, my heart skirt twirling in the wind.

I ran toward them, and as I did, I saw Walt carrying something I'd know anywhere—a red parasol with tiny flowers on it, like the one Dad had hung above my bed: the Dream Director. He pumped it up and down as he walked, keeping time. Keeping the bad dreams out and letting the good ones in. As they marched, I thought about Finny and Drew, Mom and Peyton, Betty and Dad. All of them important in some way. Doing their parts.

The pandas skipped and blurred like lines on a television as my heart felt so full, I was sure it would burst.

"You have to stay home so I have someone to bring souvenirs to," Dad said.

Walt moved forward, twirling the parasol, fading. A ghost of himself.

". . . so you can remember me."

When Dad walked out, he left holes in my heart, but he knew I'd survive. He wrote the book because, more than anything, he wanted me to learn to love the world again. Even a world without him in it.

I blinked, hard, and when I looked back, they were still there, but barely. A mass of pandas moving through the streets of Havencrest as they'd walked through my life. I thought about Drew, sitting on my porch, waiting for me. And Finny, the one who sent him. Both of them accepting me exactly as I was.

Sometimes you wore your heart on your sleeve and it fell on

the floor. Sometimes people slipped through the gaps. But sometimes, when you weren't looking, hearts stayed put and gaps closed and there you were, in the place you always wanted to be, without even trying to get there.

Things worked out, even though you never thought they would, not in a million years. I guess that was kind of the point. With all this wisdom, I should have been able to skip straight to adulthood, except I knew I couldn't skip anything anymore—not time, not places, not people. I had to be here. Dad hanging out somewhere, pandas marching away from me, Drew and Finny walking toward me.

The drums grew fainter with each roll, each step, each heartbeat. Walt turned to me, raised his paw and waved—a blur of black and white moving back and forth in the sky, which turned pink and promising with the falling sun. And then he disappeared.

"Hello!" I shouted, saying what Dad would have said. "Hello, hello, hello!"

I already missed Walt and The Cure, the baby black bears and the blackbirds. I hoped a world without them—without Dad—wasn't forever, but it was okay for now.

Maybe it was even better.

Besides, I had another mixtape to make.

ACKNOWLEDGMENTS

To everyone who ever boarded Ship Everything, I owe you my deepest thanks and gratitude. This book couldn't have happened without you.

A huge thanks to Mollie Glick, super-agent superstar. Your belief in Sophie and books with big ideas is inspiring. You keep me going, lady.

To Jill Santopolo, editor extraordinaire and champion of the book from the beginning. Thanks for your tireless work and for "going there" with me.

To the entire team at Philomel, thanks for taking a chance on a first-time author. I am grateful.

To Sherry Mendel (Harper), who helped me find my "writer" in the first place.

To Jacqueline Raphael, Luciana Lopez and Theresa Tate, who cradled the first chapters and laughed so hard I knew I had to keep going. Extra-special thanks to Jacqueline, writing partner in crime. May we always make mischief.

To Jessica Morrell. Your guidance and support have been invaluable.

To all of my writing partners, who got me through word counts with lightness and heart.

To Vanessa Veselka, true warrior and great friend. We'll always have Beulahland.

To the amazing minds of Brian Greene, Lisa Randall, Michio Kaku, Ed Whitten and all the other physicists I've forgotten to mention for playing with the mysteries of the universe and providing me with endless inspiration. You are so much smarter than I am.

To my physics adviser, Che Lowenstein, for reading an early draft and sharing the "eeeh!" of string theory with me.

To Madeleine Terry, fellow artist and adventurer of the heart.

To fellow dreamers Tim Kerr, Deanna Feeley, René Orsinger, Charity Heller, Jay Fields, and Greg Hyatt.

To my ladies, Sara Snyder, Nina Lary and B. Frayn Masters, whose friendship and generous spirits would help anyone get through the writing process. You are such a part of this book.

To Blake Nelson, whose advice, laughter and friendship reminded me to have heart and never stop writing.

To Will Bryant, who brought Walt to life.

To Jason Price, fellow spider moving sideways.

To Arie, Kai and Noah Pellikaan for never letting me get too serious.

To my grandparents—Betty and Brandon Doak—whose fabulous stories encouraged me to tell my own.

To my sister, Sandi Pellikaan, wonderful reader, amazing friend and keeper of the flame. You never let it go out. I could *not* have done this without you.

To my parents, Jim and Pegi Luna. Mom, you're the original bright light. And Dad, your big heart and persistence have always inspired me to have my own. Thank you both.

Finally, thanks to all the kids who read, dream and believe in things they cannot see. Writing for you is the very best part.